## TO THE STARS . . .

First there was the Word, then the warning—and then the war. Earth was ruined, and man had to escape from his home world to find a new destiny somewhere in the far reaches of space.

The fleet of ships that had seemed so towering and impressive while they were being built became, in the unfathomable infinities of the universe, mere flickers and sparks of life . . . precarious life that might be snuffed out from any of a thousand causes.

These were the surviving remnants of the human race, searching for a new haven, a new world, a new hope. And when they did find it . . .

*Noah II, an exciting and powerful novel of tomorrow, is now being filmed for major motion picture release. Read the book now—and watch for the great movie!*

# NOAH II

### ROGER DIXON

Original story idea by

**BASIL BOVA and ROGER DIXON**

ACE BOOKS

A Division of Charter Communications, Inc.
1120 Avenue of the Americas
New York, N. Y. 10036

NOAH II.

*Cover painting by Jack Gaughan*

Printed in U.S.A.

# INTRODUCTION:

The Mind of the Creator is infinite, far beyond the understanding of His creatures, yet this much we know—the galaxies, each containing a billion stars at least as big as our own Sun, are scattered throughout the Universe, far outnumbering the grains of sand on the beaches of all the world. This is the work of the Creator, itself beyond the comprehension of the human mind. Our own galaxy, the Milky Way, is so vast that light traveling at nearly two hundred thousand miles a second takes one hundred thousand years to travel from one side of it to the other, and not far from the outer rim is the Sun, traveling around the common center, together with its family of planets, at two hundred miles a second. It has so far to travel that it has only covered twenty-five revolutions since the beginning of time.

The Sun is a thousand times more massive than Jupiter, which is by far the biggest planet and more massive than a thousand Earths. The Sun is a controlled nuclear explosion of gigantic size which is only prevented from expanding to consume the planets by its own weight. Pouring into surrounding space light and heat of such intensity that the billionth of it which reaches us is sufficient, our parent star consumes its own body at a rate of a ton and a half for every second of its life, and has done so for the past five thousand million years. Like ourselves, one day it will die.

Yet, in spite of its immense size, not even a star can be considered most excellent in Creation, for it does not think, and passes into oblivion without knowing, even for one short moment, the glory it shares with its fellows. For that awareness we must look to Earth, the only home of intelligent life in all the solar system. Here, our story begins . . . with Man—not now, but many years from now—Man, so far from the greatest of the Creator's creatures, yet born with the ability to recognize His work. Perhaps the deepest mystery of all is that this should be of any consequence.

BOOK ONE — GENESIS

# CHAPTER ONE

In the delivery room of a Community, a young woman slept peacefully on the birth-table, the lower half of her body encased in a machine resembling an iron lung. Apart from the girl herself, the room was devoid of human beings. After she had laid there for some time, a tray slid out from the lower half of the machine bearing a newborn male child crying lustily, and this was conveyed by an automatic trolley through a recess in the opposite wall. Thus the first and last opportunity for mother and child to know one another passed unremarkably.

The child was conveyed to the ante-natal room and into a machine with a transparent cover in which it was exposed to healing and cleansing rays, which acted visibly upon it. A few seconds later the completely prepared child slid gently onto a conveyor belt which carried it toward the point where the belt divided in two directions, each leading to separate hatches; one of these was marked CARE and the other DESTROY. A counting device checked the child and the last number on the dial changed from a nine to a zero, after which the belt began again and a junction device switched so the child was carried

to the left and disappeared through the hatch marked
CARE. As soon as it passed, the junction moved back
to the other position ready to receive the next nine
successful applicants for life, the first of whom was
already on her way.

The selected boy-child was guided automatically
into one of the incubators and the process of rearing
began.

"Preston."

The boy, now five years old, ignored the voice at
first and continued to play in a corner of the padded
nursery with a group of his contemporaries.

"Preston." It was a woman's voice, kindly but
firm. "Be quiet for a moment, children."

The children quieted obediently, but without fear,
and Preston glanced in the direction of the hidden
loudspeaker. "I am ready to show you the world
now," the voice continued. "Hurry, I am waiting for
you."

The boy stood up and the others looked at him
as he walked to the door which opened as he approached it. Just before he went out, he turned to
his friends solemnly.

"Goodbye," he said. The children stared back at
him silently.

"Come along." Preston nodded, turned and walked
through the door which closed behind him. As soon
as he had gone, the moment of tension eased and
the other children went back to their play as if
nothing had happened.

Preston walked down a long corridor which
seemed enormous, but he was unafraid and the

voice seemed to accompany him. "Come along," it said encouragingly, "there's a lot to see." As he neared the end of the corridor, a door opened leading outside and, after a short pause, he walked through and stood blinking in the bright sunlight.

He found himself outside a white, single-storied building and on the roadway in front of him a Machine stood waiting. When it spoke, it used the voice he had become used to ever since he could remember.

"I will take you to your next living station," it told him. "On the way, I will show you something of the Community into which you have been accepted. Do you understand?"

"Yes." Preston nodded, and heard the door close behind him. Two steps emerged from the base of the Machine with handrails and, after a moment's hesitation, he climbed up and sat on a seat at the rear. The steps retracted and guardrails rose around the seat to prevent him from falling off, then the Machine started to move down an avenue of trees between rows of buildings similar to the one he had just left. The Community would have reminded an inhabitant from the twentieth century of an Israeli kibbutz, but apart from outward appearances there the similarity would have ended. The Machine spoke reassuringly to its small passenger as it moved along but Preston only stared most of the time, wide-eyed.

"This is the Community where you were born and where you will live all your life," the Machine told him. "It is run by Machines for the service and enjoyment of human beings, who created us long ago. Here you will find everything for your pleasure, as

11

you are prepared to accept the ultimate happiness."
Preston dragged his eyes back to the Machine.

"What's that?" he asked.

"You are too young to understand."

Preston turned back to look at the part of the
Community through which they were now passing;
if he had been older he might have noticed that not
one of the people wandering about was older than
twenty. Other Machines moved here and there but
nobody took any notice of them except the occasion-
al passengers.

"You will devote yourself to pleasure and the satisfaction of the needs of your body," the Machine
said. "You are not forbidden to leave the Community,
but outside you will only find other Communities
identical to this, so there would be no purpose. Do
you understand?" Preston nodded but turned to
stare at a grassy-banked pool where some young
people were swimming and others lay in the sun
or in the shade of fruit trees, either singly, in pairs,
or twined together like snakes. "Remember, the Machines are here to serve and protect you. They
have no other purpose."

"What must I do?" the boy asked after a few seconds.

"Nothing. Just enjoy yourself until you are prepared."

Preston frowned, then turned to look at several
young people who were standing on either side of a
Machine sucking from tubes. "Whatever you want,
you must ask," the Machine went on.

"Ask for what?"

"Whatever comes into your mind. Not until you have explored every possibility will you be ready."

Now they approached a gentle slope where another building stood open on all sides. The Machine stopped and the steps unfolded. Preston heard children's laughter and shouting from inside.

"Get down," the Machine said. "This is where you will live until you are older."

Preston climbed down and stood looking around uncertainly.

"You will sleep here at night, but you may enjoy yourself anywhere." It paused for a few seconds before continuing. "Go inside and see for yourself."

Preston walked in between two white marble pillars, stopping on the threshold of a large room inhabited by children from his own age up to the age of ten. It was identical to the nursery he had just left, only bigger, and the children were playing exactly the same games. They fell silent when they saw him, but Preston turned back to the Machine.

"I thought you were going to show me the world," he said.

"It is the same everywhere," the Machine answered.

Preston looked around in bewilderment and suddenly the older children burst out laughing.

## CHAPTER TWO

Twelve years later, Preston stood in the Administrative Center of the Community facing one of the Machines, his face flushed with determination. Although well above average height, the youth was dwarfed by the robot Administrator who faced him and experienced, not for the first time, the difficulty of knowing on which part of the Machine to focus his attention. As a result, his eyes tended to wander from the top of the Machine, where he would normally have expected to find the center of intellect, to a point three feet below where he knew the Machine's front sensor was located.

"You said I could have whatever I wanted," he went on accusingly.

The Machine paused a moment before replying; when it did, its tone betrayed anxiety, one of the emotions programmed into its original a thousand years before and which made communication with human beings more effective. "Books are difficult to obtain," it said at last.

"I don't care. You've taught me to read. Now I must have them." Preston drew himself up to his full height and took a deep breath. "I order you to get them for me," he said. "You must obey me."

"My program prevents me from acting against the welfare of any human being," the Machine agreed.

"Outside of that, you must do as I say."

"Very well," said the Machine after a few more seconds, "but I am concerned that we have failed you."

Preston relaxed and looked at the Machine more kindly. "You haven't failed me," he said.

"Then why can you not accept what we know to be for your own well-being?"

"It's not enough." Preston paused for a moment. "I can't explain," he said eventually.

"You are the only one."

"I know."

"Does that not bother you?"

Preston looked up, his eyes shining with defiance. "No," he said in a tone which ended the discussion. So he got his books, but the Machines were not the only ones disturbed by his failure to conform.

Six months after this interview, Sarah, who was a little younger than Preston, stood under a tree some distance from the pool looking down at him. He was sitting with his back propped against the trunk, a book on his lap and dozing with his head sunk on his chest.

"Preston, are you asleep?" There was no response, so the girl sank to her knees and took one of his toes delicately between her thumb and forefinger. "Preston," she said again, then watched him open his eyes and look up at her, blinking.

"Sarah!"

Sarah laughed. "You were asleep," she said accusingly, but the boy shook his head.

"No I wasn't," he insisted; "I was only thinking."

"Liar!" Sarah laughed again, then she hesitated uncertainly. "Can I sit beside you?" she asked.

Preston sat more upright. "Of course," he said. "Why not?"

"Well, we know you don't like to be disturbed." Preston shook his head slightly, while she settled more comfortably in front of him, contentedly aware of the admiration with which he looked at her naked body, and happy in the knowledge that the early summer sun had turned her skin the color of amber. This was greatly envied by most of the other girls of her age in the Community. Even though clothes were never worn during the summer except at night, Sarah was always one of the first to acquire a tan.

"You're not like the others," Preston told her. "You don't make fun of me."

Sarah immediately forgot herself in her concern for him. "They don't mean to hurt," she said, anxiously; "they just don't understand." Preston looked across at the pool where some of their contemporaries were playing and others made love in desultory fashion. Then he turned back to her.

"Do you understand?" he said. Sarah looked at him solemnly, then shook her head.

"I would like to," she said. "I don't believe what they say about you."

"What now?"

Sarah hesitated, then she shook her head. "I don't want to repeat it," she said. Preston stared down at his book for a moment, then back at Sarah's worried expression. "Preston . . . why do you do this thing?" she ventured at last.

"Read?"

"Yes."

"Because it's the only way of learning." Sarah's worried expression intensified.

"I don't understand," she said. "The Machines do everything for us. Why do you want to be different?"

"I don't know. Why do you keep coming back to me instead of preparing yourself like the others?"

Sarah looked down. "I don't know," she said quietly. "They think I'm silly not to enjoy my body."

"Perhaps you feel there's something missing from the Machine's recipe for ultimate happiness?"

She looked back at him, amazed. "How can the Machines be wrong? They know everything."

Preston paused for a moment. "Except what it feels like to be a human being," he said eventually.

They looked into each other's eyes for a long time, then bent toward one another slowly until their tongues touched delicately for a moment. Sarah sighed. "I love you," she said.

"Thank you." Preston sat back against the tree looking at her. "But don't you think it ought to mean something to say that?"

Sarah looked hurt. "I was only being polite," she protested.

"I know," he went on hurriedly, "the Machines taught us; but don't you feel any different when you say it to me?"

Sarah frowned. "I don't know," she said uncertainly.

Preston leaned forward again eagerly.

"I read that men and women lived together alone once and looked after each other."

"Without the Machines?"

"Yes. It seems strange, I know."

"How did they live? It's impossible to survive outside the Communities."

"They must have had some way," Preston said. "That's what I want to find out." Sarah shivered. "Are you cold?" he asked, but she shook her head.

"No. It's just that when you talk like this, it frightens me."

Preston paused, then he went on: "Once there were many more people, and hardly any Machines at all. They lived in great cities."

"New York is a city."

"Now it's only the name of our biggest Community; then it was a thousand times greater." He dropped his voice. "Then something happened, and nearly everyone died. The cities were destroyed too."

"Then it *is* much better now."

"I don't know." He looked at her strangely. "Sometimes I wake up in the middle of the night, as if someone had called my name. And . . . I feel . . . I almost know something everyone else has forgotten."

Suddenly some wet clothes hit him in the face, and Preston dropped the book in surprise. A group of young people had crept up on them and now moved forward, carrying them both toward the pool, laughing. Preston struggled and half managed to get free just as they reached the edge, but he lost his balance and fell in. Sarah submitted without a struggle.

When he surfaced Preston saw one of the youths standing on the edge of the pool holding his book.

"Preston, look . . . I've got your toy." Preston swallowed and tried to keep calm.

"Be careful," he warned, "water will destroy it."

"Mind. He looks angry," one of the others said.

"I'll be careful," said the first, laughing. "I won't drop it in by accident." And he winked at his friend.

"Don't be stupid!" Preston swam strongly for the edge.

"Oh, I won't."

He pulled himself out, then helped Sarah, but just as he pulled her clear, he heard a burst of laughter and turned to see the youth tearing the pages out of his book one by one and dropping them into the water.

"Stop it," he shouted furiously, and the others gave way as he rushed toward the one responsible, but the latter stood his ground, holding the book out over the pool.

"Don't come any further," he ordered.

Preston stopped, breathing hard, and Sarah came up behind him, putting her hand on his arm. "Don't," she begged, sensing his mood better than the others; but he did not hear her.

"Give it back to me," Preston said, his voice shaking, and one of the girls turned to the one who still held the book out over the water.

"You'd better do what he says," she advised, but the rest chortled with glee.

"Say . . . 'I'm mad,' " the boy with the book demanded after a few seconds. "Go on, say it." And he shook the book as if about to let go.

Preston watched in agony, knowing how long he

would have to wait to get another. He took a deep breath. "I'm mad," he said hoarsely.

Sarah tugged at his arm. "Come away," she pleaded; "it doesn't matter."

"I don't care if he does push me in," the youth boasted.

"Give it to me now . . . please," Preston said, but the other, conscious of the admiration of his friends, had not yet extracted all the fun to be had from the situation.

"Say . . . 'the Machines made a mistake about me,'" he demanded. At this his friends fell silent.

"Don't say it," Sarah begged.

But after a long pause, Preston said, "The Machines made a mistake."

"About me," the youth taunted.

"About me."

Sarah wheeled on his tormentor. "You're hateful," she stormed. "How could you make him say such a thing!"

"Well, he said it, didn't he?" the other said defiantly, but a little ashamed in spite of himself. Preston now held out his hand for the book, his face almost as white as the pages.

"Now give it to me," he said.

The youth hesitated, then said delicately, "No." And opened his hand so the book fell into the water.

Preston looked at it, then back to the one responsible, his eyes wide with disbelief. The others began to laugh but Sarah dived in at once, recovered the book and held it up to him.

"Preston. Here . . . take it," she called urgently. He turned slowly, then bent down to take it, but simultaneously the other youth came to life again and pushed him in. At this the rest doubled up laughing, but they stopped suddenly when Preston climbed out and they saw the expression on his face. His tormentor turned to escape, but Preston caught him among the trees and started to beat the life out of him with his fists.

The youth tried to defend himself but his eyes were wide with fright and the others ran screaming for the Machines. Sarah did her best to try to stop him, but Preston was almost insane with rage and battered the youth with repeated blows until he sank to the ground unconscious, with his back to the tree that had been acting as a chopping block. Sarah fell beside him to see what she could do. Then she glanced back at Preston, who looked drained of emotion, and past him—her eyes widened with horror. Preston started to turn, when suddenly he felt his arms pinned to his sides by flexible metal tentacles and he was conscious of a Machine towering over him.

What happened next was a nightmare he could only bring himself to think about many years later. Unable to move, he was carried to a building in that part of the Community where he knew the "adults" were housed, and there strapped to a self-propelled trolley with metal clamps. He was left alone in the room then for what must have been several hours. It began to get dark, then another Machine appeared and started to move around silently, apparently making preparations for a surgical operation.

"I order you to release me," Preston said desperately. But the Machine ignored him. "Don't you hear me?" he shouted. "Your program forbids you to harm a human being."

At this the Machine stopped and turned. "No one is going to harm you," it assured. "But you must be prevented from hurting others."

"You didn't see what happened."

"It doesn't matter. All we intend to do is advance your development a little early."

"What do you mean?" Preston asked, numb terror beginning to grip his throat.

"Calm yourself," the Machine replied.

"Tell me what you mean."

"You are about to become an adult," the Machine told him. "That is all."

Preston's mind whirled. "No!" he shouted, "I'm not ready!"

"It will be better for everyone."

"You can't do it to me until I ask!"

"It's unusual, I agree; but nothing in our program prevents granting the ultimate happiness whenever we consider it necessary. Now"—it looked around with apparent satisfaction—"everything is ready." It moved toward the inner door, which opened to let it through. The trolley followed automatically.

"No!" Preston shrieked at the top of his voice but it was no use.

The Machine led the way down the center of a long room resembling a large dormitory, with rows of couches on either side. On each lay a man or woman, the nearer ones in a state of ecstasy induced by wires which led from a socket in the wall beside each couch to terminals let directly into their skulls.

Preston looked from side to side in horror as the trolley proceeded down the center of the room toward the door at the far end and noticed, somewhere at the back of his mind, that each succeeding human being seemed older and progressively less active.

"Help!" he screamed. "Help me!"

The Machine paused and waited for the trolley to catch up. "Do not distress yourself," it said. "They are only conscious of the ultimate happiness. It is unfortunate that you are not fully prepared, but soon you will be content." It then proceeded on toward the door while Preston thrashed around uselessly, but with mounting desperation.

The bodies on the end couches had been there longest and were little more than living corpses. The doors at the far end opened and the Machine passed through into the operating theater followed by the trolley.

It came to rest in the middle of the room under a bank of lights and a few seconds later a high-pitched noise began. Preston found himself overwhelmed by sleep, and his eyes closed in spite of his fight to keep them open. Then, suddenly, all the lights except one small auxiliary lamp went out and the noise stopped. Preston awoke instantly.

"What's happened?" he said. "Where am I?" Then the horror came flooding back.

"Do not distress yourself," the Machine repeated. "There has been a power failure. I will go and see what has happened." It made for another door but had to push it open. As it went out, it turned slightly. "Do not hurt yourself," it advised.

In spite of this Preston struggled with renewed vigor as soon as he was left alone. A few seconds later a door opened slowly and Sarah slipped inside. She moved to his side at once but stood with her eyes closed and he realized how she must have been shocked by what she had just seen.

"Sarah!"

She opened her eyes and looked down at him. "I'm sorry."

"Please try to find some way of letting me go."

"Yes." She made a visible effort to pull herself together and began to try to force the clamps open with her bare hands.

"See if you can find something to break them with," Preston begged.

Sarah searched obediently around the room, but found nothing. "I can't see in this light." She almost wept.

"There's been a power failure. Quickly—they'll be back soon."

"I turned it off where I've seen them do it before." Almost before Sarah had finished speaking the lights came on again blinding them for an instant, and the high-pitched noise started again.

Preston gasped, "Move the trolley," feeling his conscious mind beginning to slip away. Sarah pushed for all she was worth and slowly managed to force it from under the bank of lights but the effort left her weak and breathless. "You'd better get out," he told her hopelessly. "They'll be back any minute."

"No. I can't let them do this to you. It's horrible."

"You shouldn't have come."

Sarah started to shake the trolley in helpless fury.

"Don't," Preston told her, trying desperately to master his own fear. "You must go now, Sarah, please."

Suddenly, the control panel caught her eye. "Wait," she panted. "I've got an idea!" Sarah started to press the buttons and throw all the switches one after the other. The lights went out again and shrieks of panic could be heard from the dormitory next door. Eventually the panel itself caught fire. Finally, the trolley hurled itself against the wall, but when it stopped the clamps flew open and Preston scrambled to his feet.

They hugged each other delightedly for a few seconds, then the far door burst open and the Machine reappeared; but Preston grabbed Sarah's wrist and half dragged her through the opposite door before it had time to react.

In the dormitory, people on the beds writhed in the semi-darkness, some screaming at the tops of their voices, but the two of them ran down the center aisle reaching the far end just as the door they had come through was pushed open by the Machine.

"Stop," it called after them. "You are causing great damage."

Preston tore open the door they had just reached only to find another Machine facing them, but this one clearly had no idea what had just happened and stood unmoving while they dodged past and across the preparation room to the outside door.

Once outside, Preston looked up and down the deserted, tree-lined avenue, then seizing Sarah's arm again pulled her to the left. "This way," he whispered urgently, and they both started to run for their lives. A few seconds later the door burst open again and both Machines shot out onto the road.

Once they reached the edge of the Community, Preston guided Sarah off the road into some trees. They ran a few more yards into a thicker part of the woods then rested behind some bushes trying to regain their breath.

"What are we going to do?" Sarah asked breathlessly.

"I'm going to leave."

"You can't!" She looked at him in despair, but he held a finger to his lips before she could say anything else.

Back on the road, the two Machines glided almost silently to the spot where they had left to run into the woods, then stopped.

"They have left the road here," one said.

"Should we send for a vehicle?"

"No. They are frightened enough already."

"That was a mistake."

"I know. I don't understand. We have never had that reaction before."

The other paused for a few seconds before commenting, "He was not prepared."

"Who was the female?" the companion said, ignoring the implications of the earlier remark.

"I don't know. It doesn't matter."

"Perhaps they will come back of their own accord?"

"I don't think so. More likely they will try to reach another Community."

"Then we must give warning to receive them gently."

"Yes." Then it went on more solemnly: "If they die outside it will be our fault. Then our programs will be altered."

The two Machines turned without another word and disappeared back down the road as silently as they had come.

The two young people who had listened to all this in an agony of suspense let their breath out slowly and Preston ventured a first smile.

"They've gone," he said after making sure first, but still very quietly.

"You heard what they said," she whispered. "You'll die outside."

"That's what they think."

"Even if you reach another Community, they'll be waiting for you."

"I'm not going to another Community," he told her. Sarah's eyes widened even further. "I'd almost made up my mind to leave before this happened," Preston went on. "Now I'm certain. I'm going to live in the old way . . . looking after myself."

"But you don't know how," she gasped.

"Yes, I do. The books have shown me."

Sarah looked at him a long time before speaking; then she came to a decision.

"You said it needed a man *and* a woman," she whispered. Preston looked at her, scarcely breathing; then he nodded.

"Yes." They continued to look at each other until Sarah smiled tentatively and nodded back slowly. Then Preston gathered her into his arms and they held each other for a long time, until he pushed her away again gently so he could look into her eyes.

"But how do you know the others aren't right?" he asked humbly. "Maybe I am mad!"

Sarah looked up at him, then said simply, "I think you can look after me."

Preston felt tears rush into his eyes. "I'll try," he said, as soon as he could; and when they held each other again very close he whispered, "I really will try."

## CHAPTER THREE

Preston and Sarah scrambled up the last few feet below the ridge, then stood on the crest, hand in hand, looking at the view which stretched out in front of them in the morning sunshine.

Both carried bundles of clothing and Preston had a few battered volumes tied around with a piece of rag.

The hill sloped down gently to what appeared at first sight to be an empty plain covered with waving grass. A forest bordered the plain on the left, and in the far distance the sea glinted gold and blue. They stood together in silence for a while, then Sarah turned to him.

"It's very big," she said, her voice faltering slightly. Preston nodded.

"It's the real world," he told her.

"Is it dangerous?"

"I don't think so." Then he added more truthfully, "I don't know."

Sarah looked back at the view. "It's frightening," she said breathlessly after a moment longer, "but it makes me feel something inside."

"It's beautiful."

"What is beautiful?"

Preston glanced down at her, and smiled gently. "You're beautiful," he said, then he looked back. "And so is that. It's all part of the same thing."

Sarah hugged his arm, and rested her head for a moment against him. "What does it mean?" she said.

"I don't know. Perhaps we'll find out."

They stood together in silence again for nearly a minute, Sarah shading her eyes to look into the distance, but Preston's attention was caught by the ruins of a small stone building not far from the edge of the forest.

"What's that?" Sarah asked as she pointed to the horizon. Preston followed her gaze.

"That's the sea," he told her. He paused, then grinned. "A lot of water, like a big pool."

"Oh."

"I'll show you later. Look down there." He pointed at the ruins.

"What is it?"

"I think it's an old building."

"All by itself?" Sarah frowned.

"Yes. Why not? Come on. Let's have a look at it." They started to walk down the slope toward it, but as they rounded a shoulder of the hill, they came upon a family of wild cattle. Preston held up his hand at once and they froze in their tracks. The bull took a few steps toward them out of curiosity, then stopped and grunted at them. Sarah turned to run but Preston grabbed her. "No!" he hissed fiercely.

"Let me go!" she gasped in terror.

"Stand still! If you show you're afraid they'll come after us."

"But they're horrible! They'll kill us!"

Preston shook his head, then smiled. "No, they won't," he said. "They're only wild cattle." He looked back at them. "They used to be tame once."

"Those things!" Sarah said incredulously.

"Yes. Stand still. I'm going to try something." So saying, he started to move forward slowly toward them while Sarah watched, awestruck. The bull snorted and Preston stopped. Then he started to move forward again and held out his hand. The bull looked at him uncertainly, then it tossed its head, showing the whites of its eyes and turning to make off. The cows and calves obediently fell in behind. Preston gave a whoop of glee and charged after them shouting.

After a second's hesitation, Sarah dropped her things and joined him. So they chased the cattle until they disappeared into the distance in a cloud of dust, then both of them collapsed on the ground laughing helplessly.

At last Preston recovered and stood up to help the girl back onto her feet. Then, still smiling, they went back hand in hand to pick up their things.

Soon they reached the outside of what proved to be a deserted stone cottage and, leaving their bundles outside the front entrance, walked inside to explore. The walls were substantially intact, but the roof was missing.

There were three rooms: one had a large fireplace which Preston examined interestedly, but Sarah looked around doubtfully. "Could we live here?" she asked, unconsciously lowering her voice.

Preston turned from the fireplace. "I don't see why not," he said. "It's very old. I don't suppose anyone's lived here for hundreds of years."

Sarah looked up at the open sky. "Perhaps we could get some branches from the trees in the forest?" she suggested. Preston smiled.

"That's a good idea," he said. "We can soon repair the walls."

They stood for a few more seconds, then Sarah took his hand and ventured softly, "But won't it be cold?"

Preston looked at her, then shook his head. "We'll have a fire," he said impressively.

"How?"

"I took a torch from the Machines' repair shop when I went back."

Before it got dark, the two of them had collected enough branches and leaves from the nearby woods to make a temporary roof over the room with the fireplace, and true to his word, Preston managed to build a log fire. Even so, it was a clear night and the temperature dropped so quickly they had to put on all the clothes they had brought with them. Then they sat on the floor in front of the fire and shared a bar of compressed protein he had also stolen when he went back before they had finally made their escape.

After eating contentedly together in silence for a while, Preston said: "Are you glad you came?" Sarah nodded, smiling. "I was silly to think I could have done it on my own," he went on.

"I wouldn't have let you go by yourself," she said. "No."

They finished the food, looking into the fire, occasionally glancing at each other.

"Do you want any more?" he asked. Sarah shook her head. He looked at her, then suddenly he said: "It was different for me. I knew what I was doing."

Sarah frowned for a few seconds before smiling again. "I knew you," she said simply. "You were different."

They looked into each other's eyes. "I love you, Sarah," Preston said quietly.

"I love you."

"It's not the same, is it?" Sarah shook her head slowly, and they bent forward to kiss each other.

"I'm tired," she said a moment later. "Can we sleep now?"

Preston nodded and put his arm around her; then they lay down together, close by the fire.

After a while Sarah whispered: "What will we live on, when the food we have brought has gone?"

"You'll see." He turned to her and smiled. "Starting tomorrow."

Sarah snuggled against him contentedly and they looked up at the temporary ceiling where the fire made shadows dance. Then they both fell asleep.

The following day, Preston took Sarah back into the forest and she waited while he picked some blackberries. After trying one himself, he grinned and held out the rest. Sarah took one and put it into her mouth a little warily, but a few seconds later she closed her eyes with pleasure.

"Mmm. Lovely!" she said. Then they burst out laughing and started to eat greedily until the juice ran down their chins.

Later, Preston climbed a nut tree and made Sarah stand underneath to catch the nuts while he shook them down to her. When he dropped to the ground she had already tried one without waiting for him, and without any of the suspicion which had greeted the fruit.

And so the day went by with the boy leading the girl from one tree or bush to another, until the early afternoon when they reached some wild apple trees near the edge of the forest where both of them jumped to catch the lower branches and swung backward and forward until a shower of unripe fruit cascaded to the ground; but as soon as each of them had taken a bite, their expression simultaneously turned to disgust.

"Ugh!" Sarah threw hers away at once, but Preston examined his.

"I don't think it's ripe," he announced.

"Ripe?"

"It's not ready to eat yet. Not old enough."

"I don't want any more anyway," Sarah said, shaking her head. "I'm full."

"There are trees like this near to the house," Preston told her. "Later in the year, when it's nearly winter, we'll be able to eat them, without having so far to go."

Sarah looked around and sighed contentedly. "Let's go back now," she said.

"All right." Preston nodded, then bent down to pick up a bunch of wild parsnip. He took her hand and they walked the remaining few yards to the edge of the wood. Sarah glanced down at the things in his hand.

"What did you say you were going to do with them?" she asked.

"Cook them. Put them in hot water from the fire. They'll be nice. You'll see." Sarah made a face.

"They look horrible," she said.

They paused for a moment when they came out of the trees, watching the waves of grass rolling across the plain, then suddenly Preston gave a shout and, letting go of Sarah's hand, ran forward.

"Sarah . . . look!" he called out, and bent over a patch of bewhiskered wild barley growing some twenty yards away. It was short and growing very thinly, but barley just the same.

"What is it?" she said without bothering to follow him.

"Come and see for yourself."

After a few seconds, Sarah wandered over languidly. "I'm sleepy," she said. "Let's go back."

"Look at this first!" He pulled an unripe head toward her, and she looked at it without interest.

"It's only grass," she said.

"Yes, but it's a special kind. You see these whiskers? That means it's barley. We can make bread out of it when it's ripe."

"Everything has to be ripe!" Sarah said, making a face. "The Machines could make bread whenever they wanted."

"Well, I'm not a Machine."

"You sound like one sometimes!"

Preston looked at her. "What do you mean?" he said sharply. Sarah shrugged.

"The way you keep talking about waiting for things to be ready. It sounds like the way they used to talk about preparing us to be adults."

Preston straightened up. His face had gone very white.

"Don't say that!" His voice shook with anger. "Didn't you see those people?"

"Yes."

"It was horrible!"

"But they asked to be made like that," Sarah said defensively.

"I don't care. I want to forget. Don't ever speak of it again."

Sarah looked at him, alarmed. "All right," she said eventually. "I'm sorry. Please go on. What were you saying?"

After what was to her an agonizing few seconds, Preston bent down again and the color began to return to his cheeks.

"Look," he said gruffly. "I'll show you something wonderful." He tore off the ear from one of the stalks and rubbed it between his hands; the grains did not separate easily but well enough. "These are seeds," he said, turning to show her. "When they're ripe, you can put them in the ground and a whole

lot more will appear." Sarah looked at him in astonishment.

"Out of the ground?" she said.

"Yes. Much more than you put in. So much, you
can eat most of it and need only save a very little
to start again."

Sarah laughed in amazement. "That's something
the Machines couldn't do!" He shook his head and
smiled.

"No," he said. "But you'll see. We'll come back
in the autumn and collect them all so we can put
them in the ground nearer to the house."

"Then we shall always have enough to eat," Sarah
said.

"Yes."

They heard a thundering sound behind them and
turned to see a group of wild horses galloping into
sight, led by a gray stallion.

"What are they?" Sarah whispered excitedly.

Preston didn't answer, but watched spellbound as
the leader tore past them quite close, followed by
the group, which contained several young colts.
The stallion stopped about fifty yards away on the
top of a slight rise in the ground; he looked briefly
in their direction, whinnied, then charged off again
with flashing hooves and tossing mane, his wives
and children charging after him. Suddenly, as if
caught by the same spirit, Sarah struck Preston's
hand from underneath so the grains of barley flew
high into the wind, then she raced away along the
edge of the wood. After recovering from his surprise, Preston shouted with glee and set off in pursuit, but he was amazed at how fast she could run.

He really had to exert himself, but was just about to catch her when Sarah suddenly changed direction and plunged back into the trees. Preston followed and found her waiting for him with her back to the trunk of a tree. He rushed forward and put one hand against the trunk on either side of her so she could not escape, but the next instant she threw her arms around his neck and kissed him passionately, straining her body to his.

They set up house together and throughout the summer lived easily on the food they found in the forest. Preston discovered a stream deep enough to swim in half a mile north of the house; here they went on hot afternoons when Sarah had finished her housework, and it was too exhausting to go on with the garden which now surrounded the house and which they increased by a few yards each day. After cooling their bodies in the water, they would lie on the grassy bank, and sometimes they would make love passionately, and sometimes tenderly; and both of them were very happy.

At the end of an Indian summer, Preston at last picked one of the apples from the nearest tree to the cottage, judging it to be ripe, and took it inside for Sarah to try. He didn't find her in the front room, which they had also turned into a kitchen, so he pushed open the inner door and went through into the bedroom, where he found her lying face downward on their bed. He went to her side and knelt down quietly, holding the apple by its stalk so she could see it as soon as she turned her head.

"Are you asleep?" he whispered. "Look, I've got

a present for you." Sarah stirred without looking up.

"What is it?" she said, her voice muffled.

"See for yourself. You can eat it now. Look!"

Sarah sniffed, and after a few seconds turned around. She had obviously been crying but he was so taken with the apple he did not notice. He put it in her hand and she took a bite; then, after chewing for a while, she swallowed and nodded. "It's very nice."

Preston took it from her. "Very nice. Is that all?" He took a huge bite and munched contentedly. "It's delicious," he said, grinning through the apple. Then he noticed her expression and the smile faded at once. "What's wrong?" he said.

Sarah tried to brush the tears away. "I'm going to have a baby," she said. Her voice shook slightly.

"A baby!" Preston repeated stupidly.

"Yes." She looked at him, exasperation mastering her fear for the moment. "It's not so surprising, is it?"

"No, but . . . How will we . . ." His words petered out as the implications grew on him.

"We should have thought of it before," Sarah said hopelessly, and suddenly her features contorted as she tried not to weep.

"Preston . . . I'm frightened!"

He took her in his arms and held her silently for a long time, then he said quietly, "You'll have to go back." Sarah looked up at him quickly.

"Back where?" she said.

"To the Community. So the Machines can look after you safely."

"Is that what you want?"

"Of course not, but it wouldn't be safe to have the baby here."

Sarah hesitated before asking, "How did women have their babies before the Machines?"

Preston shook his head. "I don't know," he told her.

"Their husbands must have looked after them," Sarah went on.

"I suppose so."

"Then you must look after me." She turned back to him.

"But . . ."

"I can't help being afraid," she interrupted, "but I trust you."

Preston looked down; suddenly he found it difficult to say anything at all, and Sarah put out her hand to him, forgetting her own fear. "Don't look like that," she whispered; "we'll just have to look after him ourselves."

After a few seconds, Preston looked up with a wry smile. "What makes you think it's going to be a boy?" he asked.

"I just know," she said softly. "And we'll call him Jem."

"I never heard that name before."

Sarah smiled. "It just came to me," she said. "He'll be born in the spring."

The Indian summer came to an abrupt end. First with days of rain, then biting winds that tore the remaining leaves from the trees. For a while, Preston and Sarah continued to live well enough on the food they collected during the summer, but it did not last as long as he had planned, and soon the snow began to cover everything. A month later, the last of the food ran out and they began to starve.

Preston dragged the bed into the kitchen and put it in front of the fire. Here they would at least keep warm as long as he had strength enough to go out for more wood, but Sarah was soon so weak she could hardly stand and became more emaciated each day as the child growing inside her consumed what reserves she had left.

The day had begun the same as any other, with Preston going out to get some wood for the fire and boiling the bark which he had stripped off some trees the previous afternoon. This "soup" did little to nourish them but he felt sure that without it they would have been dead more than a week ago. As it was, he found it increasingly more difficult to drag himself out each day, but he knew that once he was too weak to keep the fire going their end would come quickly. Preston sat looking into the fire thinking, occasionally glancing in the direction of the girl who dozed fitfully on the bed. Sometimes he almost wished they could die quickly so the agony would be over.

The morning passed, and the early part of the afternoon, until it was time for him to go out again for wood and to bring some more bark for the following day. Preston got up and put the last log on the fire, then he started to wrap himself in his outdoor winter clothes. Sarah opened her eyes and looked up.

"Where are you going?" She asked weakly.

"Just outside," he told her, but she shook her head.

"Don't go," she whispered. "At least stay in the warm. It's not worth it."

Preston looked down at her, and suddenly the apathy into which he had been sinking during the past few days was stripped aside and he felt the desperate need to do something for her. She was here because she had put her trust in him. He could not let her die.

"I've got to try," he said abruptly, and turned for the door without knowing what he could do that he had not done before, but determined to go on trying until he died in the attempt.

"Don't be long," Sarah called after him. "I hate it when you're not here."

"I won't be long," he promised, and went out, closing the door behind him.

Once outside, the cold gripped him as if he had been plunged naked into a tank of cold water, and the shock almost stopped his breath; then he began to shiver, and this involuntary action opened the capillaries of his skin, holding back the cold. Preston picked up the stick with the sharp pointed end for stripping off the bark and trudged off in the direction of the forest.

He moved from one tree and bush to another seeking yet again any trace of food he might have overlooked before, probing the snow desperately with his stick, but there was nothing. Finally he sank to his knees in exhaustion, his eyes closed.

When he had been in this position for a while, Preston suddenly heard a shriek from a few yards further into the wood and this, in all probability, saved him from dying of exposure then and there.

He rose to his feet in alarm and looked around; then, after a few seconds' hesitation, moved warily in the direction of the sound.

He arrived at a small clearing just in time to see a fox making off with a dead hare in its mouth. He stared at the blood and the bits of fur on the snow, then a fantastic idea began to form in his mind. He looked down in wonder at the stick which he still carried, then turned on his heel and hurried back to the edge of the forest.

Preston emerged from the trees and surveyed the snow-covered plain; then he froze as he saw a small herd of wild cattle, so far away there were only black dots on the snow; but even at this distance, he could see the group included a young heifer, who probably could not run as fast as the others.

They allowed him to get within fifty yards before starting to move away and at once Preston broke into a run. Almost immediately he tripped and fell into the snow, but picked himself up and continued, throwing into the chase all his reserves of energy, knowing that if he was unsuccessful now he would never manage to get back.

The older cattle outdistanced him easily and so would the heifer, but by some miracle she stopped and looked back. Preston got within five yards before she made off again and, seeing her start to draw away, he threw the club as hard as he could. He missed her head, but she tripped over the club and fell to the ground. Preston flung himself upon her with a cry and seized her around the neck with his left arm. In spite of this, the animal struggled to her feet but he managed to pull her down again and this time near enough to snatch up the pointed stick and plunge it into her neck. The heifer threw him off, but when she stood up blood was pouring down her sides onto the snow. The stick fell to the ground but Preston snatched it up and his next blow killed the dazed animal outright.

He stood panting for a long time, looking down at the gory mess he had made of such a beautiful creature; then he retched, but his stomach was empty.

When he recovered, Preston staggered back to the cottage to get a knife. When he returned the next time, his arms were full of food, enough to keep them for the next two weeks.

As Sarah had predicted, the child was born in the spring.

Preston leaned over the bed where she lay. There was little he could do but bathe his wife's face from time to time and he felt thoroughly frightened, but in between the spasms of pain she seemed completely sure of herself. After what seemed an eternity, it was over.

Preston picked up the child and put it into her arms. Almost immediately, it began to cry and Sarah looked up at him, her eyes shining.

"Jem!" she breathed. Preston nodded, smiling with joy and relief.

Sarah looked at the baby, then up at him again. "Fetch some warm water so I can wash him," she told him. He hurried to do as she asked, but when he reached the kitchen, he let out an uncontrollable whoop of joy. Sarah smiled. "Quietly," she called after him, and was amused by his readiness to do as he was told. She knew it would not last for long!

Later that afternoon, Sarah slept with the baby tucked up beside her. Preston watched for a while then, unable to stay still and be quiet, he tiptoed out of the front door.

The melting snow had almost disappeared and the front of the cottage was bathed in sunshine. He looked around, not knowing quite what to do with himself, when he suddenly noticed a haze of green over the barley patch where only two days before had been bare earth. He rushed forward to look more closely, then bent down and lovingly fingered the new shoots.

"It works! It really works!" he shouted; he stood up and called out: "Sarah," and dashed back in through the front door calling her name again; but he stopped at once, seeing she was still asleep. For a few seconds Preston looked at his wife and son sleeping peacefully, then he turned and went out, shutting the door behind him quietly.

He paused for a few seconds, but suddenly he felt himself caught up in a tidal wave of emotion and began to run away from the cottage, leaping into the air and laughing. He ran to a rise in the ground some hundred yards from the house and stopped on the top, out of breath, looking around.

In front of him, the land stretched into the blue distance. The wind blew the grass in waves across the sea of the plain, and the shadows of individual clouds raced toward him.

His mood began to change. The laughter faded and he looked around again in wonder. Everything was the same, but different; he felt for the first time the presence of someone waiting patiently for his understanding. Hardly knowing what he was doing, Preston raised both arms high above his head and put his head back to shout at the sky.

"Father!"

The clouds seemed to race toward him even faster, and Preston followed them with his eyes to the horizon, slowly lowering his arms to his sides. Then he saw out on the plain, standing almost at the focus of the wind, the tall figure of a man.

The stranger stood waiting while the boy walked toward him—not looking at Preston at first—but when he was less than twenty yards away, the other turned to look at him directly and smiled.

Preston froze, his heart almost stopped with awe, for there was something about the other which was both human—yet more so: a quality of goodness he felt he could amost reach out and touch. Power was there too, beyond his understanding, and a sense of authority he knew instinctively to be entirely without human arrogance.

"Preston." The stranger held out a hand toward him. "Do not be afraid. My name is Vicro."

# CHAPTER FOUR

At the end of thirty years, Vicro told Preston to build a high stockade around the site he had chosen for the work of construction. At first only Preston and his family, and those who had followed their example, were available, but the hills surrounding the New England valley were rich in timber and the twenty-foot-high fence was nearly half-finished before the others began to arrive.

There were to be just over ten thousand of them in all. Everybody knew, because Vicro had said so, but some had to travel from the other side of the world. The drought would not begin until the last of them were safely inside, but time was short and work on the ships that were to carry them to safety must begin as soon as possible.

It was now mid-May. The day had started chilly with a mist rising from the floor of the valley and decorating the still half-leafed branches of the beech trees with garlands of dew, but Ham, Preston's second son, had been in charge of the gang which had worked through the early part of the night so it was nearly eleven o'clock by the time he woke up, and the sun, having brushed aside the morning haze, was beginning to bake the ground hard, making it more difficult to drill fresh holes for the new trunks.

Ham looked up at the bare wood ceiling. The room was in one of the many hastily erected rest buildings which had been sited as far away as possible from the area cleared for construction of the ships. By training he was a mathematician, which would make him invaluable to the safety of the fleet later, but now he was only useful for his contribution to the unremitting grind of cutting down trees, dragging them into position and sinking them deep into the earth so that, when the time came, they would stand firm against the tide of desperation which would threaten to engulf the few who had listened. At first, he had fallen into bed every night almost faint with fatigue and aching from head to foot in muscles he never knew until then he even possessed; but it was the same for everyone and there were to be no exceptions, not that Ham would have had it otherwise. In time their bodies had hardened and, as he worked most of the day stripped to the waist, his skin had become the color of polished bronze. When he awoke now, he felt marvelous.

Although fully alert from the moment he opened his eyes, Ham liked to allow himself the luxury of a few minutes of stretching slowly and enjoying the feeling of sheer animal well-being. His eyes ran quickly over the rest of the room, all of which was of the same rough and temporary nature as the ceiling. There was very little furniture, and what there was had been largely improvised. If he had awakened in the room without having seen it before, he might have imagined he had traveled back in time, as far, perhaps, as the second millennium, whose video recordings had somehow survived, to the time when men had feared death by war rather than boredom.

Everything in the room was a bare necessity—they were to leave so soon there was little point in anything else—everything, that is, except the large mirror which he had rescued from their house near the farm where he had been born and where he had spent his childhood with his two brothers Jem and Jacy. Ham had taken it originally from one of the Communities which had fallen into disuse when its human inhabitants had died out and the Machines had moved elsewhere. He had carried it back carefully to the house he had been building so that he and Valla could have a place of their own, and fitted it against the wall to one side of the window just over the low chest of drawers. He had made a stool out of some logs and the bottom of a large round wooden carton, which had once contained artificial butter, then he had sat on the stool in front of the mirror to test the whole arrangement for size and alignment. Only then had he allowed Valla into the room to see what he had done for her.

Ham had realized the whole thing was crude in the extreme, but when he saw her surprise and happiness, and when she fetched her brushes and put them on the chest of drawers in front of the mirror, just like the real dressing table the Machines had given her in the Community where she had been brought up, he had felt as proud of it as anything he had done in his whole life.

Valla—one thought led to another, and now he turned to look at her, still sleeping peacefully beside him. With the elimination of disease, beauty in woman was not uncommon; but even so, Valla was beautiful in a way that never ceased to surprise him, or make his heart turn over whenever she walked toward him with that easy swinging stride of hers. She had as much reason to be tired at the end of the day as he—working with Sarah to help the dozens of newcomers still arriving daily to settle in—but, like her husband, Valla spent most of her time out of doors, and if she was beautiful before, the early summer sun had also done its best by turning her light brown hair the color of pale honey and her skin to gold. The blinds were drawn but Ham could hear the pulsating sounds of activity in the distance. He ought to be getting up but when he looked at her again, he longed to stay by her side just a few moments longer.

Valla slept on her back with one hand above her head. The breeze had blown a wisp of hair across her face and after a few seconds Ham put out his hand and delicately brushed it away so that it would not go into her eyes. He looked at his watch, then bent down and kissed her gently on the forehead. For a moment her expression remained unchanged then he saw the beginning of a smile.

"Valla, it's no good," he whispered. "I know you're awake."

Valla changed her position slightly and answered without opening her eyes.

"What time is it?"

"Eleven o'clock."

Valla's eyes snapped open in alarm.

"It's all right," he hastened to assure her. "We worked late. Remember?" Valla sighed.

"Oh, yes!"

Ham waited a few seconds, then he said: "Are you hungry?" Valla didn't answer at once but she turned to him.

"Only for you," she whispered. Ham took her in his arms and they kissed; then he held her close to him, but after a few seconds he felt her whole body shaking, and realized with surprise that she was laughing.

"What's so funny?" he demanded. Valla tried to stop.

"I just remembered something your brother Jacy said yesterday."

"What?"

"He said if Alison got any more freckles she'd look like an over-ripe apple."

Ham frowned. "What's so funny about that?" he said.

"It wasn't what he said so much, it was the way he said it." Ham snorted. "You know how he can make faces," she went on.

"Jacy has a clever tongue but he's not always as kind as he might be."

"Alison didn't mind. She laughed with the rest of us."

"She's too good-natured."

"I know. He doesn't deserve her." Valla looked at him. "Any more than I deserve you." Ham smiled in spite of himself.

"Don't be silly," he said and bent down to give

her a quick kiss. Then he swung his legs over the side of the bed and padded across to the window.

"It's a lovely day," he said after a few seconds, "but it means the ground will be hard again." Valla sat up, smiling.

"Why do you become embarrassed whenever I say something nice?" she teased.

"Because it isn't true," he retorted.

"Does that matter so much?"

"Yes." Ham went on watching the scene outside. Everywhere he looked trees were being felled and dragged manually or by horses toward the last gap where dozens of others were digging holes in the ground to take the remaining trunks. There was a small lake in the center of the compound which was fed by an underground stream and acted as a reservoir.

The area enclosed by the stockade was two square miles. This was necessary for, in addition to the human inhabitants, it contained a thousand animals, mostly domestic but numbering at least two of every other species they had been able to collect. Observation towers had been built at eight points along the perimeter of the fence and catwalks were being constructed just below the top of the inside to facilitate defense, but the largest area inside the enclosed space was still unoccupied, for here the twenty ships needed would be built.

Valla got out of bed and came up behind her husband, putting her arms around him.

"Well, it so happens it is true," she said. Ham looked down at her, puzzled, having forgotten the thread of their conversation. Valla rested her head against him and went on: "You're worth more than all the rest of us put together." Ham turned and took her into his arms.

"You shouldn't say things like that," he said.

She smiled up at him. "I thought you didn't mind if it was true." But Ham shook his head.

"There's only one person who's worth all the rest of us put together."

"Father? But he couldn't manage without the three of you."

"You forget how things have changed. When he and Mother started, there was nothing." Ham shrugged. "Everyone thought he was mad, but by the time we were old enough to help, the farm already existed; animals had been retamed, and several others had already followed his example."

Valla frowned slightly. "Not enough," she said; then she went back to the other side of the room and began to dress.

"Without him there would be no chance at all," Ham pointed out.

"How do you know?"

"Because Vicro said so." Valla didn't answer immediately and when she did, she avoided looking at him directly.

"Nobody else has ever seen Vicro," she said. "We've only got your father's word for it."

Ham looked at her sharply. "Valla!"

"All right, I'm sorry. I suppose I believe, really. But it's more difficult for the rest of us."

Ham went and sat on the edge of the bed looking at her. "I don't understand," he admitted. "I just know Father is right. He always has been."

"Most of the time."

"What do you mean?"

"He's not right the way he favors Jem at your expense."

"Jem is the eldest," Ham said reasonably. "It's natural for a man to value his firstborn above all others."

"And your mother dotes on Jacy, her youngest." Valla told him.

"Perhaps."

"But I say he's wrong. You'll be the one who will most truly follow in his footsteps, and take his place when the time comes."

"I don't want to take anyone's place," Ham said.

"I know that, but you'll see. As far as Jem's concerned, your father's blind." Ham stood up again.

"I don't like it when you talk like this," he said. "You forget how he's worked for us all our lives. Even when we were old enough to help him more, he made us go into the City, to the old library so we could learn. Even then he must have known we should need that knowledge one day." Valla began to brush her hair.

"I never went to the City," she said, thoughtfully. "Now I never will."

Ham began to dress. "It wasn't pleasant," he said after a few moments. "But it was necessary. There were people there who dominated the Machines; but not in a good way. They left us alone, though they thought we were crazy."

"Like they thought Preston was when he went to warn them."

"Yes, and they threw him out; but somehow the

word spread to those who would listen in spite of it all."

Valla paused for a moment then she said, "I was lucky. I don't think I would have been any different if I hadn't met you."

"We are all lucky."

Valla smiled. "Except Alison," she said.

Ham paused, then nodded briefly. "Yes. She was the only one to set off on the same path completely by herself. That's why Father thinks so much of her."

"What she saw in Jacy, I'll never understand!"

The young man concerned, short but quite good-looking, stood under a tree in another part of the compound lecturing a group of twenty young men and women with the aid of a diagram of a wiring circuit and a pointing stick. Alison moved among them, demonstrating what he was saying with pieces of an electric motor.

"It's difficult for most of you who were brought up in the Communities," he was saying impressively, "but you must remember that although the Machines perfected the science of electronics in some respects, there were whole fields they ignored completely." One young man raised his hand.

"Sir, how can we hope to learn enough in the time left to be of any help?" he asked.

Jacy smiled a little patronizingly. "We know you can't learn much before work on the ships must begin," he said. "But you can still be of considerable help."

"There are so few of us," Alison put in, "even if

you just understand what's meant when we want a particular thing done . . ."

"Exactly," Jacy interrupted. "Just what I was going to say. When we know what's required ourselves, we'll break the work down into simple stages."

"But we must all be able to speak the same language technically," Alison finished for him. Jacy looked at her irritatedly, then another young man put up his hand.

"Sir, what I don't understand is how Vicro is going to bring the things we need when the stockade is finished."

"They will be brought in ships similar to the ones we are to build," Jacy told him.

Up on the ridge overlooking the compound Preston and Sarah stood together watching a large pine tree quiver under the annihilating blows of an ax before crashing to the ground.

Sarah turned to her husband. "It always makes me feel sad," she said quietly.

Preston looked down at her and smiled. In middle age, the contrast between them was even more marked for he had filled out into a bull of a man who towered over everyone except Jem, his eldest son. His face was rugged but handsome and crowned by a mop of iron-gray hair. By contrast, Sarah was almost frail. Her eyes were still beautiful and her face had acquired a serenity with the years. When she spoke her voice was strong and her menfolk listened to her with respect: they had reason, for she was the first woman to take up again her responsibilities as a wife and a mother. But her life had been hard and it had sapped her strength.

A man came hurrying up. "Sir," he said urgently, inclining his head at the same time to Sarah, "we have hit some rock." He pointed in the direction of the stockade.

"And you want me to fix up one of my levers?" Preston asked.

"As soon as possible, please." He paused for a moment, then added, "The people are afraid the drought will begin before our defenses are ready."

Preston put a hand on his shoulder. "Don't distress yourself," he said. "Vicro promised the drought would not begin until we could defend ourselves." Then he glanced briefly at Sarah. When she nodded he took her hand and together the three of them started down the track. "I may not be as ingenious as my sons," Preston said with a grin, "but I think I've learned a thing or two."

"Without you, there would be no hope," the man said earnestly; but Preston shook his head.

"It was God's will," he said, "not mine. Just as it is that the drought will not begin until the stockade is finished." The man looked up at him.

"Then Vicro will come again?" he asked, and Preston nodded reassuringly.

"Yes, then he will come bringing materials and plans so we can build the ships we need to carry us away from here to a new Earth."

## CHAPTER FIVE

On one of the catwalks a young man wound a device which emitted a high-pitched wailing sound. Jem stood beside him, dressed for battle. He was a younger version of his father and closely resembled him but was even taller and physically more impressive. Beside anyone else, he was a veritable god of a man, and knew it.

On hearing the warning, the defenders ran to their appointed weapons racks, which were placed in strategic positions throughout the compound, and snatched up the sharpened wooden poles which would act as spears. The able-bodied men ran toward the stockade and climbed the catwalks while the young women and older men also armed themselves but made for the center of the compound as did the older children. The rest, consisting of old people and young children also hurried to the center but without collecting weapons, and there they were surrounded by a double row of those others, who thus formed an inner sanctuary.

Jem strode along the top of the catwalk urging those not already in position to hurry, while Ham marshaled one of the two reserve forces consisting of a hundred young men into an area in the center of the eastern half of the camp.

Jem looked at his watch. The shouting began to

die down and the warning sound faded. From where he stood, he could see that everyone was now in his place, even the youngest child motionless and silent, waiting. He turned and looked along the nearest row of defenders.

"Just under two minutes," he called out. One of the defenders turned around, smiling. It was Preston who nodded approvingly.

"Not bad for a practice," he said, and Jem suddenly grinned boyishly. Then he raised his spear high above his head and shouted so that the whole camp could hear him in the silence.

"Stand down!" At once the tension collapsed in talk and laughter as everybody went back to their work.

As the ranks of defenders broke up, only Valla remained looking in the direction of Jem, her lips parted. After a while he became aware of her gaze even from the distance and turned to look back. Seeing he had noticed her, Valla closed her eyes and took a deep breath.

About a year ago he had almost stumbled over her sunbathing in the woods beyond the farm. She had made a bed for herself in the bracken and had been half asleep, lulled by the warmth of the sun, the drone of insects and the song of birds calling to each other in the depths of the wood. He had stood looking down at her, his breath stopped.

When his shadow had fallen across her face, Valla had opened her eyes quickly to see who it was.

"Jem!" She let out her breath, then smiled. "You startled me."

"I'm sorry." But he had not returned her smile. Instead his eyes had consumed her lightly clad body.

Valla had looked up at him. Her smile faded and she got to her feet. "Don't look at me like that. It frightens me."

"I can't help it," Jem had answered. "I'm in torment."

Their eyes had locked together and, without looking, he had sensed the soft warmth of her skin, and her breath which raced now to match his own. They had been drawn together slowly as if by a magnet until, at the last second, Valla had suddenly put out a hand.

"No!"

The word itself had pierced him like a dagger, then she had turned and run away through the trees out of sight, afraid to look back.

Jem had dragged himself back to the farm. They had not seen each other again for two days, and when they did meet there was no change in her outward behavior, but from then on he was aware that Valla made sure never to be left alone with him again.

When the pain of his longing for her became too great, a love he could scarcely admit to himself, let alone his family, Jem would escape to one of the Communities, and there forget himself for a few hours with one of the many young women who were flattered to be chosen by the tall red-headed stranger whose skin was burned by the sun and whose muscles were iron from work in his father's fields; but when the fire of love-making had burned itself out and the girl had laid by his side half dead with the strength of him, the longing would return as strongly as ever.

That night, Preston called a meeting of all those to whom he could look for immediate help in the task of building the ships themselves. This included his family as well as Simon Bryant and most of the other Scots who had come from one of the outer islands which had escaped both the ravages of old wars and the subsequent care of the Machines; it also included David, the only son of one of the first couples to follow Preston and Sarah's example. They had been killed when a storm blew a tree down on their house; the boy himself was staying over at Preston's farm at the time.

As his father talked, Jem glanced in Valla's direction but she pretended not to notice.

"The last of the ten thousand has arrived, and the stockade will be completed by dusk tomorrow," Preston told them. "After that it will be impossible for anyone to get in or out—but that doesn't matter: we have an ample supply of food and water to last until the twenty ships are completed."

At this a murmur ran through those listening. Preston paused to look around before going on: "Most of us gathered around this fire now are the lucky ones. Fortunate enough, for one reason or another, not to have lived under the suffocating care of the Machines or, perhaps worse, in the shadow of what remains of once great cities; it is to us the rest must look to bear the major burden.

"Each of us has some skill vital to the construction of the ships that will carry us away from here,"

Preston continued; "to the flight itself, or to the beginning of our new life when everything is left behind and we have to rely completely on our own resources. And remember this, our burden may be greater because, in addition to doing our own share of work, we must help teach others to be able to do theirs. In some respects, however, our task is easier, because we do not have to start completely from the beginning."

Jem looked across at Valla again but she stared determinedly into the fire in the center of the clearing.

"Remember that for those raised in Communities, the idea of work is difficult to grasp," Preston went on, "and we must be patient." He then turned to face the Scots. "Simon Bryant over there will be in charge of constructing the ships' hulls from the materials and plans Vicro will be bringing to us soon. He and his friends have built many kinds of craft in the past, and I am sure they will give us the start we need." Bryant nodded briefly and Preston turned back to the rest. "The large area of empty ground on the south side of the compound is, of course, set aside for that purpose. As for the rest of us, well . . . there will be plenty of time to organize who does what. I'm afraid my own skill is confined to agriculture so, to begin with, my family's contribution will come primarily from Jem, who—as most of you will have realized after this afternoon, if not before—is in charge of our defense." There were a few laughs at this and Preston allowed himself a brief smile. "With regard to this," he said, "I have no doubt that some of you feel too much effort is going in that direction. To those, I can only repeat Vicro's warning that once the drought begins, and the truth of the message he gave becomes apparent, a tide of despair from outside will threaten to engulf us all . . . and only these measures can avoid our being swept away." He paused to let this sink in before continuing. "Once the ships are completed, Jem will assume command of the fleet under my authority, and my second son Ham will be responsible for navigating the course given to us." He paused once more before concluding: "One last thing before we go to our evening meal: Vicro has commanded that we rest for three days as soon as the stockade is completed. This order, as all others, will be strictly obeyed." He looked around. "Are there any questions?"

Simon Bryant took half a step forward. "Sir, will we see Vicro?"

Preston shook his head. "No."

"Then . . . when will he come?"

"After the period of rest is over."

"Immediately afterward?" Bryant persisted, and Preston frowned slightly.

"I don't know," he said. The Scot paused then, feeling that perhaps he had said too much already, smiled pleasantly and inclined his head in thanks.

Preston looked around and, as there were no more questions, he said: "Thank you for listening to me. I will try not to take up so much of your time again." He smiled, then turned to Jem and the two of them began to walk away, talking, while the others broke up separately or in groups. Valla turned to Ham.

"I don't want to eat with the family tonight," she said.

Ham looked concerned. "Aren't you feeling well?" he asked.

"I'm all right. I just don't feel like company."

"All right. Let me bring you something; we can eat by ourselves."

"No. You go. Your mother expects you."

They started to walk away. "She expects both of us," Ham persisted. "But of course she understands we want to be alone sometimes." Valla stopped and turned to face him.

"For a clever man, you can be very stupid sometimes!"

"Valla!"

"Can't you see I want to be by myself? Leave me alone!"

So saying, she turned and walked off quickly into the darkness, leaving Ham standing there looking both hurt and puzzled.

As Preston had predicted, the stockade was finished the following day.

It never rained again.

# CHAPTER SIX

The sun beat mercilessly out of a sky the color of brass and the vegetation began to wither; but there was still an empty space where the new ships would be. There was also little sign of movement.

On the stockade, Jem paced about restlessly, avoiding the looks of the other sentries perspiring in the heat. Suddenly he saw Valla in the distance walking past some buildings, and after glancing quickly at his companions, who were talking among themselves despondently, he climbed down the ladder and dropped to the ground.

After a few seconds, Valla sensed that somebody was following her and stopped to turn around, but when she saw who it was, she immediately broke into a run.

"Valla!"

Jem ran after her but she quickened her pace and vanished around a corner. A moment later, he reached the place where she had disappeared and found himself some fifty yards from where Ham was giving a lesson under the trees to a depressed looking group of young people; Jem was out of breath and angry.

Valla walked up to her husband and gave him a quick peck on the cheek, then she sat down nearby and tried to ignore Jem glowering at her in the distance. Ham was unaware of his brother's presence and after a brief smile at his wife continued talking; but even he seemed to have been affected by the heat, and his usually interesting teaching voice emerged in something of a drone.

Jem stood watching for a while, then he turned away and found himself facing Simon Bryant. The two men looked at each other, then Simon spoke the words all of them were secretly harboring in their hearts.

"When?"

Jem looked at him with irritation and moved to walk past, but the Scot put out a hand to restrain him.

"It's been three weeks," he said. "The people are beginning to wonder."

"Why don't you ask my father?" Jem snapped.

"You know he doesn't like to think we doubt his word."

"Then don't."

Bryant paused, looking at him. "Don't you?" he said eventually.

"I'm his son."

Bryant smiled thinly. "Yes, of course," he said. "I was forgetting."

Jem gritted his teeth. "Be careful," he warned. "I'm in no mood for an argument."

Bryant glanced over at Ham, then back to the one who towered over him. "It's only natural to wonder," he said more reasonably. "We have all come a long way."

Jem looked at him. "If you came from the Moon,

you would have traveled no distance at all compared to my father," he said.

Bryant looked puzzled. "I thought he was brought up in a Community near here?" Jem smiled for the first time.

"That's because you don't know him," he said, then walked away down the avenue between the buildings while Bryant stood watching.

Not far away Preston and Sarah sat in the shade of a tree while he read to her. Sarah looked at him fondly, perhaps a little wistfully.

"That was the first book the Machines gave you, wasn't it?" she said when he had finished.

After a few seconds, he nodded. "I think it was the only one they could find at the time." He looked up at the hills and she knew him well enough not to be fooled by the front he put on for everyone else, including his sons.

"Don't worry," she said softly. He turned back to her.

"It's not that I don't believe Vicro will keep his promise," he said after a moment. "It's just that sometimes I doubt my own ability to live up to what's expected of me." Sarah nodded gently.

"It's good that you should feel that once in a while," Then she looked down at the book on his lap. "Read it to me again," she said.

Preston smiled, then he dropped his eyes:

" 'I rescue all who call on me,' " he read, and Sarah closed her eyes to listen.

" 'I protect whoever knows my name.

I am with them when they are in trouble

I bring them safety and honor.

I give them life, long and full.' "
He looked up at her, knowing the last line by heart.
" 'And show them how I can save.' "

Sarah opened her eyes to look into his. She was filled yet again, as she had been so often recently, with the bittersweet realization that she loved him even more, now that she felt her life drawing to its close.

A moonless night full of stars. No wind stirred the drying leaves drooping from the branches of young trees on the hillside too small to have been of any use. In the camp, lamps flickered but no one stirred, and only the sound of a solitary cicada broke the silence. All the sentries had fallen asleep. In their room, Ham slept peacefully, Valla fitfully, as far away from him as possible.

Preston stood alone to one side of the open space looking up into the night. He felt that something tremendous was about to happen. After a few seconds, he turned his head slightly:

"Vicro!"

A single point of light, many miles above the earth, grew in strength, and twenty beams of light reached from it to the ground. Preston covered his face with both hands but still the intensity of the light grew until his body became invisible in the glare, and with it a sound beyond description that both horrified and exulted him. Then, just as suddenly, the light faded and the sound ceased.

Preston lowered his hands slowly and looked at the recently empty space in wonder.

The following morning found him standing in almost the same place facing a crowd of all the people within the stockade, except those on guard. They packed the perimeter of the open area staring at him in awe, and beyond, past his shoulder.

Suddenly Preston raised both arms in a gesture of welcome. "See for yourselves!" he shouted, and swung around to face the space which, from then onward, would be known as the construction ground.

Where before there had been nothing, now lay distributed mountains of materials, tools and machinery. Preston stood to one side smiling broadly, and at once the crowd surged forward laughing and shouting to see what Vicro had brought.

Amid the hubbub, Preston led the way, followed by his family and the other leaders he had spoken to earlier. Eventually he stopped in front of a large black cube measuring twenty feet down each side and touched it briefly before turning to the others.

"In here are two machines for our use," he told them, "but we must accept them as being beyond our understanding."

Jacy frowned. "Why, Father?" he asked.

"Because that's what Vicro told me," Preston said, looking pleasantly at his youngest son, but with a directness that silenced him. Then he turned to the others. "The first is for cutting the material in accordance with the plans which are also inside. No other tool can do this." Bryant and Fearson, his right-hand man, exchanged quick looks at this, but Preston went on: "The second is for plotting our course, once we start."

Jem stepped forward to take a closer look.

"Do we know where we are going yet?" he asked, and his father turned to him.

"No," he admitted. "Our course will be given to us the night before we leave—but there is a lot to do before then." He turned back to Bryant. "Simon . . . I suggest you and your men start here. You will be the first to have to learn to use the cutting machine, so you might as well begin at once." The other nodded.

"Very well, sir."

"The rest of you come with me."

Preston moved on and now, wherever he walked, people reached out to touch him, their faces shining with relief and joy.

Ndrew, one of Bryant's younger men, turned to their leader as they stood watching Preston walk away.

"Well," he said, "what have you got to say now?" The older man shook his head.

"He's a remarkable person, all right," Bryant admitted. "I've always said so." Then he looked around at the others. "But if anyone expects me to believe all this stuff just arrived from outer space, like that . . . !" He finished the sentence with a shrug.

"Then where did it come from?" Ndrew persisted. "We all slept."

"I'm not saying I know how he did it."

"Then you don't believe Vicro was sent to help us?"

"I believe what I can see," Bryant retorted obstinately, and pointed after Preston. "He was sent to help us," he said. "I believe that, or I wouldn't have come. But, well, if he likes to have us all believe this was done by somebody else, it's all right with me.

It doesn't make any difference anyway now, does it?" Ndrew grinned and Bryant turned to the others: "Well, come on," he said sharply. "Don't just stand there gawping. You heard what he said—let's commence by starting at the beginning!"

Bryant allowed himself a thin smile and the others burst out laughing. Then they set to work opening the cube.

Within three weeks, the hulls of half the ships had already been laid and others were soon to follow.

According to the plans, the completed ships would be gigantic crystal-shaped objects with thirty-two facets and measuring two hundred feet in diameter; but when the first was finished, Ham discovered that the internal capacity exceeded what would be expected from such external measurements by ten times. After many hours of frustration, they eventually had to admit that there was no alternative but to accept this paradox as one more product of a civilization which had advanced beyond the understanding of the human mind in its present stage. There were others; one was the black material from which the ships' hulls were made; another was the cutting machine left to shape it to the required size.

Preston stopped to watch a new plate being raised into position and fixed into the side of one of the new hulls by a perspiring gang of Fearson's men using a block and tackle. Then he walked on, past where Alison and Jacy were wiring up control panels, assisted by several of their students; and further, where Ham argued with David and several others over some diagrams which were laid out on a table. Preston arrived, eventually, at the place where Ndrew was using the machine to cut more plates, which were being marked out on the rough material by others using templates. They all worked cheerfully but showed signs of the oppressive heat. Preston stopped beside Ndrew, smiling.

"Have you found out how it works yet?" he asked, and the younger man looked up, grinning.

"No, sir, but you were right. Nothing else touches the material, but this glides through it like butter." Preston frowned slightly.

"You tried something else?" he questioned. "Didn't you believe me?" The young Scot looked uncomfortable.

"Yes, sir. We just thought we'd see how ordinary tools would do."

"You should have more faith," Preston said reprovingly.

"Yes, sir."

Preston hesitated, then his curiosity got the better of him. "How did they do it?" he asked. Ndrew picked up a small piece of the material and turned it over in his hands.

"This stuff's so hard, not even the glass-cutters could make a scratch."

"What about the new glass . . . for the observation windows?" Preston asked.

"Exactly the same," Ndrew confessed. "I don't know what it's made of, but I have a theory that the stuff of which it's composed is held together by a force we know nothing about."

"And the cutting machine?" Preston persisted.

"I don't think it cuts as we understand the word at all."

"How does it work, then?"

"This force, whatever it is," Ndrew said, "I think the machine has the power to suspend it along a given line so the material just falls apart." Preston nodded.

"That's very clever," he said. "Maybe one day you'll tell me what that force is?"

Ndrew smiled again. "I hope to, sir." Preston nodded approvingly.

"We'll have plenty of time to study, once our journey begins."

During this exchange a boy, about six years old, came up behind Preston and stopped, listening, so that when Preston turned to move on, he found the child standing in his path looking up at him with an anxious expression.

"Sir, when will we see the Sun again?"

Preston smiled. "We shall see the Sun," he promised, "when our journey begins." Then he sat on his haunches so that his face was on the same level with the boy's. "You see, God decided to punish the people who refused to obey Him by stopping the rain," he said. "Do you understand?"

The boy nodded. "I know that's why we must leave," he said.

"Good." Preston pointed up at the thick layer of cloud overhead. "So all the water that would have fallen as rain is being held up there in the clouds. That's why we can't see the Sun, although it's so hot. They act like a sort of blanket." The child paused, thoughtfully.

"Will it rain after we have gone?" he asked, and Preston smiled.

"I don't know," he admitted. "God doesn't tell us more than we can understand; but He sent Vicro to save us." The boy frowned.

"Who is Vicro? Why don't we ever see him?"

"He's just a person, like you and me," Preston told him. "Only the world he comes from is much older, and the people there chose to follow God's will."

"Is that why he knows what God wants?"

"Yes. But why he only shows himself to me, I don't know," Preston said a little wistfully. "Sometimes it makes it very difficult."

Then he went on, more cheerfully: "I was just on my way to see if the animals we are taking with us are all right. Would you like to come too?"

The boy nodded eagerly. Preston laughed and picked him up easily, then walked away carrying him on his left arm and listening to the questions which now burst out of him in a flood—doing his best to answer some of them.

## CHAPTER SEVEN

In the middle of the construction ground, Ham finished the lesson he was giving and rolled up the diagrams while nodding at a remark one of his pupils had just made.

"I think that's enough for the time being," he said. "As soon as the navigation computer is installed in the command ship, you'll be able to see more clearly."

The class nodded but Ham glanced around curiously. The whole afternoon he had sensed they were not paying as much attention to him as usual. "Is anything bothering you?" he asked after a few seconds. "Apart from the heat, I mean!" Some of them smiled. "I get the feeling most of you have something on your minds."

One of the young men glanced around, then he ventured respectfully: "Sir . . . when will the attack come?"

Ham paused, then he sighed. "I see."

"It makes it difficult to concentrate, not knowing," one of the others put in.

"If there was only some way of finding out," said a third.

Ham looked up at the hills, then he turned back to the worried faces of his pupils. "There is no way," he told them. "If it was intended for us to go outside the stockade, a gateway would have been made."

"Perhaps it will never happen," one of the others said hopefully.

"I wish you were right," Ham agreed.

"Sometimes there are sounds outside the stockade at night," said one of the girls. "I've heard them." The others nodded and looked at each other.

Ham thought quickly, trying to decide the best way to calm their fears, then he took a deep breath and paid them the compliment of complete frankness.

"I'm sure those outside will try to take the ships from us sooner or later," he said quietly, "but try not to worry." He smiled briefly. "I know that's easy to say," he went on, "but Vicro knew it would happen —that's why he told us to build the stockade first. So now we're ready for anything, whatever it is, whenever it comes."

He glanced back at the ridge overlooking the camp before turning to assure them. "As long as we do what Vicro commanded, we shall come to no harm. I'm sure of that."

At that moment Ngle, the general in command of the City's army, was studying the camp's defenses from the cover of some trees at the top of the hill. An artist squatted beside him, making excellent sketches of the camp's layout and the construction of the stockade; behind them stood a guard of half a dozen men. The general was already holding some of the sketches, which he compared with what he could see, nodding his approval.

The artist completed another detail of the stockade with approximate dimensions marked, and Ngle took the last sketch from him.

"That should be enough," he said. "You have done well."

"Thank you, sir."

Ngle turned to those behind him. "The rest of you stay here," he ordered. "I'm going down to have a closer look." He handed the sketches to his second in command.

"Guard these with your life."

"Yes, sir."

The man took the papers and held them gingerly as the general turned to go, but the artist took a few steps after him.

"General Ngle, sir . . ."

Ngle paused. "Well?"

"You won't forget me," the man pleaded, "when the time comes. You promised."

Ngle smiled briefly. "So I did. Well . . . we don't need you any more. It's a long journey back to the City, and water is scarce." the man's eyes widened in horror as the general turned to the guards. "Dispose of him," he said curtly. The soldiers grinned.

"Yes, sir."

"No!" The artist shrieked and fell to his knees, but Ngle had already started to walk away.

"You promised," the wretch screamed after him. "You said I could come with you— Ahh—!" His words ended in a cry of agony as three of the soldiers almost simultaneously thrust sharpened poles into his body.

Jem paced restlessly up and down on the catwalk, while a guard leaned listlessly against the top of the stockade looking up over the hill. Both started and froze as they heard the cry in the distance; but it was not repeated, and after a pause they both let out their breath and looked at each other. Here the sounds of construction were muffled.

"What was that?"

Jem's eyes swept the hills before answering: "I can't see anything." he said eventually.

"We never can." Jem compressed his lips, but after

a few seconds he started to walk along the catwalk. The other man watched in silence for a few moments. "It's beginning to get on everyone's nerves," he went on. "This waiting—not knowing when to expect an attack." He shrugged. "If an attack's coming at all."

"It's coming, all right," Jem said, turning and starting back toward him.

"I was talking to some of my friends last night. They were saying the work of building the ships is being affected." Jem stopped in front of him.

"In what way?" he asked.

"It's difficult to keep your mind on what you're supposed to be doing, when all the time you've half an ear cocked for the alarm," the other told him. "More mistakes are being made, the longer it goes on. Some of them can't sleep. They see fires burning in the distance at night and . . . hear things like that." He jerked his head in the direction of the hills. "It slows everything down." He hesitated for a few seconds. "If only we knew what was going on out there," he finished.

Jem stood looking at him a moment longer, then suddenly he made for the top of the ladder.

"Stay here," he ordered. "I'll be gone for a while."

"Yes, sir."

"And don't go to sleep!" Jem threw over his shoulder as he started to climb down.

The man came to the top of the ladder and watched him drop to the ground and hurry off toward the northern part of the camp.

In one of the larger buildings, Sarah was supervising the preparation of the evening meal; she was assisted by many of the other women, including Valla. She looked around, then turned to the girl by her side.

"We need some more salt."

Valla nodded. "We seem to be using a great deal," she said.

"I know; but in the heat it's necessary in order to stay healthy. Father and I found that out our first summer. We couldn't understand why both of us were getting cramps so much."

Valla smiled. "I'll get some," she offered.

"Thank you. There's plenty in the store."

Sarah watched the younger woman turn and walk toward the storeroom door, then she called after her: "Don't forget to shut the door." Valla looked around. "All this steam!" Sarah added by way of explanation, and the girl nodded with a smile; then she opened the door and went through, shutting it behind her.

The storeroom was almost as big as the kitchen, dimly lighted and with avenues of supplies piled to the ceiling. Valla walked between the rows, looking for the salt, but stopped and turned when she heard the door open and close again, although she couldn't see who it was.

"Sarah? Mother?"

On getting no reply she frowned and walked to the end of the row, then caught her breath when she saw who it was standing just inside the door.

"Jem!"

"I had to see you," he said.

Valla took a deep breath to stop her voice from shaking.

"What for?"

"I need your help." Jem took a step toward her. "I've decided I must do something," he said tensely. "I'm useless until the first ship is ready to test."

Valla looked up at him. "How can you say that?" she protested. "What is more important than our defense?"

"Exactly," Jem went on, moving closer. "But what good am I doing standing around behind the stockade waiting? We must have information . . . and who better to get it than I?"

Valla's eyes widened. "No!"

"You must help me," Jem said urgently. "If you care for me at all." Valla looked away. "You're the only one I can trust not to go running to Father."

Later that night Jem stood at the top of a ladder helping Valla up the last few rungs onto a deserted part of the catwalk. When she was safely on, he straightened up and adjusted his belt, where he had a water bottle strapped next to his sheath knife. "It's all right," he told her. "There's no one else here, but we haven't got long." He bent down quickly and picked up a rope which was already tied to the top of the stockade, and threw it over so it dropped to the ground outside.

"All you've got to do is pull the rope up when I've gone," he said. "So no one from outside can use it to climb in. Then get away from here before anyone comes." Valla looked at him.

"Jem, I'm afraid."

"There's nothing to be frightened of. I've left a note for Father which he won't find until he goes to bed, explaining why I've gone. There's no reason why you should know anything."

"But New York is such a long way."

"Forty miles to be exact. That's why I couldn't take anyone else—except Ham—and he's busy."

"But what will Preston say?" she pleaded. "You know he's forbidden anyone to go outside the stockade."

"I suppose he'll be angry," Jem admitted. "But he'll get over it when he sees me back safe and sound."

"Are you sure you're doing the right thing?"

Jem smiled. "Quite sure," he said. "Father put me in charge of defense, didn't he?" Valla nodded.

"Besides, you know it's no good arguing with him."

"Nor you," Valla said, allowing herself a faint smile.

"But I'm convinced that if an attack is to be launched, it will be made from the City," Jem went on. "The best thing I can do is find out when and how."

Valla shivered. "How long will you be gone?"

"Five days . . . a week at the most." They looked at each other in silence for a few moments, then Jem said; "I must go. David will be coming soon."

"Be careful."

Suddenly they were in each other's arms.

"Valla!"

"Don't let anything happen to you," she begged. "I couldn't bear it."

Jem shook his head. "I won't." He pulled his head

back and looked into her eyes for a few seconds, then kissed her again. A moment later he broke away and moved quickly to the rope.

"Don't forget what I told you," he whispered.

"Jem!"

Valla rushed to the edge as he climbed over the side and watched him slide to the ground. He looked up at her for a moment, waved, then disappeared into the darkness.

Two hours later Preston found his son's note and immediately called a meeting of the family and other leaders. They had never seen him so angry.

"None of you knew about this?" he demanded of those facing him. Most shook their heads, but Ham glanced sideways at Valla, who was standing beside him. She was gazing fixedly into the fire as if she heard nothing.

"Very well," Preston went on, "I shall see him on his return. Son or no son—and whatever his intention—I will not tolerate the flouting of Vicro's instructions."

He paused, looking around, then went on more quietly but with great intensity.

"Who are we to question the one without whom we should all be destroyed? And must it come to that before we accept that we cannot understand everything?" Preston paused again before going on: "The only real contribution we can make is to have faith in those who would save us . . . and I pray to God that too much harm has not been done already by my son's arrogance."

He looked at each one of them in turn and Ham

glanced at his wife, who was still staring into the fire as vacantly as before; but Bryant turned to Fearson and the two men exchanged a secret smile.

## CHAPTER EIGHT

Preston's farm, where Jem and his brothers had been brought up, lay on the direct path to the main highway which ran south to New York, and which was now used almost exclusively by the Machines. Jem reached it after two hours and decided to spend the rest of the night; he awoke early next morning, having slept on a pile of hay, in the corner of his old room.

Jem yawned and stretched, then he stared at the ceiling. After a few seconds he frowned, then his brain cleared and he got up to look out of the window.

Everything was bone dry. A wind stirred small whirlpools of dust between the buildings, and the forest behind was barren. Jem turned away from the window and pulled out his water bottle, from which he started to take a long draught. After a few seconds, though, he stopped himself and shook the bottle to see how much was left. He shrugged, then replaced the bottle in his belt and brushed a few strands of hay from his clothes before turning to go outside.

Jem stopped outside the front door to look around. He found it difficult not to be depressed by what he saw. On impulse, he walked to the side of the house where there used to be a pond and found it completely dried up, then he came back to the farmyard and tried the hand pump, but this was dry also. He stood for a moment, looking around for the last time, then shook his head and set out over the plain in a southerly direction.

It was still overcast but already hot as Jem waded through the sea of dry grass. After about an hour, he came to a slight rise and turned to see the way he had come. He paused to take a sparing sip from his water bottle, then turned to go on, but now he saw the land on the other side of the ridge for the first time, and the sight made him stop in his tracks.

There had once been a small lake in the area directly in front of him, but the bed was now cracked and hard. What added horror to the scene were the desiccated corpses of hundreds of animals who must have staggered from miles away to this last water hole, and there died fighting over the remaining few drops of precious liquid. The last survivors had torn up the ground in pursuit of the vanishing spring until they too had fallen where they stood.

In a workshop at the compound, the night after Jem had left, Jacy flung his screwdriver to the ground and wheeled from the half-completed control panel to face Alison.

"All right!" he shouted. "If you think you can do so much better, go ahead and do it!"

"I didn't say that," she protested, trying to reason with him. "You know you're much cleverer than I am."

"Ham doesn't think so," her husband retorted.

"We're not talking about Ham," Alison said.

"But you don't mind talking to him about me, behind my back."

"That's not fair. He just comes to help us whenever he can spare the time."

"We don't need his help," Jacy said sharply.

"We need the help of anyone who can give it." Alison sighed. "So few can," she added.

Jacy looked at her, then deflated visibly. "How can I concentrate on anything when I can't sleep?" he said plaintively. Alison moved toward him.

"I'm not blaming you," she said. "Everybody makes mistakes." She put her arms around him. "But it has to be put right, hasn't it?"

"I suppose so," Jacy muttered. "I'm just so tired."

"Poor Jacy," Alison said, mothering him.

"It's bad enough without Father keeping us up half the night," he complained.

"You can't blame him."

"I don't blame Jem either."

Alison hesitated. "He shouldn't have gone," she said eventually. "It was stupid."

"Why? Because Father said so?"

"No. Because he doesn't really know what he's doing."

"Jem always knows what he's doing," Jacy said loyally, and Alison smiled.

"And you always stick up for him," she told him.

He was about to make some retort but then stopped and gave a long sigh. "At least if he can find out what is going on, it will be one less thing to worry about," he said. Alison nodded.

"Let's hope so."

Jacy moved back slightly and sagged on the panel they were working on. He had never been one to suffer in silence, but looking at him now Alison had to admit to herself that he really did look tired.

"Look," she said, "why don't you go and take a nap? There's no point in making yourself ill. Please!" Jacy glanced down at the panel.

"What about all this?" he said.

Alison smiled. "It's not so bad," she told him. "It won't take long. By the time you wake up, I'll have it fixed."

Jacy looked at her. "What about you?" he asked.

"I feel fine." She put a hand on his arm. "Go on, darling. We depend on you."

Jacy started to move. "Well, all right. If you're sure you don't mind."

"Of course I don't."

Alison went with him to the door and kissed him just before he went out. "Go on," she said. "It's time I did my fair share." Jacy opened the door but turned back to look at her. He knew she was just as tired but she seemed lighted from within by some extra force.

"You do more than your share already," he said soberly. "And you know it."

"Nonsense!"

Jacy shook his head. "No." He paused for a moment, then he said, "I don't know what I'd do without you sometimes." Alison bent forward and kissed him again lightly.

"I don't know what I'd do without you," she said softly, "so it's just as well neither of us have got to." Her husband smiled wearily, then nodded.

"All right," he said, "don't try to do too much."

"I won't."

"It can wait."

"I'll see how I get on," she promised. "Go on." Jacy nodded and disappeared through the door, yawning and closing it behind him.

Alison sighed, then went back to the panel and began pulling out wires from the back, shaking her head but smiling. A few seconds later, the outer door opened and Ham came in. He stopped just inside, looking around.

"Where's my brother?" he asked.

Alison held her finger to her lips. "Ssh!" she said. "He's having a rest."

Ham looked surprised. "Resting?" Alison shrugged. "He was overtired."

Ham raised his eyebrows. "What about you?" he said.

"I'm all right," she told him.

He looked at her more closely. "You look pretty tired yourself," he said eventually.

"I'm fine, really." She went on working, then Ham suddenly realized what she was doing and moved to her side.

Alison shrugged. "We made a mistake," she said in answer to his unspoken question.

Ham glanced at the inner door pointedly. " 'We'?" he asked.

"That's what I said," Alison replied defensively.

Ham paused, then realizing further comment from him would be both pointless and unwelcome, he smiled. "All right," he said, "what can I do to help?" Alison looked at him gratefully and nodded in the direction of another panel.

"You can check that one we finished yesterday," she said. "We haven't had a chance yet."

"All right; where's the diagram?"

"On the table." Ham looked across the room, then walked over and picked it up. He put out his tongue at the door of the room where Jacy was resting, but he smiled as he walked over to start his allotted task.

Jem reached the main highway, climbed up the embankment, then paused for a short sip from the water bottle. He glanced up and down the road which, at first sight, seemed to be deserted but, as he was replacing the stopper, he suddenly noticed a shape by the roadside about a quarter of a mile to the south. Jem tucked the bottle back into his belt and began to walk toward it. After a hundred yards, he stopped and stared. He could see now the shape was a motionless Machine. He hesitated for a few seconds, then started to run forward, grinning and shouting.

"Hey, you there! Machine! Wait a minute!" He eventually stopped in front of it, slightly out of breath. "Thank you for waiting," he panted. "I want to go to New York."

Jem paused, waiting for the Machine to let down its steps so he could get on behind, but it remained motionless and silent. He looked at it, puzzled.

"Didn't you hear me?" he demanded. "I want to go to New York. I order you to take me there." The Machine still did not react, and Jem moved closer.

"What's the matter with you," he said, and pushed it impatiently, but it was too heavy to move. "Are you dead too?" He spoke the words in exasperation, but almost immediately the real possibility hit him, and he stood staring at it, a little awestruck.

"You really are dead, aren't you?" he said quietly, after a while. "One of the great Machines, lifeless as a dead cow!"

Jem paused a few moments longer, poking the Machine here and there but nothing happened. Finally he stepped back.

"Oh well," he said. "I'll have to walk after all." He raised his hand in mock salute. "It would have been nice knowing you." Then he turned on his heel and started off down the road.

The highway passed through heavily wooded country and the trees, although devoid of leaves, pressed in so thickly on either side that Jem couldn't see many yards into them. He walked on all that day, pausing to rest from time to time but passing two more inert Machines with scarcely a glance. Eventually it began to get dark and he decided to find somewhere to rest for the night; after walking on for another few hundred yards, he found an opening in the trees and plunged off the road to flop down with his back to a treetrunk.

He paused for a while, enjoying the rest, then

reached into his pouch and produced a tin. He took two pills from it and swallowed them with a few gulps of water, then leaned back against the trunk and closed his eyes.

He woke up and heard screaming and shouting in the distance. He jumped to his feet and, although it was now completely dark overhead, he could see a glow in the sky, further into the wood.

He could not see it yet, but the light was the reflected glare from the burning buildings of a large Community. Most of the buildings were already a blazing inferno and the bodies of men, women and children lay everywhere about, slain in the battle which had just finished.

Jem advanced cautiously through the trees, then froze when he heard something crashing through the undergrowth toward him. He drew his knife and backed into the cover of a large treetrunk. Seconds later two women and a man came racing past —their eyes lighted with terror. They did not see him; indeed, they were oblivious to everything except the need to put as much distance as possible between themselves and the horror behind them. After they had disappeared Jem paused, listening, but he could hear nothing except the sound of the fire so he sheathed his knife again and went on toward the blaze.

He emerged from the trees and looked around, sickened at the sight which met his eyes. His first reaction was to turn back, but a thought struck him, and he got out his water bottle, looking toward a group of buildings on the far side, as yet untouched by the blaze. Possibly there would be somewhere he could refill it.

With this idea in mind, Jem decided to have another drink before moving forward to investigate, and this action nearly cost him his life. As he stood, his body outlined against the flames, a man carrying a spear crept out of the wood behind him, his eyes fixed desperately on the bottle. He raised the weapon, advanced a few more steps, then threw; but in his haste the spear went wide, just missing Jem's right shoulder.

Jem sprang around, dropping the bottle and unsheathing his knife in one movement, to find his attacker almost upon him. With a cry, the man reached for Jem's throat, and ran straight onto the knife. The two men looked at each other, their eyes only a few inches apart, both equally shocked, then the stranger sank to the ground and died.

Jem bent down to retrieve the bottle, still clutching the cork in his left hand, and found that the remaining contents had spilled into the earth. He sheathed the knife after wiping the blade clean on some dead grass and tucked the bottle back into his belt; then he moved hurriedly, but with care, in the direction of the yet untouched buildings.

After picking his way across the bodies of the slain, Jem found himself outside a building with large double doors. The building next to this caught fire as he watched, but he found an outside tap just to the right of the doors and, after looking around quickly to make sure no one else was about to spring on him, he removed the cork from his bottle and bent down eagerly . . . only to discover the tap was dry. Jem swore as he straightened up, then he decided to try inside and pushed open one of the two doors.

The ground floor had been the repair and re-charging room for the Machines servicing the Community. The roar of the fire was muffled inside, but Jem could see by the reflected light from the build-ing opposite. A smell of burning confirmed his im-pression that it would not be long before this build-ing too shared the fate of the Community as a whole.

On one side of the room several large Machines containing complex circuits for the servicing of their fellows were surrounded by a crowd of others. Jem could see that the bigger Machines had connected themselves to the charging points and the whole pic-ture told him what must have happened. Each Ma-chine was capable of working for several days be-fore it had to be recharged; when its reserve power fell below a certain level, its program directed it to return to the charging point, where it was checked by the supervising Machines and reactivated for another work period. Obviously the main power supply had failed. Machine after Machine had re-turned for recharging but none were able to leave, until finally the supervising Machines themselves had run down. Jem could imagine the effect this would have had on the Community, but a bang and a loud crackling from above told him that fur-ther speculation would have to wait.

An elevator-shaft led to the room above which, if the design of this workshop was typical, would have been used for storing spare parts. The elevator was out of action but, in any event, it was highly unlikely that any water would have been stored up there. Jem turned for the door, but a tiny sound above the muffled roar of the flames caught his attention. He hesitated, decided his mind must be playing tricks, and was about to leave when he heard it again. A cry for help: somebody was in the room above.

Jem looked around quickly. There was a trapdoor in the ceiling but no ladder. The building had evidently been built when there was at least some human participation in the work of running the Community, for no Machine had ever used such a thing. Another cry from upstairs was followed by a second crashing sound.

He ran outside to see if there was another way up, and narrowly missed being hit by one of the falling timbers. Jem saw that the whole top of this building was now on fire and he only hoped there was some kind of ceiling between the person upstairs and the blazing roof.

As the exterior of the building offered no encouragement, there was no alternative but to plunge back into the lower room, which was now beginning to fill with smoke. In desperation Jem disconnected one of the larger Machines and tried to push it directly underneath the trapdoor. It was hard going against the dead motor but he finally managed it, then scrambled to get on top. The trap was still six inches from his outstretched fingers.

Jem leaped to the ground. He could reach the trap with a jump but he had to find something to knock out the door from below so he could catch the sides of the opening. He could still hear cries from above, although by now the roof must be a blazing inferno.

He found a discarded spear and remounted the Machine, blessing the steadiness which had previously made it so hard to move. The trapdoor gave easily and through it he could see the ceiling of the room above beginning to give way—the draft from below adding fresh impetus to the flames. He jumped and pulled himself up, then crouched at the edge of the hole above, panting with effort, unable to remember quite how he had managed it, but that wasn't important.

Sweat poured into Jem's eyes, making it even more difficult to see through the smoke, but eventually he was able to make out several rows of bins containing odd bits of metal—he'd been right about one thing anyway—but apart from this, the room was empty.

The heat was now intense, and he was about to lower himself back through the trap when he heard another sound and saw for the first time a door at the far end of the storeroom. Whoever it was must be in there. The door was heavily built and apparently locked on the inside, but he managed to smash it open with his shoulder. The room beyond, which in all probability once acted as an office, was furnished now like a small bedroom or cell. The something on the bed proved to be the body of a young girl, whether still alive Jem hadn't time to establish, as the collapsing ceiling in the room behind reminded him. He snatched her up and swung around for the doorway, but almost immediately he was brought to a halt. Someone had chained one of her hands to the metal bedpost with an old-fashioned hand-cuff.

Jem's gorge rose in anger at whoever had done this. The wrist was red-raw where she had tried to get away and now, as a result, in a few seconds the ceiling above the bed would collapse and she would be destroyed. He felt his way back into the store to see if there was anything to break the chain but he couldn't see for the smoke; it was hopeless.

He blundered back and stood for a moment look-ing down at her. Perhaps she was already dead? But, at that second, the girl opened her eyes.

Part of the ceiling above the bed collapsed and lay smoldering on the bottom of the bed, only a few inches away from her bare feet. In another sec-ond the rest would follow and then it would be too late.

The knife appeared in Jem's right hand with the practiced movement of one who had spent a boy-hood running wild in the woods surrounding his father's farm. In another second he brought the ra-zor-sharp edge down on the captive wrist as hard as he could. The girl gasped and fainted—but she was free.

Jem made for the trapdoor, which was now sur-rounded by burning timbers. He kicked them to one side, only faintly conscious of getting burned him-self in the process. He laid the girl's body near the edge, with her good arm hanging down through the trap. He lowered himself through to the Machine below, then reached up and pulled her after him. A few seconds later he was on the ground and mak-ing for the open air. He didn't stop until he reached the edge of the wood, where he put the girl down gently with her back to a tree and turned just in time to see the building collapse into an inferno of blazing wreckage.

Jem examined the stump. The girl had already lost a good deal of blood and if he didn't do something he would have saved her only to watch her bleed to death. He took the strap from his water bottle and bound it around her lower arm as tightly as he could. He was relieved to see that this reduced the bleeding to a slow seepage. The amputation was clean enough but he knew he dare not leave it like that. Something would have to be done so the strap could be removed. He got up and walked back toward the fire, then around the various buildings until he found what he was looking for: a bar of metal almost white-hot at one end where it still projected into the fire, but cool enough at the other to pick it up by wrapping it around with his tunic. Jem carried it carefully over to where the girl still lay unconscious. It had probably served once as a supporting strut for a window, or something similar, but now it had a more vital role to play.

The smell of burning flesh made him sick as he cauterized the wound and afterward he threw the bar far away into the bushes with revulsion, as though it were responsible for the mutilation itself. He released the strap, gently at first, saw that the bleeding had stopped altogether, then bound up the blackened end with strips torn from his shirt.

He looked down to see if she was still breathing. He was too tired to take in more but saw that, although she looked very pale, this was so. At least she had felt no pain and that was one blessing. There would be pain enough in the morning, but now she slept. He dropped to the ground beside her; he didn't even know her name.

In a few more seconds he was sound asleep.

Jem woke up feeling cold and thirsty; the sensation of having swallowed a handful of nails reminded him that stomach walls cannot grind against one another indefinitely on the strength of energy pills. It was already light, and the day greeted him with the gray, dry heat of an airless boiler room. He struggled to stand up, holding onto a tree for a few seconds while the wave of dizziness passed. He remembered the previous night and the girl—where was she? He found her standing on the edge of the clearing some twenty yards away staring at the smoldering ruins, then at the charred stump of her left arm. The bandage had either come off or she had pulled it off, and she was shivering violently. Jem cursed. Once he had found somewhere to refill his water bottle he needed to go on to reach the City and get back again before it was too late; but he couldn't leave her like this.

When he touched her shoulder, she turned slowly to look at him and he saw for the first time how beautiful she was—in spite of the fever and her smoke-blackened skin. In spite of her mutilated hand and the tunic which hung around her shoulders in rags; in spite of everything she was beautiful with the wistful appeal of a child, although he could see she was nearly full-grown. Her blue eyes suddenly rolled up and she pitched forward onto the ground before he had a chance to catch her.

Jem found one building still intact, a room on the edge of the forest away from the others, which had been used to store playthings. Here by some miracle was an inflatable mattress, some chairs and several rugs. He laid her down gently on the blown-up mattress and covered her with a rug.

Eventually Jem found an underground cistern with a small amount of water left in the bottom. He drank deeply himself, after which he felt stronger; then he filled his water bottle and carried it back to the girl. She drank eagerly and he bathed her face but she was in such pain he thought it better to leave her undisturbed as much as possible.

For the rest of the day Jem sat beside her on one of the chairs, leaving only briefly once or twice to refill the water bottle and to see if he could find any pain-relieving drugs among the wreckage, but it was no use. He did find some partially damaged cartons of powdered protein, however, and although it couldn't have been less appetizing eaten just with water, it did stop his stomach from grinding. He even managed to persuade the girl to swallow some in one of her few lucid moments, but most of the day she lay on the bed gripped with pain and burned by fever. All he could do was give her water whenever she asked and see she did no harm to herself.

Once, when he was wiping her face with a cool, damp cloth, it seemed the fever left her for a few seconds and she stared at him curiously from eyes which seemed enormous, now that her face was not contorted with pain.

"Hello!" he said, smiling. "Are you feeling better?" The girl continued to stare at him without answering, then it was as though a flood of pain which had been temporarily checked swept over her with redoubled force. She opened her mouth to scream but managed to bite it back into a moan.

Jem continued to nurse her as best he could, keeping an anxious eye on the stump, but it showed no signs of becoming diseased. He had read about such things and knew that the risk was not as great as it might have been owing to the Earth's atmosphere having been systematically purified of all harmful germs and viruses by the Machines some five centuries earlier, but the risk of death from shock remained. Fortunately, he instinctively did the right thing in keeping her quiet and warm.

The fever burned itself out at last toward evening on the following day. Jem, having had little sleep the previous night, had fallen asleep in the chair by her side. The girl raised herself on an elbow and looked around. She felt weak and her left arm throbbed mercilessly, but now her mind was clear. She sat up, paused for a moment to look at the sleeping figure beside the bed, then stood up. She had to grab for the back of the chair in which Jem slept to stop from falling over, but the dizzy spell passed and she found she could let go after a while and stand without support. Jem stirred uneasily but did not wake up. The girl stood looking down at him for a few seconds more. There was an old game club in the corner but he looked very strong. She might not kill him with the first blow, then it would be too late.

Jem woke up about ten minutes later. He rubbed his eyes wearily and was about to go back to sleep when he saw that she was gone. He jumped to his feet and ran outside, but there was no sign of her. He was looking around, trying to make up his mind as to which was the most likely direction she could have gone, when he heard a sharp cry from the forest slightly to his left. He plunged into the undergrowth in that direction.

The girl had tripped and fallen, hurting her injured arm but, hearing Jem crashing through the bushes toward her, she staggered to her feet and started to run; after another few steps, she fell down again.

Jem reached her side a few moments later and was about to bend down to help her up when he saw something flash and drew back his hand just in time. His own knife, which she must have taken while he slept, thudded harmlessly into the ground. He sprang back and before she could pull it out for another attempt, put his foot across her outstretched hand, causing her to yelp with pain.

Jem bent down for the knife and, having retrieved it, backed away a few paces to look down at her. "What's the idea?" he demanded angrily. The girl didn't answer but continued to stare at him as though she expected him to use the knife on her in return.

"Don't you know it was me who got you out of that building?" he went on.

He saw the girl glance at her left wrist and his

tone softened. "I'm sorry I had to do that," he said, "but you were chained to the bed. In another few seconds you would have been burned alive." Now she seemed to be peering at him in a strange way.

"Who are you?" she said, eventually. "I don't know your voice." Jem paused for a second, then he realized what was wrong. The big luminous eyes—the way she was looking at him. Of course . . . she was shortsighted! He laughed suddenly for the first time in days. The girl frowned.

"I can't see anything funny," she said irritably.

"I'm sorry." Jem smothered his amusement. "Where are your glasses?" he asked.

She looked even more annoyed, but his laughter seemed to have stilled her immediate fear.

"Era took them."

"Who is Era?"

The girl sighed and looked away. "He is the man who took me," she said, then added, "when the Machines stopped."

"Why did he do that?"

"To stop me from running away, of course." She looked at him as though this was so obvious he must be the world's worst idiot to ask such a question. Jem decided to try another tack.

"Why did you run away from me?" he said.

"Because I don't want to belong to anyone." The girl stressed the last word fiercely.

"I don't want to own you."

"Then why did you come running after me?" she demanded.

"Because you'd been sick for two days ever since . . ." He pointed to her left side. "I've been looking after you," he went on. "You didn't know what you were doing, so I thought . . ." He finished the sentence with a shrug. Then as an afterthought he added severely, "Fine thanks I get. I'm in a hurry to get to the City. I stop to save your life and you try to stick me with my own knife." He glared at her but she looked so vulnerable it was impossible to stay angry.

"What do they call you?" he asked more gently. The girl looked up and now he could see her eyes were swimming with tears.

"Aura," she whispered, then she moved to bury her face in her hands before realizing this was no longer possible. She looked so devastated at being deprived of even this limited sanctuary, that Jem felt an agony of pity for her, and while she remained frozen with indecision, he came forward and picked her up gently.

"Come on," he said quietly. "It's getting dark. I've got something we can eat." Aura didn't say anything but accepted his authority by resting her head on his shoulder and closing her eyes.

Jem carried her back to the outbuilding and put her down again on the bed. Then he fetched some more water and made her eat some of the synthetic food, after which she asked him to leave her for a while.

Jem sat on a fallen tree outside thinking about the City and what might be going on there. He had already lost two days and still had to decide what to do about Aura. He couldn't very well leave her, but it was equally obvious she was too weak to travel. Apparently it left him no alternative: he would have to wait until she was stronger.

During the next few days, while Aura rested, Jem was able to unearth some cartons of dried meat and vegetables, which made their meals considerably more interesting. They kept the wound covered most of the time, but it seemed to be healing well, and as the days went past it became progressively less painful.

Jem buried the bodies in a pit he found nearby in the forest, and Aura continued to recover. She found a new tunic and tidied herself up; she even produced a hair brush, and Jem was amazed how the scarecrow with a beautiful face was transformed into a lovely young woman. Soon she felt strong enough to try to fill in the gaps in her story, but it had all been such a nightmare she found it difficult to give him a clear picture. Nevertheless, the facts which did emerge had considerable bearing on what he had set out to discover, so the delay became less frustrating.

With the decline in world population, hydropower facilities for generating electricity became sufficient to meet all needs and other systems were abandoned; but during the fourth month of total drought, the rivers feeding the reservoirs were reduced to such an extent that there was no longer enough head to drive the turbines.

The Machines carried on for about a week after the power failed, then everything ground to a halt.

At first the Community had been reduced to panic; then one man, Era, regarded before as slow-witted because he had not fitted in with the butterfly existence followed by the other young men and girls of the Community, took command.

Era foresaw that it would not be long before the main pipe which distributed water from the plant in the City ran dry, and he ordered that every tank should be filled and that new pits should be dug to act as additional reservoirs. To begin with, only a few agreed to help, but the rest woke up one morning to discover that he had commandeered all the food, and that his followers were guarding it with sharpened poles. Two of the young men continued to laugh at the new leader, as they had in the past, and tried to push their way through; but when their dead bodies were thrown back at the feet of the waiting crowd, the others prepared to take the situation more seriously.

From then on, anyone who wanted food or drink had to earn it and that meant doing what Era and his lieutenants decreed. Almost overnight, the situation changed so that, apart from a privileged few, the Community inhabitants found themselves the new Machines.

The few chosen by Era enjoyed their new situation immensely. One thing the Machines had never been able to give them was the respect of their fellows, and now they had not only this, but fear into the bargain. Another grievance had also been that although the young people of the Community had always mated in complete freedom, and permanent liaisons were discouraged, no rule of social behavior had required a girl to accept anyone against her will. Hence, as in the past, the physically beautiful were favored; but now the favors went to those with power over life and death.

At first a few had tried to run away but these were easily caught and put to death; but a week before, the food and water reserves had fallen so low that Era had seen no alternative but to drive away all but the selected few.

When the dispossessed had found there was no means of reaching the City except on foot—and this was impossible without food and water—they had torn branches from the trees and made weapons for themselves to attack the Community under the cover of darkness. Superior numbers and surprise had carried the ensuing battle; and when as much food and water as could be carried was taken, someone had the idea of setting fire to the buildings in case any of Era's supporters were still in hiding.

Aura had always despised Era but he had never wanted anyone else. In the past he had hung around the periphery of her circle hoping, in time, that she would tire of her companions and turn to him, but no matter how bored she became, it never happened. As much as anything, it was these years of bitterness which gave him strength when the time came, and the certainty that if he became leader she would come to him.

He had given her time to choose of her own accord, and no matter how many friends urged her to accept the privileges he offered—as much for their sake as hers, for he was a far worse tyrant when angry—she refused, preferring to work with the rest rather than become his private property. Finally his patience had broken and Era took what had always been his to take by force. Aura was dragged to his quarters and there she remained under the threat of death until almost the end; but no matter how often he forced her to submit, she had always managed to deny him the full satisfaction of possession, even when she lay in his bed, her body clasped in his arms.

Era knew how successfully her hatred drowned his joy, but, in return, he treated her like an animal, keeping her confined to his room most of the day and making her undergo any obscenity his fevered imagination could devise for the amusement of his friends—and to assuage the mounting hurt that would not be stilled. Aura knew that, given the least encouragement, his attitude would change at once, but she could not bring herself to pretend when she felt such loathing, even though she knew the time could not be far off when he would kill her in one of his rages.

It had been Aura's eighteenth birthday on the night of the attack. Era and his friends had been drinking with their women, and she had been forced to drink so much herself she had become sick and had begged to be allowed to lie down, but Era had refused. He had even been on the point of making her take still more, when the attack came.

In the confusion, he dragged her up to the loft where Jem had found her. He had fastened her to the bed and taken away the ladder so she could not escape, but this had proved his downfall for, in doing so, he became separated from the others. A group of attackers found him hiding the ladder and they killed him with their spears.

The night after Aura finally told Jem the whole story, he lay awake, trying to imagine the horror she had been through. Now that she was almost fully recovered, Aura was as beautiful in her own way as Valla, but they were utterly different. Valla was perfect with the heady quintessence of a woman, which made him want to forget himself forever in her arms; but Aura, with the smooth lines of a young faun and eyes that flashed with gaiety, aroused in him an ache to guard and protect her—something he had never experienced before.

Valla lay awake also, beside her husband, staring into the darkness. After a while she turned and saw that he was awake too, looking at her.

"Can't you sleep?" he whispered. Valla shook her head, then flopped on her back as far away from him as possible. Ham turned on his side toward her and put out a hand to stroke her hair.

"What's the matter?" he said. "You seem so unhappy." Valla didn't answer. "I wish you'd tell me." But after a few more seconds Valla turned her back on him.

"There's nothing the matter," she said. "Go back to sleep."

"There must be something."

"Just leave me alone!"

Ham pulled his hand back as if he had been stung.

## CHAPTER NINE

On the fourth morning—the sixth, counting the two days she was delirious—Aura was well enough to travel. It was only fifteen miles to New York and Jem decided to take it in easy stages, which meant they had to carry food and water for two full days, and a reserve in case they found the City in chaos, and had to return at once. He cut up some fabric from the chairs to make rough pouches, which were supported with improvised straps, and a two-gallon can was padded so it could be similarly slung. Having done this, they hid the rest of the food and water under some bushes in the forest for the longer journey back.

Aura's wound had continued to heal and she had learned to manage so well that Jem tended to forget she had any handicap at all, particularly since she had pinned the end of a long-sleeved tunic over her wrist and the pain had subsided to the extent that she wasn't constantly having to bite her lip to keep it under control.

The journey was slow to begin with, but this was due largely to Jem's insistence on holding back every twig which might otherwise have banged into her left side. Even so, Aura tired quickly, but she gritted her teeth, and after another mile managed to get her second wind. The leaden feeling began to lift and she even chuckled at the sight of her huge companion trotting along in front, looking like an old peddler from a history book.

The heat was oppressive; Aura's wrist began to throb, and the woods were dry and lifeless, but she was happy—these days with Jem were the first good times for what seemed like ages. She was touched by Jem's obvious devotion to her. He was so different from the fair-haired, golden-skinned boys with whom she had grown up. He was big and hairy, and dark-skinned in a way that was slightly repelling, but she supposed he couldn't help that. Jem couldn't help what he looked like, any more than she could help what she felt about it. She would not dream of hurting him, but it was a pity all the same.

Eventually they reached the road, which was as deserted as before, and Aura had a rest while Jem built a small pile of stones to mark the spot. There would be no fire to guide them next time.

Now that they were able to walk alongside each other, Jem was careful to shorten his stride and to stop frequently so that Aura should not become overtired. Even so, they made good progress, and by the time he decided to call a halt for the night they were within four miles of the City.

During the course of the afternoon they came across two Machines that had run out of power, but saw no sign of life. Sometimes they walked in silence, and sometimes they sang songs which Aura tried to teach him; but mostly the quarter tones of the melodies defeated Jem and more often than not their duets would end with them both having to stop for a while helpless with laughter. In the Communities all art forms had been taken to a degree of sophistication any child born to them could master, but to Jem the poems Aura recited and the point of the jokes she told him were as incomprehensible as the split harmonies and broken tempo of the songs. Even so, he enjoyed the day immensely and tried to explain, in turn, why it was so important they undertook this journey; but although he explained patiently about Vicro and the way they had built the ships, she soon lost interest and interrupted him to ask how much further they were going that day.

When they did stop, they were on top of a hill and could see the City in the distance. The forest ended a few hundred yards down the slope and the country from then on consisted of a flat, rather desolate plain.

"Well, that's it." Jem said, pointing. "New York." Aura stood behind him, looking impressed.

"I've never seen it before," she said. "It looks enormous."

"Until recently, a hundred thousand people used to live there," he told her, "but once it was a thousand times bigger." Jem paused, then he went on, half wistfully: "Gigantic buildings touched the clouds, and underneath the ground were great roads, and machines which carried hundreds of people faster than you can imagine." Aura turned to him.

"What happened?" she asked. Jem frowned.

"It was destroyed," he said. "Then the Machines took over and finished what men had started."

"How do you know?"

Jem turned to look at her. "You wouldn't understand," he said. "Not yet."

Aura nodded. "Thinking makes my head buzz," she agreed, and Jem smiled.

"You'll get used to it."

"But all I want is for things to be like they were before," she said plaintively.

"How can you say that?"

"I was happy. The Machines did everything for us."

"That's not living!"

"It was very nice."

Jem began to look angry. "Well, it's never going to be like that again," he said, "so you might as well forget it."

"Don't shout!"

They glowered at each other for a few seconds, then Jem looked around. "We'd better find some shelter," he said gruffly.

Not very wisely, Jem built a fire in a clearing just off the road to cook some of their food; then except for the light from the fire, it was dark, and whenever he poked it with the blunt end of his staff a shower of sparks drifted up into the branches of the tree above their heads like a cloud of fireflies.

After they had eaten, they settled down on either side of the fire to go to sleep, but after a few minutes, Aura broke the silence.

"Jem are you asleep yet?" she whispered.

Jem turned to look at her, then shook his head. "What is it?"

"Tell me some more about the farm." Jem didn't

move for a few seconds, then he raised himself on one elbow to face her and picked up a piece of dried twig which he threw into the fire.

"I can't tell you much else," he said eventually. "We looked after ourselves and the animals . . . sometimes it was good, and sometimes it wasn't." He shrugged. "Only my father and mother had known anything else so it didn't make much difference either way."

Aura also raised herself so that she could look at him more easily. "And he made you learn things when you got older?" she asked. "Your father, I mean."

Jem nodded. "Yes. We weren't very willing to begin with, but he made us, all right." Jem smiled.

Aura thought about this for a while, then she said a little wistfully, "Will you teach me to learn things one day?"

"If you want."

Aura nodded. "Yes, I think I'd like that." She lay back and looked up at the tree, then she whispered, "Jem."

"Yes, Aura?"

"The idea of a man and a woman staying together without anyone else . . . it seems strange."

"It always does to someone raised in a Community."

"But you think it's strange too," she said, turning again to look at him.

"Of course not; why do you say that?"

Aura shrugged. "Well, you have no wife like your . . . brothers." She stumbled over the last word.

Jem frowned. "I just haven't found anyone I wanted to keep yet," he said.

"But you are the eldest."

"I know that."

Aura hesitated before going on, then she ventured: "Perhaps you found someone and couldn't have her."

"You ask a lot of questions," Jem answered huskily. "Why don't you go to sleep? I thought you were tired!" It had been a shot in the dark, but Aura congratulated herself on being so near the mark.

"Perhaps you should choose me," she said softly; then she stood up silently and unbuckled the belt of her tunic so that when she walked across the space separating them it swung open.

Aura knelt beside him. She put her injured arm behind her back and her right hand softly around the back of his neck; then she pulled his head gently against her breast and felt him shudder as his mouth crushed against her skin. She bent over and kissed his hair, then she pulled his head back and opened her mouth to receive his kiss.

They reached the barricade just after midday. It was nothing more than a wall of all kinds of debris stretching from one side of the street to the other, leaving a small gap in the middle. This was guarded by soldiers wearing the distinctive black armbands of the City forces emblazoned with the head of a goat. Jem and Aura adopted a servile manner and stopped in front of them.

"What do you want?" snapped the one who appeared to be in charge. Jem put on a whining voice.

"Sir, we are the only survivors from the Harad Community twenty miles to the north."

"You look all right to me," one of the others commented, coming up to inspect them.

"Yes," said a third, "most of those arriving here are starving."

Jem nodded and opened his hands in a gesture of explanation. "We had plenty of food," he said.

The one in charge looked at them more closely. "Where was this?" he said.

Aura took half a step forward. "The Harad Community," she told him. "We were attacked five nights ago and everything was destroyed."

"But we managed to escape," Jem put in.

The second soldier turned to the one in charge. "He looks big enough to look after himself," he said, but the leader shook his head.

"No," he answered scornfully. "Community people are all the same: helpless as babies and just about as much use." The others who had now gathered laughed at this.

"He's probably telling the truth," one of them said. "I seem to remember a few arrived from Harad some days ago."

The senior one turned back to Jem. "Where have you been in the meantime?" he demanded.

Jem shrugged stupidly. "Wandering," he said plaintively, and Aura nodded.

"We got lost," she said.

Their interrogator nodded and turned to the others. "What did I tell you?" he said. "Helpless." And he spat on the ground in front of them, while the others chuckled again. "And now I suppose you want the City to look after you?"

Jem looked at him appealingly. "We've nowhere else to go," he said.

"Just like all the others," commented the one standing next to the senior guard, who nodded again.

"Yes, they all arrive here sooner or later. All right, we'll see to you." He gave a sly wink at the others, then pointed at the man beside him. "Go with him," he ordered; "he'll show you where to go." Jem nodded eagerly, bobbing his head.

"Thank you, sir. Thank you."

"Many times," Aura added.

"All right." The third soldier poked Jem with his spear. "Follow me."

Jem gritted his teeth but managed to retain his servility.

"Yes, sir."

Their escort turned and walked through the gap in the wall of rubble. Jem followed, and Aura moved to do likewise; but before she could pass through, one of the soldiers grabbed her by the shoulder and swung her around to face him. He reached out to touch her breast, but instead of trying to avoid him she pushed her still-blackened stump through the end of her sleeve and held it under his nose. The soldier's face contorted with disgust, but his companions were convulsed by this and, while they were still laughing, Aura made her escape.

They were conducted through the front entrance of a large gloomy building where Jem's staff, water container and food pouches were taken from him. Then a door was flung open and they found themselves at the top of a short flight of steps leading down to a large hall packed with what must have been almost a thousand refugees standing so close together that anyone who fell would almost certainly have been trampled to death. There were one or two windows high out of reach, and these had to suffice both for light and ventilation, but the atmosphere was stifling and the room was in permanent gloom.

As soon as they appeared at the top of the steps, everyone began to clamor for the guard's attention, and he had to shout to make himself heard:

"Be quiet . . . all of you!" The babble half subsided to a murmur, like hens in a battery house. Jem and Aura looked on the scene below them in dismay.

"Go on, you're not allowed to wait on the steps," the soldier told them.

"Why not?" Jem asked, turning to him. "Surely we—"

"Don't argue," the other interrupted savagely, and suddenly pushed Jem, catching him off-balance and sending him crashing down the steps into the crowd.

The mass at the foot of the steps probably saved him from breaking his neck, but three or four people collapsed under him shrieking. The soldier laughed; but when Jem struggled up and started back up the steps, the grin vanished and he raised his spear to defend himself. When Jem stopped the point was barely a few inches from his throat. It would have been easy for him to take the spear away, but his head regained control; that would have spoiled everything.

The soldier's face twisted into a relieved snarl of

triumph as Jem backed down, and he jerked his head at the girl beside him. "Go on," he shouted. Aura moved to obey. "And make your friend behave himself if you know what's good for him."

He raised his head to the others who had now fallen silent. "You won't have much longer to wait," he told them. "They are nearly ready to receive you."

The words should have been reassuring, and they were to most of those listening, but to Jem they sounded more like a threat. Before he could say anything, the soldier had backed out and the door slammed shut.

At once the clamor began again and Jem helped Aura to a safer place against the wall. "You stay there," he told her, then he turned to help those whom his fall had knocked down.

No one else seemed to care. In fact, those nearby trod all over the ones on the ground without even bothering to look down and Jem had to use all his strength to force a space to enable them to struggle up.

"Move over, can't you?" he shouted, then pushed again to help one young woman to her feet. "Are you all right?" he asked; but she didn't answer, and a few seconds later was lost in the crowd. Jem then hauled an older woman to her feet but she collapsed immediately, and he had to risk being knocked over again in order to pick her up. This time he laid her on the steps and turned to dive back into the fray when he heard Aura call out:

"Jem, help me!"

Waves of pressure rippled up and down the room as everyone fought to breathe, and Jem turned to see Aura being crushed against the wall. Even he had difficulty reaching her, but when he did, he put an arm against the wall on either side of her and braced his back to form a frame. She was sobbing with fright.

"Don't leave me, please don't leave me!"

"I won't," Jem reassured her.

He struggled against the pressure and saw the steps and small platform at the top fill up in spite of the soldier's orders to the contrary. The minutes passed and eventually Jem began to doubt even his ability to shield Aura much longer. Then a door at the top of some steps at the other end of the room opened and two soldiers appeared. They shouted ineffectually into the din to begin with, but finally the clamor settled enough for one of them to be heard.

"We are ready for you now," he announced. "You will be taken one by one for questioning, then you will be allocated work."

As those at the other end left, the pressure noticeably lightened, and after an hour it was even possible to sit down.

Two hours later, Jem and Aura were the only ones left, apart from the bodies of a dozen unfortunates who had either suffocated or had been trampled underfoot. The door opened and a soldier looked in. He glanced from one to the other, then pointed at Jem.

"You're next," he said. Jem glanced quickly at Aura, who looked up at him round-eyed, then he turned to the soldier.

"Can I wait for the girl before starting work? We want to stay together."

The soldier grinned. "You can wait for her," he said.

"Thank you." Jem turned back to Aura and bent down to kiss her. Then he said in a voice too low for the soldier to hear: "Don't forget what I said."

Aura shook her head almost imperceptibly, then Jem mounted the steps and followed his escort through the door, which was banged shut behind him.

Jem was led toward an archway of light down a long, dark passageway in which their footsteps echoed and the figure of the man moved in silhouette in front of him. Finally they reached the end and emerged into a large open space at the rear of the building. The soldier stepped to one side and Jem also stopped, blinking in the strong light.

The first thing he saw was a long double line of soldiers forming a pathway from where Jem stood to the center of the open ground. Each soldier was armed with a drawn spear.

"Go on," the one at his side ordered. "Walk!" Jem found himself being prodded down the line and noticed, first, a huge mound of earth some fifty yards beyond the last soldiers. Laborers with shovels squatted there, grinning at him. Next, about half-way between the mound and the end of the line he saw a great pit, on the edge of which two soldiers stood grinning and beckoning, their bodies spattered with blood and their spears stained to the hilt.

Jem realized what was happening: the City authorities had no intention of stretching their limited supplies any further—nor were they going to risk being surrounded by starving bands of refugees who might overwhelm them if their numbers became too great. He had already been propelled almost to the edge of the pit, and at the bottom he could now see hundreds of bodies of those who had preceded him, who had obviously been killed by the two executioners standing on the edge. Some still writhed on top of the others, but no doubt their hosts reckoned five feet of earth would put a stop to that. Jem swung around.

"Murderers," he shouted, at the same time realizing the futility of what he was doing. "What have you done?"

The soldiers burst out laughing and forced him to continue, but at the last second he pulled himself together. They had not thought to take his knife—probably because the art of weaponry was only just being rediscovered.

Almost at the edge of the pit, he pretended to stumble, and one of the two slaughterers, whose turn it was, checked his thrust, waiting for him to stand up again so he could run him through more easily. Jem sprang upright, the knife miraculously finding its way into his left hand. With the same movement, he ripped the soldier's belly open to the top. It was so quick the man barely grunted, then he stood looking down at his now exposed intestines in sheer disbelief. The other soldiers were stunned with surprise—just long enough for Jem to push his victim back over the edge and seize the spear of the man on his right with his right hand while bringing the knife around in a curving blow which carried it between the man's lower ribs and into his heart, killing him instantly.

The second executioner fell backward as he died, the way of his previous victims, leaving the spear in Jem's right hand; by the time the other soldiers recovered, their two companions had disappeared and in their place stood a ferocious red-bearded giant with a spear in one hand and the thing which had caused so much devastation in the other. The time taken for this transformation was approximately five seconds.

"All right, who's going to be next?" Jem shouted.

They came at him in a rush. He sidestepped the first wave and three were carried past him over the edge by those behind. Of these, one fell on his own spear, one broke his neck and the other scrambled out the other side and ran away. With the pit at his back, they could only come two at a time, and to begin with Jem had little difficulty keeping them at bay. Within two minutes, he had killed ten, not counting the original two and the two who had fallen into the pit. Then they withdrew, giving him a breathing space.

Jem knew it was only a matter of time before he began to tire or a chance thrust caught him. In any event, he thanked his lucky stars it didn't occur to them to try throwing their spears, which he could never have evaded, but now he might be able to escape. He turned to run, but stopped almost immediately.

*Aura!* Jem swung back to look at the building from which he had just emerged. He couldn't leave her.

The guard commander stood to one side of the building, urging on reinforcements who ran through the narrow gap between this building and the one next to it. These men, although dressed similarly to the extermination squad, were obviously of a higher caliber, some of them being almost as tall as Jem himself. They moved into a rough semicircle around him about thirty yards away, so that now, even if he was to change his mind, it was too late to escape. He turned to face those nearest, then the commander stepped forward and gave the order to attack.

The two largest soldiers advanced within ten yards, then they stopped for a moment and Jem saw that the upper parts of their bodies were encased in some thick material, probably strong enough to withstand a thrust from a spear. The two exchanged a few words quietly, then split, each moving to the edge of the pit on either side of him, but still out of reach. Jem realized that now he couldn't face one without turning his back on the other. He was finished and they knew it, moving in with experienced confidence so different from the mindless rush he had faced before.

In the split second available, Jem did the only thing he could think of, which was to jump outward away from the pit and turn so that he could face both of them again at the same time. He was conscious that, in doing so, he was turning his back on the others, but a brief glimpse of the expression on the commander's face told him the man was amused by the exhibition and fully confident the two he had assigned were competent to deal with the situation without help. Jem made a thrust at the nearer soldier but the man turned his blow easily and he had to parry savagely with the knife in his other hand to avoid a counterthrust from his companion.

Now Jem had to fight as never before in his life, constantly having to break at right angles to prevent one of them from closing in behind. Once, he slipped and fell into the pit himself, but his adversaries realized he could cross the diameter and climb out at any point before they could reach the other side, so they did not hurry or risk becoming separated through being caught in two minds. Instead they let him pick his spot and climb out, thus tiring a little more, before closing in on him from opposite sides as before.

To Jem the struggle seemed endless—parry, thrust, parry again, then leap to a new position, always wondering if he had been quick enough or if, at last, he would feel one of their spears sink into his back. Suddenly he caught sight of Aura standing at the edge of the onlookers with a guard on either side of her.

"Aura!" The momentary distraction was all his enemies needed, and before he realized what had happened, his right shoulder was pouring blood and the spear dropped from his hand. In spite of himself, Jem glanced over again to where he had seen her, but this time Aura had vanished.

Jem looked back at his opponents, feeling giddy with loss of blood. He could only see one of them. He tried to blink the sweat from his eyes and concentrate on what he was doing, but there must be something wrong. . . . Why couldn't he see them both any more? Then everything went black as the second soldier stepped up behind him and hit him over the head.

Both soldiers stood grinning as Jem collapsed into the pit and a roar of triumph went up from the onlookers, who rushed forward with spears poised, but the commander reached the edge of the pit first and blocked their path, spear upraised.

"Stop!" he shouted. "The first to cast his spear will die."

The soldiers came to a halt, and began murmuring among themselves, but the commander silenced them. "The Council will have better use for him."

A few hours later, two elders followed the guard commander through a series of underground stone passages dimly lit by oil lamps and they, in turn, were followed by two guards. At last they reached a particular door, outside which stood another guard.

"Open up!" the commander ordered. The other nodded and took a key from his belt, which he fitted into the lock. The first elder glanced at his companion anxiously. They wore the distinctive dark robes of Senior Council members, but both were men of small stature.

"Is he dangerous?" He turned back to the commander, but the other smiled reassuringly.

"Not at the moment, Lord."

The guard opened the door and stood back, whereupon the commander entered the cell followed at a safe distance by the others.

The room was barren, except for a wall lamp and a low bed on which Jem lay unconscious, both hands secured to the wall above his head by hasps and chains. The commander looked down at him, smiling grimly, then he glanced at the doorway where the two elders stood just inside.

"It's all right," he told them. "He's still unconscious." The elders moved to the foot of the bed and looked down at Jem, their nervousness being replaced by satisfaction.

"You have done well," the first said after a few seconds.

The commander smiled ingratiatingly. "Thank you, sir." The second elder then turned to him.

"There's no doubt the girl was telling the truth?" he asked.

"No, Lord. That is the eldest son."

"What is he called?" asked the first.

"Jem."

"Jem?" the other repeated. "That is a curious name."

"The girl told us everything," the commander assured him.

"In exchange for her life, I presume?"

"Yes, sir."

The first elder glanced down at the unconscious figure on the bed, then he asked pointedly, "What do you propose doing with her?" The commander grinned.

"I thought perhaps . . . if the elders would permit . . . I would keep her myself for a while." The other two exchanged grins at this.

"I don't see why not," said the second. His companion nodded.

"I agree. He deserves a reward." But he turned to the commander sharply. "As long as you don't try to bring her with us." The other shook his head hurriedly.

"Of course not, Lord! She will be killed as soon as we are ready to leave."

"Then that's all right." They all turned back to look at Jem.

"You say he was wounded?" the first asked after a moment.

"Yes, sir. That is being attended to."

"Good. Whatever happens now, he must be kept alive."

"There's not much danger; he is abnormally strong, but I will see to it." The first elder turned to face him.

"We shall hold you responsible," he said, adding menace to the nasal, sing-song tone of a life-long City dweller. The other did not answer but a look of fear crossed his face, then the second elder turned for the door.

"I wonder what General Ngle will say."

His companion suppressed a smile. "He should be pleased," he said innocently.

"It will certainly mean we are not so dependent on his soldiers overcoming Preston's defenses."

"Yes." The other nodded, then glanced swiftly at the commander.

"You will say nothing of this," he ordered.

"No, Lord. My loyalty is to the Council of Elders." They both looked at him for a few moments solemnly.

"See you don't forget," the second said quietly.

## CHAPTER TEN

The hulls of the ships stood on the construction ground like twenty enormous black crystals, their hatchways open, and with hundreds of people swarming up and down the ramps like bees entering and leaving a hive.

Inside the command ship, Ham and Simon Bryant led Preston down one of the corridors which cut at right angles through the concentric circles of lateral passages to the center of the ship. At first, all the corridors were full of people either working on the internal fittings or hurrying from one place to another with materials and tools, but presently these were left behind.

Bryant turned to Preston. "Once the hulls were completed, we started at the center of each ship and worked outward," he said. "That's why this area has all been finished."

They came to another intersection, took a left turn, then turned right again after ten yards. Preston smiled at Ham resignedly.

"I'll never find my way around," he confessed.

Ham returned his smile. "You had too much to do

outside, Father," he said. "You'll soon pick it up."
Bryant nodded.

"Of course."

They came to the end of the passageway where it joined the inner corridor, which ran around the chamber at the very heart of the ship—a relative radius of thirty feet. There was a low inner door in the white wall opposite on which was painted the words: DANGER—ANNIHILATION BOX. Ham turned to his father.

"This corridor goes right around and comes back here," he told him. Preston smiled.

"Like the center of a puzzle?"

Ham nodded. "That's right. For all our newly acquired knowledge, that's just what most of it is." He turned to the door. "Inside here is the power plant which generates electricity and keeps all the environmental systems going. I expect you'd like to see inside?"

Preston nodded. "Very much."

Bryant got out a key and started to unlock the door. "Don't worry about the notice," he said. "It's for their own good; but you can't come to any harm inside as long as you don't start playing around with things you don't understand."

Preston smiled. "I'll take your word for it," he said. Bryant ducked and went through the low doorway, while Ham stood to one side to let his father go in next.

An iron catwalk led all the way around inside the cylindrical chamber. Bryant stepped to the left to make room for Preston, then Ham squeezed in on his father's right. An iron ladder led down to the center of the room, in the middle of which was a huge spherical tank made of the transparent material used for the windows, and containing a colorless liquid with the viscosity of glycerine in constant motion. Thick cables led from four diametrically opposed anodes, and shafts of brilliant blue light projected from just inside each to a central point where there was a single focus of such intensity that it was impossible to look at it directly for more than a split second. There was no other source of light in the chamber and the moving liquid projected constantly changing patterns on their bodies and on the walls behind them.

Ham pulled the door shut and the three of them stood silently, shielding their eyes from the direct glare with their hands. After a while, Preston spoke quietly:

"This provides power for everything?"

Bryant nodded. "Yes."

"What about fuel?"

"That's the liquid in the vessel," Ham told him. "What you can see will keep everything going for at least a hundred years." Preston turned to him amazed.

"How?"

Ham shook his head. "We only half understand," he admitted. "Matter is solid energy. They used to make power, centuries ago, by turning one kind of material into another, but this annihilates it completely, one atom at a time."

"That's the brilliant point of light in the center," Bryant put in. "One atom turning itself into pure energy; and no matter how close you looked or how powerful the instruments you used, you could never really see what was happening any more than a telescope can resolve the light from a distant star."

Ham nodded. "In a way, that's what you can see," he said. "A star . . . but on an infinitely small scale."

Preston paused for a few seconds, then he looked around the chamber in wonder. "Enough energy to power the whole ship from a single atom!"

"But not to drive the ship in space," Ham interjected. "The power here only works the control panels on the outside." Preston looked at him, puzzled. "I think we'd better go up to the flight command deck," Ham went on. "It will be easier to see."

Ten minutes later they joined Alison and Jacy, who began to explain the flight controls. As usual, it was Jacy who insisted on doing most of the talking.

While trying to absorb everything his son was saying, Preston's eyes wandered around the now completed cabin. It was some thirty feet across and had a band of observation windows following the circumference of the ship and extending from three feet from the floor almost to the ceiling. Immediately in front was a bank of flight instruments and controls with two seats, the first of which was to have been occupied by Jem, but no one mentioned his name now as Jacy sat down to illustrate the points he was making. The second was for David, who had proved the most outstanding of the new young pilots, and who had fully justified his appointment as second-in-command of the command ship. In fact, he could have commanded a ship of his own but, as the Preston family was to travel in the first ship, he had elected to serve under Jem. Immediately behind the pilots' seats was the most important single instrument they carried, the navigation computer, and on the left of this was the table at which Ham would interpret the computer's instructions for the benefit of the flight crew. Finally, to the right was the communications equipment, which on this ship would be operated by Jacy himself.

"Each of these thirty-two keys will operate one of the panels on the outside," Jacy was saying, and Preston dragged his mind back to what his youngest son was telling him. "They can be operated either singly or in groups, depending on the instructions from the navigation computer over there. They won't work at the moment because the delay switch is on, but when you press one down like this"—he demonstrated—"the vanes on one of the panels on the outside open up, driving the ship in the opposite direction."

"One is enough, or even one partially open," Alison added.

Preston nodded, then he said: "What if all the panels on one side are opened at the same time?" Jacy looked at his brother momentarily.

"That can only happen once we're clear of the Earth," Ham said.

"According to Ham's figures, each extra panel squares the power of those already open," Jacy went on, "so a third panel gives four times the power of two, and a fourth, sixteen times the power of three and so on."

"Then the power given by sixteen must be unimaginable." Preston observed.

"It is," Jacy said airily, "particularly when you think that five is enough to drive the ship up to the speed of light."

Ham smiled a little ruefully. "What happens after that, we aren't sure," he admitted. "Obviously the rest are intended to be used."

"We don't even know where we're going yet," Jacy said without thinking. Then they all looked at each other in silence for a moment. Finally Bryant spoke.

"There's one point no one seems to have made," he said. "We haven't the faintest idea what makes the ship move." Preston looked at him, then over to Ham, who nodded.

"That's right," he agreed. "When we were in the annihilation chamber, I told you the power there only controlled the vanes covering the panels, apart from generating electricity." Preston nodded.

"Well, that's all it does—cover and uncover the panels."

"Then what *does* drive the ship?"

Ham paused, then he said quietly, "We don't know. We can only think the panels must harness some force we don't know anything about. We don't understand what it is or how it works."

There was another moment's silence which Bryant was again the first to break. "That's not to say it's supernatural or anything like that," he pointed out. "After all, electricity existed for millions of years before anyone realized it was there."

Preston nodded. "That's true," he said quietly. "God

puts many gifts into the hands of those who learn how to use them. The miracle is that we've been given the use of something we have done nothing to deserve." He looked around and smiled. "Thank you for showing me. Now I have something to tell you. I shall be taking two of our younger men on a short trip outside the stockade."

"Outside?" Bryant said, more sharply than he'd intended. "I thought that was forbidden." Preston nodded pleasantly.

"It is," he admitted, "but this is an exception to the rule."

"But, sir, how can that be?"

"The one who makes the rules can change them," Preston told him.

The following day, Preston and Ndrew stood at the foot of the stockade on the outside watching David slide down a rope to the ground. Preston steadied him when his feet touched earth.

"All right?"

The young man nodded. "Yes, thank you."

"Good." Preston looked up to the several faces peering down at them and called out "Okay." The rope was hauled up, then he turned to his two young companions. "Follow me," he said, and started off in a southerly direction into the woods and up the hillside at such a pace the other two almost had to trot to keep up with him.

The two sentries watched the trio disappearing into the trees but, just before they were lost to sight, Preston turned and waved encouragingly. One of the sentries responded, then he turned to the other with a worried expression on his face.

"I don't like it," he said. "First Jem, now Preston."

"He said he'd be back before nightfall," the other pointed out.

"But what if something happens to him too?" The two men looked at each other.

Preston scrambled up the brow of the hill, then paused to allow the other two to catch up.

"I'm not going too fast for you, am I?" he asked.

David shook his head, almost winded, but the young Scot managed to gasp: "Not at all." Preston nodded.

"Good." He turned and made off again.

The other two glanced briefly at each other in agonized fashion, then hurried to catch up.

Half a mile further on, Preston paused on a spur to glance back at the compound before following the ridge, which now ran in a southwesterly direction and would take them out of sight. He turned to the two who stood beside him trying to regain their breath.

"The going should be easier from now on," he said. David nodded without answering and Preston smiled. "Do you want to stop for a rest?" David was just opening his mouth to say "Yes, please," but Ndrew cut in first.

"Not at all, sir," he said. Preston nodded approvingly.

"It's about a mile along the top of this ridge," he said, and David shut his mouth.

Preston led them to the point where the ridge suddenly fell away five hundred feet in a sharp escarpment to the dried-up plain below. In this position they could see right across the flat, open country to the beginning of the forest which stretched from there almost all the way to New York.

"If an attack comes, it will be from that direction —from the south," he told them, after they had stood in silence for a while. "From here you can see halfway to the City, but it might not be possible to observe an army on the march until it emerges from the forest about six miles from here." He pointed. "In particular from there, where you can see a gap in the line of trees." David turned to him.

"Why from there?" he asked.

"That's where the main highway runs," Preston told him. "It would be easier to come that way; but don't concentrate there to the exclusion of other directions," he added, turning from one to the other. "They might try to take us by surprise."

The young Scot looked all around. "In that case they might strike from the east or west," he said, "or even from the north." Preston nodded.

"Quite right. That's why I said that, although it's the most likely spot, we must not ignore the other possibilities." He paused for a few seconds before continuing. "They must come from the south originally. I don't think it would be possible to deploy to the east or west before they emerge onto the plain."

"What about the north?" Ndrew asked.

"The whole land between here and the City reservoir is dry," Preston told him. "I don't think they could carry enough water to march right around us. It is not a possibility we should ignore completely, but as far as you're concerned, I want you to concentrate mainly on the land you can see in front of you."

"Yes, sir."

"You have marked this position well?"

"Yes, sir." The two young men nodded.

"Then you will take it in turns to keep watch. You have water and provisions enough for three days, then you will be relieved by two others I shall bring. You understand?"

"What if we see them coming?" Ndrew asked. "The army, I mean." Preston glanced back instinctively in the direction of the forest.

"One must come and warn me at once," he said. "The other stay and try to follow their progress."

"Very well."

Preston looked from one to the other again and seemed satisfied. "I'll leave you now," he said, "and bring others to take your place in three days' time. In the meantime, remember how much may depend on this. Watch day and night. Never sleep at the same time!"

The heavy door of the underground cell flew open with a crash as the guard commander strode into the room. Jem was standing at the far end, his arms and legs shackled with chains.

"Come on. The Council wants to have a look at you."

"What for? Why are you keeping me here?"

"Don't start all that again. We know who you are."

Jem gritted his teeth. "The girl lied to save her own skin," he said.

"Tell that to the elders." The commander gave a

savage push which sent Jem staggering toward the door. His wounds had healed, but he had not yet regained his strength or he might have given a better account of himself in the confined space, even though his hands and feet were restricted.

He was escorted back along the labyrinth of passages and finally up some stone steps which led to the anteroom of the main Council Chamber, a large hall around which sat fifty of the City's rulers. Behind them, armed guards stood among marble pillars and, at the far end, a little apart, General Ngle sat, resplendent in dress uniform. He was flanked by a troop of soldiers who exchanged hostile stares with the Council guards nearest them.

Jem was pushed into the room so violently he lost his balance, with his feet being shackled together, and fell on his face, where he lay panting with rage and frustration. The elders stared down at him with curiosity—several with unnatural interest—while the guard commander turned toward them.

"The man I spoke of, my Lords."

When Jem raised his head he found himself surrounded by four guards in addition to the commander.

"Make the prisoner stand up," the first elder demanded in a high, piping voice.

"Yes, sir." The commander poked Jem roughly with his spear.

"You heard what the elder said," he ordered. "Stand up!"

Jem nodded. "All right," he muttered hoarsely. "Leave me alone." Eventually he struggled to his feet. A murmur rose from the council as he stood up.

Bowed as he was under the weight of chains, Jem was still a gigantic figure compared with the men next to him.

The first elder looked around triumphantly. "What did I tell you, my Lords? He even looks like Preston."

"It must be him," another agreed.

"I saw Preston when he came to the City that time," said another.

"I did too," said a fourth.

"What does General Ngle think?" said one of the others, turning to the man at the far end who, until now, had sat silently staring at their prisoner. This was taken up in an excited buzz which died as the general rose to his feet and slowly walked up to Jem. He looked him up and down without expression.

"I hear you know how to fight," he said eventually.

"A desperate man may do many things," Jem answered carefully; but the commander stepped forward eagerly.

"Not like that," he said. "You should have seen him, General. He—"

"Silence! I didn't ask for your opinion." Ngle turned back to Jem. "Do you deny being the son of Preston?"

"Yes."

"In which case you will not object to teaching my men the secret of your new weapon," the other said evenly. Jem looked at him, puzzled.

"What?"

"The sharp thing, which cuts flesh." Jem's frown lessened.

"You mean the knife?"

"Yes. Where did you get it?"

Jem hesitated, then he said, "I found it."

Ngle smiled briefly. "You may be an accomplished warrior, but you are a poor liar. There's not a man in my army who could have fought as you are reported to have done."

"I told you—" Jem began, but Ngle held up his hand.

"Yes. I know what you said." He turned to the elders. "I saw Preston as close as I am standing to this man now, when he came to warn us. We should have listened then; but I agree . . . this must be his son." He glanced at Jem briefly.

"Then you agree to our plan?" the first elder asked, trying to keep his voice from revealing his satisfaction. Ngle looked at him for a moment, then nodded.

"I don't believe an ordinary man would respond to what you propose," he said, "but as we have found to our cost, Preston is not an ordinary man."

The second elder nodded. "He speaks the truth."

"The army is almost ready to move," Ngle went on. "All we are waiting for now is the supply wagons to be completed." He moved further into the center of the room. "I propose that the army move into position as if the original attack were going to take place," he said. "But we will try your idea first. If it fails, the storming of the compound can proceed as planned originally."

His audience murmured among themselves for a few moments, then one of them said: "That sounds like an excellent idea."

"The only trouble is," whined another, "that by the time the soldiers have all been given places on the ships, there will be so few left for our friends. The other way, we could leave the army behind."

Ngle turned on this angrily. "I cannot agree," he began, but the first elder interrupted him sharply.

"If that's what the Council decides, you will have to obey." The two men glared at each other.

"At least we are guaranteed of being saved this way," said one of the others diplomatically, breaking the silence, and the man to his left nodded in agreement.

"That's right," he said. "If the first elder's plan fails, and the army is not in a position to attack immediately, Preston's ships might leave before a new assault could be organized."

One of those sitting on the far side rose to his feet and looked around. "I propose we adopt Ngle's plan," he said in a thin, high-pitched voice, "except that two elders should travel with the army, and a sufficient number of guards—just to"—he hesitated, then smiled—"keep an eye on things," he concluded. Most of the Council members nodded approvingly, and the general smiled grimly, looking around.

"What is the matter, my Lords? Don't you trust your military leader?"

This was a great joke and everyone laughed. There was not one who would not trample on the next to save his own skin and they all knew it, but Jem stared at them in disgust. He spoke when the laughter faded.

"What do you plan to do with me?" he demanded.

"Why . . . exchange you for half your father's ships," the first elder told him, giving a wink to those on the other side of the room.

"You must be mad," Jem said angrily. "Preston would never betray those who put their trust in him." Ngle stepped forward.

"Then you do know him!" he said. Jem bit his lip. "It will be interesting to see, I agree," the other went on.

"Even if I were his son, which I deny . . ." Jem began. The others started to laugh again.

"I very much hope you are mistaken," the first elder told him, raising his voice to make himself heard. "If only for your own sake. You see, after the offer has been made, you will be pegged out on the ground just outside the stockade, and every five minutes we have to wait, some member of your body will be removed." Jem looked around the room in a daze. This only made the others laugh even harder.

"The offer will remain open as long as you are still alive," his tormentor went on, "but I hope your father is the sort of man who makes up his mind fairly quickly." The elders doubled up, almost helpless with mirth, and the first elder had to shout his last remark.

"You'd better scream as loudly as you can from the beginning. It would be a pity to delay a decision!"

Jem was returned to his cell.

Forty miles away, on the edge of the ridge, Ndrew and David stood up when they saw two of their friends coming toward them. They picked up their things and went to meet them; then, after exchanging a few words, the four separated: Ndrew and David to walk back to the compound, the two newcomers to settle down and keep watch over the plain —empty now, except for dust devils and the dark edge of the forest beyond.

During the ensuing days, Ngle brought the ten thousand soldiers under his command to a peak of training which ended with a demonstration attack on a mock-up of the stockade, identical in every respect to the one around the compound—even to the buildings immediately behind. The elders watched as drums throbbed and the first contingent of shock troops carrying ladders and grappling ropes with hooks flung themselves against the fence. They were backed by others who twirled balls of fire on the end of short ropes which they hurled over the stockade onto the buildings behind, and these were soon ablaze.

A spirited defense was made by other soldiers using staves with blunt ends but one wave of attackers followed another and eventually the defenders were overwhelmed. Ngle turned proudly to the group of elders standing on the dais beside him.

"When the rivers dried and the big generators stopped," he said, "they thought we would grind to a halt with the Machines. Now look at them!"

Most of those listening nodded with admiration, but a few exchanged apprehensive looks.

A soldier came running up and stood just below them.

"Pardon, sir." He saluted the general.

"What is it?"

"Cam presents his compliments and would inform

you that the last wagon has just been completed."
Ngle turned to the elders expansively.

"Did you hear that, my Lords?" he demanded.
"You have just witnessed our last rehearsal. Now for
the real thing."

## CHAPTER ELEVEN

Preston walked alone through the deserted meeting hall of the command ship, which was also de-
signed to be used as a dining room; then through
the library and a long intersecting corridor with
dormitories and smaller rooms on either side, turning finally toward the main entrance.

Against the brighter light from outside, Ham stood
in the hatchway, his body in silhouette, peering into
the ship. "Father?" he called tentatively. Preston
walked toward him, quickening his step.

"Are you looking for me?"

"Well, yes," Ham said, as his father joined him.
"Everyone is at supper; we all wondered where you
were."

"Preston nodded apologetically. "I'm sorry."

Ham looked at him. "Aren't you hungry?" he asked.

Preston shook his head. "Not just yet," he said.
"Would you ask Mother to put something to one side.
I'll have it later."

Ham hesitated. "Is something wrong?" he asked.

"No, I just want to do some thinking." Preston paused, then he said quietly, "These are not easy days for any of us."

"It's Jem, isn't it?" Ham said after a few seconds."

"He is never far from my thoughts."

Ham nodded. "We all think about him," he said gently. "But there is nothing we can do, is there?"

"No, you're right." Preston put his hand on his son's shoulder. "Don't bother about me," he said. "Go and finish your supper. I'll be along presently."

"All right, Father." Ham hesitated a moment longer, then he turned and walked down the ramp; but he stopped at the bottom and called back: "We ran out the temporary power lines today. By tomorrow night we should have those lights fixed on the stockade—then at least they won't be able to sneak up on us in the dark!" Preston smiled and raised his hand in acknowledgment; then he watched Ham turn and walk out of sight.

The smile faded from Preston's face and he lifted his eyes to the ridge overlooking the camp. After a while he prayed:

"Dear Lord, if it be not against Thy will, let my son return to me alive. Forgive his disobedience, I beg; or if he must bear the consequences of his own foolishness, let his death be quick and painless."

Chained to the rear axle, Jem staggered along behind one of the supply wagons which rumbled and crashed its way toward the gateway out of the City. Twenty men pushed and cursed, and the noise from

143

this and the other wagons in the narrow street was almost deafening.

General Ngle, mounted on the only horse, was the first to pass under the gateway which led out onto the main highway leading north. Behind him marched company after company of men wearing protective padding and carrying spears, until the whole column stretched away across the plain into the distance, creating great clouds of dust. In the first wagon to thunder through the gateway the two senior elders rode, surrounded by a contingent of Council guards, led by the guard commander. The next was the one to which Jem was chained; then eight more carrying food and water. Many swayed and crashed into the sides of the restricted exit but they were solidly built and it was the gateway itself which splintered as they emerged. In one instance, a soldier pushing one of the wagons was crushed to death as it passed through, but no one took any notice and his place was swiftly taken by one of the two gangs of relief hauliers who walked alongside each vehicle. Columns of men followed, each carrying six or seven unlighted fireballs, and finally the elite troops, almost as big as Jem, brought up the rear to make sure that nobody dropped out. By the time these had passed through under the eyes of the rest of the Council watching from above the gateway, the head of the column was well over a mile away.

The elders watched the army disappearing into the distance, then one of them noticed a man with crazed eyes also watching from the corner of a deserted building nearby. He turned and shouted at once to one of the soldiers, standing immediately below them, who had been left to guard the City.

"Guard!" The man turned to face him.

"Yes, Lord."

The elder pointed. "There's someone over there who seems to have escaped your attention." The soldier and his companions turned just in time to see the man's head disappear.

"We'll deal with him, Lord."

The soldier spoke briefly to his nearest companion, and the two of them set off in pursuit. They rounded the corner into a deserted street and paused, looking around. After a few seconds one of them saw a movement at the end of a side street, seventy yards away, and they set off again.

The soldiers ran into the side street and saw that it was a dead end; their quarry was trapped. They stopped running and started to walk toward him, grinning with anticipation; but just after they had passed a grating in the roadway lifted and four men emerged behind them, two carrying spears. They were filthy and their clothes were in rags, but they stalked after the soldiers in silent determination, despair giving edge to their courage.

The soldiers cornered their man, who backed against the wall and shrieked as they speared him to death, but a few seconds later the soldiers themselves cried out in agony and pitched forward. The two men with spears bent down and picked up the dead soldiers' weapons, which they handed to their two unarmed companions; then all four, grinning grotesquely, began to drag the three bodies to the hole and drop them through one by one. The four followed quickly, and the last pulled the grating back into position.

The street was as deserted as before.

The leading supply wagon reached the bottom of the hill where the forest began and Ngle came riding back; he shouted orders for the gangs who had pushed the wagons across the plain to stand down and the first of the two relief gangs to take their place. When this was done, the first wagon started to move again—painfully slowly, but it did not occur to the two elders riding on top to get down and lighten the load. The second wagon also started up the hill with Jem staggering behind, followed by all the rest.

In spite of the team leader's shouted encouragement, the first wagon came to a halt again and the new hauliers had to strain for all they were worth to stop it from rolling back.

"All right, the rest of you who haven't done anything so far come on," the first leader shouted to the second relief gang. "Lend a hand . . . hurry up now. . . . Push!"

With the additional effort, the wagons started to roll again as similar orders were echoed back down the column. Ngle drew level with Jem and reined in his horse so that it walked beside Jem for a moment.

"You help push as well," he shouted, "unless you want it to roll back on you. Go on!" The guards marching on either side of Jem prodded him with their spears until he obeyed.

When the first wagon reached the top of the hill, the hauliers instinctively relaxed for a moment, but the road dropped away to the other side almost immediately and the wagon started to roll forward under its own weight. The elders sat bolt upright in alarm.

"Get hold of it, you fools!" they shrieked. "Quick!" Everyone rushed forward obediently, but the wagon gathered speed so fast that not enough men could reach it in time, and some of the most determined, including the leader, disappeared under the wheels, screaming.

The gradient increased and the wagon broke away completely, accelerating down the hill at terrifying speed just as Ngle reached the crest. He saw the wagon leave the road at the first bend with the elders still on it, fly into the air, turn over almost in slow motion, then crash into the trees. The general watched impassively, then he turned to the others, who looked up at him fearfully.

"Help the second wagon," he said calmly, and turned his horse to meet the wagon just as it was appearing over the crest. "None of you let go when you reach the top," he shouted. "Stop, but keep hold." He then moved on to the rear of the wagon as the team leader took up the order and the survivors of the first wagon gang hurried forward to help.

Ngle reined in his horse, then turned again and rode beside Jem until the wagon drew to a halt. He shouted at the Council guards, who still stood at the top of the hill looking where their masters had disappeared: "You—come here; and you—and you two." The four ran forward and stood in front of him, trembling. Ngle pointed at Jem.

"Unchain him from the wagon."

"But, sir . . ." the senior guard began to protest.

"Do as I say," Ngle thundered. "He's too weak to do you any harm. I want two of you to walk on either side of him. Fasten the chains to your belts. We don't want to lose him too."

"Yes, sir." The guard nodded to the others and they hurried forward obediently.

They were more careful on the hills after that, but most of the time the road was reasonably flat and the column swung along at full marching pace. Jem walked more easily now, in spite of the two soliders chained to him on either side. He knew they were frightened of him and would occasionally glare at the two nearest, gaining some small satisfaction from the looks of terror which flickered across their faces.

Ngle sat on his horse at the roadside watching the end of the column pass and waiting for the guard commander, who came running up with four of his men and stopped in front of him, panting. He looked down at them with distaste.

"Well?"

"They were both dead," the commander gasped. "We could do nothing."

"I told them it would be safer to stay behind," the other said, without interest. "You'd better join the rest of your men guarding the prisoner." The commander nodded.

"Very well."

"Very well, *sir*," Ngle barked. The two men looked into each other's eyes, but the man on the ground gave way first.

"Very well . . . sir," he conceded, and turned to

move away; but Ngle was not letting him off so lightly.

"You're under my command now," he said. "See you don't forget."

The commander turned back, putting on the most respectful look he could muster.

"No, sir, we will obey your orders."

Ngle nodded curtly. "Get on with it, then."

The commander gave an order and the five of them began to run to catch the end of the column. Ngle allowed himself a brief smile, then he kicked up his horse and galloped after them so they had to jump to the side of the road to avoid being ridden down.

In the late afternoon of the following day, David lay in the grass on his back asleep, while Ndrew sat beside him staring into the distance across the plain. Suddenly Ndrew stiffened and, after a few seconds, put out a hand to shake his companion awake without shifting his eyes from their point of focus. David sat up beside him, rubbing his face.

"What?"

Ndrew pointed, and David followed his gaze to where columns of dust could be seen rising above the trees above a mile into the forest.

"They're coming," Ndrew said simply. "There must be thousands of them to make such dust. Run and warn Preston. I'll stay here."

"Right!" David scrambled to his feet.

"Be careful."

David nodded. "I will," he assured him, then set off at a brisk trot.

Ndrew watched him go for a few moments, then he stood up himself and walked to the very end of the ridge, where he stood leaning on his spear looking south, as still as a heron. Shortly afterward it began to get dark.

The news of David's return ran through the camp like fire. Preston immediately called a meeting of leaders and David reported what he had seen.

They stood silently for a few seconds after the younger man had finished, then Preston put out his hand and touched David's shoulder briefly.

"You have done well," he said, then he turned to the others. "We must stand to immediately, but it's unlikely they'll try to attack before dawn."

Jacy grinned nervously. "Particularly now that the lights are staring them in the face," he said, and Bryant nodded.

"Father, may I make a suggestion?" Ham took a step forward and Preston turned to him.

"Well?"

"We know they're coming—that's something; but wouldn't it be more valuable if we knew their exact strength?"

Preston nodded. "I was just coming to that," he said. "Ndrew should remain on the ridge for another hour. I intend to join him and see for myself." There was a worried reaction to this and Ham glanced around briefly before turning back.

"With respect, sir, that's not what I had in mind; nor do I think it wise." Preston looked at his son keenly.

"Are you doubting my judgment?"

"If anything happened to you," Ham said solemnly, "we would be lost. Surely it would be better if someone else went? Me, for instance. Under cover of darkness, we could get close enough and be back here in less than four hours." Preston paused for a few seconds, then he smiled a little ruefully.

"Perhaps you're right," he admitted. "It's true Ndrew and yourself together might move faster, much as I hate to admit it." Then he hesitated, wanting to say something else without knowing how, but Ham looked at him and understood.

"I will keep my eyes open," he promised, "and let you know what I see."

It took Ham less than half an hour to gain the end of the ridge and there he stopped, looking down at the plain where the lights from campfires blossomed like a thousand orange flowers.

"Ndrew . . . where are you?" he whispered, and was relieved to hear the other answer immediately.

"Over here." A few seconds later, he saw the young Scot as a blob of darkness against the skyline and walked toward him.

"Ham!" Ndrew put a hand on his arm for a moment, then both of them turned back to look at the plain.

"Do you know how many?"

Ndrew shrugged. "At least ten thousand," he said. "The same as us."

"But they'll all be fighting men. Three times as many as we can muster."

Ham smiled in the dark. "Let's go and have a closer look," he said. The other nodded and together they turned and set off down the southern slope.

When they had made camp, the commander had ordered the chains to be removed from the four guards so the prisoner could be attached to one of the now stationary wagons. "I'm going up to report," he told them, "but I'll be back soon." He walked out of the firelight in the direction of Ngle's headquarters.

The senior guard spat as soon as he had gone. "He's changed his tune quick enough," he said, and the others nodded; but they were glad to remove the chains from their belts, although Jem was standing with his head bowed, looking completely exhausted.

"He doesn't feel safe now that the elders aren't here to hold his hand," one of them said, taking up the thought voiced earlier. "If you ask me, Ngle arranged the whole thing." His companions grinned as they unwound their ends of the chain.

"Don't let him hear you say that," one more cautious than the others warned, but the first guard spat again contemptuously.

"Why not?" he demanded. "There's never been any love between the general and the Council."

His friend nodded. "They need him."

"But they're scared stiff he'll take the ships and leave 'em all behind." They all chuckled at this.

"Well, I don't care for one," began the other, as he bent down to attach his chain to one of the wheels. "As long as he—" But he never completed the sentence as Jem suddenly came to life and jumped back, tearing the end from his grasp.

Jem wheeled around, using the loose chain as a weapon, and brought the rough metal links crashing across the necks of the two men still holding him

by the other. The one furthest away caught the full
force of the impact and dropped his end with a
scream. He staggered back, clutching his face while
blood spurted between his fingers from the empty
socket where his left eye had been not a second earlier. The other soldier dropped the chain as well,
and Jem was free to run, but in the heat of the moment he made the mistake of swinging again at the
comparatively uninjured man as he backed away.
He was too close and the chain wrapped itself
around the man's neck. Jem struggled to pull free
and his luckless opponent tripped and fell to the
ground with the chain still around his throat. The
jerk broke his neck and he lay still, but the dead
weight pulled Jem forward suddenly and he fell to
his knees.

When the senior guard felt the chain tear from
his grasp he swung around, then froze at the sight
of Jem, who had now turned into a terrifying attacker. A spear lay near to hand, but he kept his
head and picked up a thick stick from a pile which
had just been collected to feed the fire. He waited
for Jem to turn his back, making sure to stay out
of range in the meantime. When he saw the prisoner
dragged to his knees, he jumped forward and brought
the club down hard on the back of his neck.

The fourth guard, reacting more slowly and less
intelligently, cast his spear at the kneeling figure;
but as Jem collapsed a split second before the
spear arrived, the weapon instead caught the man
with the club full in the stomach.

A few seconds later, the guard commander came
running with four more soldiers behind him, just

as the sole survivor snatched up another spear to finish off the now unconscious prisoner.

"What do you think you're doing?" he screamed.

The other stared back at him wildly. "He broke loose. He's killed all of them."

"Fool!" The commander fetched the man a savage blow across the side of his head. "Do you think I care how many of you die? It was your fault for letting him go."

"He pretended to be exhausted, Lord," the other whimpered; "you saw for yourself. He took us by surprise." His words ended with a yelp.

"Think yourself lucky I'm back in time or it would have been your screams we should have enjoyed before setting off tomorrow." The guard fell to his knees sobbing. "Pah!" The commander looked down at him contemptuously, then turned to the four who had accompanied him and nodded at Jem's prostrate figure.

"Bind him to the wagon before he wakes up," he ordered.

"Yes, sir." They moved quickly to obey him.

"And make sure nothing else happens. I still have to make my report." He turned to move away, then hesitated and turned back. "Mind you . . . we shall say nothing of this."

When Jem regained consciousness he found the chains had been removed and he was now tied hand and foot with ropes. As his eyes focused, he became aware that one of the soldiers was squatting beside him with a short club. It was the survivor from the original four whose head and pride were still smarting from the humiliation meted out to him.

"Every time you move, I'm going to hit you with this, see," he said savagely and gave Jem's head a sharp tap, which made his brain scream in protest, but not enough to knock him out again. He closed his eyes and groaned while the other grinned.

"That's right," he said, "you carry on. You've got a lot to answer for." Jem smelled blood for the first time. The front of his tunic was soaked but, apart from his head, he seemed to be uninjured. He decided the wisest course was to keep his mouth shut.

The soldier looked disappointed. After a few seconds, he gave Jem's head another bang, but on still getting no response, he said, "You think that hurts! You wait till we get going on you tomorrow morning." He grinned for a moment, then gave him a savage thump.

"Leave him alone!" When Jem's vision cleared, he became aware that one of the other guards was standing a few feet from his head. "His brains'll be like jelly if you go on tapping his head like that."

Jem's tormentor looked up and gave a grin. "I'm not doing any harm," he said. "Just keeping him dizzy so he can't give us any more trouble."

"Give it a rest. Don't you want any supper?"

Ham parted the bushes carefully and by the light of the fire saw two guards bending over the man lying on the ground about twenty yards away. Ndrew peered over his shoulder.

"Come on," he heard one of them say, "you can't fight on an empty stomach. There won't be time in the morning if we have to move as early as he said." So saying he turned and walked back to the others, who were sitting down eating their supper.

The other glanced back at the man on the ground, then he stood up and nodded. "All right," he said, and moved to follow, so their victim's face was seen by those watching from the bushes for the first time.

"Jem!" Ham started, and Ndrew quickly put out a hand to steady him.

The last to join the group put down his club and picked up a bar of compressed protein, which he started to stuff into his mouth, looking back and grinning at Jem lying on the ground.

"I told you to leave him alone," the first one said.

"Don't worry, I wouldn't let him miss the fun to-morrow for anything!"

One of their companions sauntered over and stopped beside Jem, looking down at him. "Do you believe they'll open the stockade to save him?" he asked after a few seconds. Jem's tormentor walked across to join him, still stuffing food into his mouth.

"I hope not," he said. "Nothing would give me greater pleasure than to see him cut into small pieces.

"What about us?" one of the others called across. "I hope the plan succeeds. If they all fight like he does many of us will die."

The first guard spat. "Ah . . . you're all too soft," he said, and turned to give Jem a resounding kick. A second later a spear embedded itself in his back and he turned to the man beside him, eyes wide with disbelief and his mouth open in a silent scream.

Ndrew and Ham sprang from cover, Ndrew carrying a spear and Ham armed with a long knife. They killed two of the seated guards almost before they had time to move, then Ham snatched up a spear from one and caught the other one who had been standing over by Jem in the stomach as he rushed in to attack. One of the others started to run, but Ndrew caught him before he had left the clearing and Ham pounced on the survivor—but not before he had thrown his spear.

Ham pulled the spear from his opponent's body, then turned to see Ndrew staggering toward him; as he watched, his friend's knees buckled and he collapsed into the fire. Ham rushed forward to pull him clear, but found a spear was sticking into his back. He must have died before his body reached the ground.

After making sure Ndrew was really dead, Ham turned and ran to his brother, who looked up at him, his eyes filled with amazement.

"Ham!"

Ham unfastened the ropes as quickly as he could and helped his brother to sit up. "How do you feel?" he said anxiously.

Jem shook his head, trying to clear his thoughts. "Not good," he replied, "but I'll be all right."

"Wait!" Ham held up a hand, listening. "I don't think anyone heard," he said after a short pause, "but let's get out of here."

"Right."

"Can you stand?"

"Of course." Ham helped him to his feet, which were shackled together with a chain.

"All right?"

Jem nodded. "Just a bit giddy." Then he looked

down. "But what about these?" he said. "I can't go back like this."

"I'll try to get them off on the way back," Ham told him. "Come on." He turned to lead the way.

"No, wait."

Ham turned back. "What?"

Jem put out a hand to restrain him. "There's something we should do first."

Ham glanced at the body by the fire. "Ndrew's dead," he said simply, but Jem answered impatiently.

"Not him," he said. "Something else." Then he gave a wicked grin.

They found the five water wagons sufficiently separated from one another to be able to dispose of the guards, one group at a time. Then it was simply a question of opening the tanks and remaining long enough to see that no one interfered during the time it took for the last drop to drain away.

They stopped when they reached the foot of the ridge, and Ham managed to prise open the hasps with his knife while Jem sat on a rock. Then he straightened up and threw the chain into some nearby bushes. Jem stood up.

"Thank you."

"That's all right." Ham turned to look down at the lights of the army flickering in the distance. "I wonder how long it will be before anyone realizes."

"Not long."

Ham turned back to look at his brother. "Perhaps they will go back," he said, but Jem shook his head.

"They can't. There's no water between here and New York."

"Then let's go. Father will be waiting." But Jem suddenly put a hand on his brother's wrist:

"Don't tell anyone," he said quietly, "I don't want Father to know." Ham looked at him. "I don't mean about my being captured," Jem went on, "or what we did just now."

"You mean about the plan to use you as a hostage against us?"

Jem nodded. "There's no point in upsetting Father. In any case, I'd have died first."

"How?" Ham looked at his brother more closely, but Jem couldn't answer. "You know how much he loves you," he said.

"You don't think he would have agreed?"

"I think the choice would have killed him." Ham looked at Jem a few seconds longer, then half turned away. "But you're right," he said. "He's been distressed enough." He started to climb the hill and Jem fell in behind. They didn't speak again until they reached the top, when they paused for a few seconds to regain their breath.

"We'll say we ran into each other just after I escaped," Jem said.

Ham turned to look at him. "You escaped?" he said amazed.

"Yes. It would be better for morale if we said that."

"Whose morale?"

Jem paused. "The ordinary people," he said at last.

Ham nodded grimly. "Of course."

"That is, unless you want to play the big hero," Jem said pointedly.

"No, Jem, I don't want to do that." Ham paused

for a few seconds, then he sighed. "All right, but what about Ndrew, who died saving you?"

"We'll say he was killed by one of the soldiers guarding the wagons." Jem looked away to avoid Ham's glance. "Well, it's near enough the truth," he said. "Come on, they'll be needing us."

He set off without looking back and, after a few seconds, Ham followed.

The loss of the water was discovered before the two brothers had regained the stockade, and at first panic broke out; but Ngle moved among his men, calming their fears, and at first light he had them all gathered in ranks before him, and spoke from the top of one of the wagons. He held a spear in his right hand and, although nothing like the size of Preston, he dominated them with his words.

"You all know what has happened," he began quietly. "Luckily, most of us have full water bottles; but even if we were to start back to the City at once, leaving everything behind, the majority would die from thirst on the way." A rumble of agreement rolled through the ranks, and Ngle held up his left hand. "But there is no need to despair," he told them. "We shall not die, because all the water and food we need lies just on the other side of those hills." He pointed over their heads.

"We have trained hard for months to become the finest fighting machine the world has ever seen," he went on, deliberately raising his voice, and a low cheer broke out while some began to grin at each other with mounting confidence. "I never believed in the elders' plan to use Preston's son as a hostage," he continued, catching their mood. "His escape has simply rid of us a distraction from our true objective—the storming of the enemy's stronghold." He raised the spear above his head now, and this time a real cheer answered him. "We have everything we need to succeed," he went on with growing intensity. "Courage, skill, weapons . . . and now, to put a final edge to our endeavors, a choice between life and death." He paused, then dropped his voice dramatically. "Remember, once inside, the ships and a future for ourselves and our chosen companions are ours." The rumble of enthusiasm gathered momentum and, once again, he raised the spear. "We could always succeed, if we had the will. Now we can, because we must."

The cheers became deafening, and Ngle pointed toward the ridge in the distance, shouting at the top of his voice to make himself heard:

"Take up your positions!"

The soldiers turned and ran to form themselves into columns as before, only now on a broad front several hundred yards wide. Ngle looked down and saw the commander leading his horse forward. He mounted and moved to take up a position in front of the army; then he turned in the saddle and raised his spear.

"Forward!" The soldiers raised their weapons in an answering shout which was heard by the remaining lookout on top of the ridge several miles away. To the throb of drums, the army started to roll across the plain like a juggernaut.

## CHAPTER TWELVE

The stockade was fully manned and the two reserve detachments under Ham and Simon Bryant were in position.

The old people and younger children filed into two of the central ships, which were surrounded by a guard of young women and older children.

Jem stood beside his father on the catwalk behind the southern stockade; both men watched the crest of the hill for the first sign of the advancing enemy.

"Perhaps they will not come," Preston said after a while.

Jem shook his head. "They have no choice," he said, and his father sighed.

"All we needed was another two weeks."

The two stood in silence again, both alone with their own thoughts, then Jem said: "If we can hold for a while, lack of water is bound to tell in the end."

Preston nodded. "Yes," he agreed. "You did well. They will never return if we defeat them now."

Jem turned his head to look at him. "Then I'm forgiven?" he asked quietly.

Preston turned to him. "You are my son," he said simply.

Jem smiled. "You have three sons, Father."

"Yes." Preston nodded slowly.

The last of the old people led the remaining

children inside the two ships and the hatchways were closed. Valla was one of three young women guarding the ramp of the ship nearest to where Preston and his eldest son stood talking quietly; her eyes rarely wandered from Jem to the crest of the hill above the stockade, which was the focus of attention for practically everyone else. Suddenly the girl to her right stiffened and pointed half a mile along the ridge.

"There they are," she called out. Her cry was immediately taken up by others and Valla looked quickly in the same direction where a man on a horse had just ridden into view and stopped, looking down at them.

Jem turned to Preston. "It's Ngle, commander of their army," he said tensely. "He's the only one with a horse."

Ngle turned in the saddle slightly, looking to his left, then he made a gesture urging those behind to spread out further to the west.

David glanced at Ham urgently. "Where're the rest of them?" he whispered, and Ham nodded briefly.

"You'll see in a minute," he said.

The general stood in his stirrups to signal the attack. A few seconds later the defenders saw the whole crest of the hill engulfed by the first wave of soldiers, who were immediately followed by a second, and a third . . . and so on, seemingly endlessly, as those in front started down the slope, until the whole hillside was alive with the advancing enemy. The front ranks reached the belt of trees separating the bottom of the ridge from the stockade and disappeared from view, but still the army poured over the crest and down the nearside like water over a dam.

The two girls on either side of Valla looked thoroughly frightened, but her face was expressionless. Now they could hear the distant sound of cheering.

Preston grasped his spear more firmly. "Here they come!" he shouted.

The front rank of attackers came running out of the trees carrying ladders and grappling hooks, followed by a second, similarly burdened. Then wave after wave of assault troops, yelling at the top of their voices, burst out of the wood as the front and second ranks crashed against the stockade, holding their ladders in position and casting hooks as they had practiced many times before. A few seconds later the assault troops arrived and began to swarm up the ladders and ropes laid for them.

As fast as the ladders were dislodged by the defenders, more arrived and some enemy soldiers managed to get onto the catwalk. Preston and the others fought like demons to throw them off, but for every two they killed or pitched over the side, three seemed to take their place.

Preston saw they would have to do something and shouted to one of the young men beside him: "Call one of the reserves."

"Yes, sir."

Out of the corner of his eye Preston saw one of the attackers coming and turned to parry the thrust just in time, bringing the hilt of his spear around to smash it into his opponent's face. "Go on!" he shouted. "Tell the others to watch the north side."

The young man half fell down the inner ladder

while Preston turned without a second glance to pick up the inert body of the man at his feet and throw him over the side, seemingly without effort. Then he sprang to deal with two enemy soldiers who had trapped one of the younger defenders against the nearest watchtower.

The messenger ran for all he was worth toward the reserve detachment led by Simon Bryant. When he arrived, he was too out of breath to speak but pointed in the direction of the main attack. Bryant nodded at once and led his men away at a run while the young man stood breathlessly looking after them.

A moment later, an enemy soldier seemingly appeared from nowhere and, surprising his exhausted opponent, killed him easily; but when he withdrew the spear and turned, he found himself facing Valla and the two other girls who had seen what was happening from the nearby ramp.

Out of sight, over on the other side of the camp, David turned to Ham impatiently. "We should go help," he said, but Ham shook his head.

"Not yet."

"But . . ."

"Do as you're told!" Ham snapped at him.

Ngle sat on his horse looking down at the battle with satisfaction: it was obvious that the defenders of the southern stockade were about to be overwhelmed. His smile faded when he saw Bryant and the rest of his detachment swarm up the ladders into the attack, leaping past their exhausted companions and clearing the catwalk of the invaders.

The enemy soldier lunged at one of the girls and she shrieked, falling to the ground as the spear pierced her breast. Without thinking the second girl at once bent down beside her fallen companion and was killed instantly by the solider's next thrust. Valla then had to fight for her life.

On the hillside, Ngle pointed with his spear to the east, fresh waves of uncommitted assault troops ran to attack this flank, where they gained an immediate foothold against the less experienced defenders; but this had not gone unnoticed.

"The east side!" Ham shouted. "Follow me." And he set off at a run.

Valla defended herself as best she could, but she was no match for the enemy soldier who was one of the elite Jem himself had found so testing. Desperate, she looked around for help, only to see Ham and the others disappearing into the distance; in the breathing space made available by Bryant's arrival, however, Jem looked across and saw what was happening. Without bothering to use the ladder, he vaulted to the ground and ran as fast as he could, but Valla was tiring quickly. She managed to dodge a thrust but in doing so tripped and fell against the foot of a door. The soldier moved in for the kill.

Valla winced but the thrust never came; a spear thudded into the door instead, just missing her attacker, who wheeled around to find Jem facing him, now without a weapon.

The enemy soldier rushed at him, but Jem sidestepped and felled him with a blow from his bare hand on the back of the neck. Then he sprang to pick up the enemy's spear, but Valla, who had picked herself up, cast her own weapon first, killing their opponent instantly. They stood for a few moments, looking at each other, then Valla threw herself into Jem's arms with a sob.

The enemy withdrew to regroup, and the defenders rested, out of breath and exhausted. Sarah and Alison led some of the other women in dressing wounds, and the bodies of the fallen were removed.

Preston looked across anxiously at Jem, who was just climbing up the ladder back onto the catwalk. "That was close," he admitted. "What happened to you? I was afraid you were hurt."

Jem shook his head. "Some of them got into the center of the compound."

Preston looked even more anxious. "Was anyone hurt?" he asked.

"Two of the girls were killed . . . Valla nearly. I got there just in time." Jem glanced briefly up at the hill, then he went on: "Ham had to go to the east side; they nearly broke through, but not quite."

"Is he all right?"

Jem nodded, then he looked around. "Where's Jacy?"

"On the north side."

Valla climbed onto the catwalk with a large skin of water and started to give each of them a drink.

"I thought you'd be thirsty," she said to Preston when she reached them.

"Thank you." He took a deep draught, then said, "Jem said you had a narrow escape."

Valla looked at him quickly, then at Jem. "If he hadn't come, I would have died," she confessed.

Preston nodded. "Ham will be grateful," he said, and smiled at his son. "So am I." Then he tipped back his head for a second draught, while Jem and Valla looked at each other in silence.

"Ah . . . that's better!" Preston wiped his mouth with the back of his hand and handed the skin back to Valla. He glanced toward the woods. "I hope they're feeling as thirsty as we are!"

Valla moved along the catwalk to the others, and for a while the two men looked up at the surrounding country without speaking.

"Do you think they'll try again?" Preston asked at last.

"There's no sign of them leaving."

After a few seconds Preston nodded. "If we can hold them once more, we'll have won," he said.

Jem looked at him. "Why do you say *if?* You used to be so sure?"

Preston answered without turning: "We rely on God's mercy," he said. "We have no right to presume anything."

They lapsed into silence again for a few more seconds, then Preston said, "Tell Ham to pull his detachment back into reserve."

"Yes, Father." Jem turned and climbed down the ladder while Preston straightened up and looked along the catwalk to where Simon Bryant and some of the others were resting.

"Simon, when you have all had a drink, I want you to send half your men to the north side." Bryant stood up and came toward him.

"Do you think they'll try there?" he said, stopping in front of him.

"It's possible; in any case, we've lost too many to hold both detachments in reserve."

The second attack was almost identical to the first except that once the defenders had been engaged fresh troops burst from the woods behind, swinging fireballs, which they lobbed onto the catwalks and the roofs of the nearest buildings. On the northern side of the camp, Jacy and the others looked over to where several fires had already begun to burn.

"Should we go across and help?" one asked, but Jacy shook his head.

Under Alison's direction, teams of boys and girls dealt with the fires as best they could, organizing chains to pass buckets of water. The stronger ones climbed onto the most vulnerable roofs to flick the fireballs off with whatever implements came to hand, but none of them fell near the ships. Even if they had, there was little danger as long as the hatches remained closed.

Under the pall of smoke and the distraction from the opposite side, a large enemy attacking force ran up to the northern stockade in complete silence and, while the defenders were trying to peer back through the smoke to see how the battle was going, the new assault force scaled the fence without opposition and poured onto the catwalk. Taken by surprise, the defenders were quickly overwhelmed and only Jacy and one or two others managed to jump to the ground and escape.

Jacy came staggering through the smoke toward

Ham's detachment, gasping, and the other ran to meet him.

"What happened?"

Jacy pointed back over his shoulder, coughing.

"They've broken through," he wheezed.

"Go tell Father." Ham turned to the others and shouted: "Come on as fast as you can." Jacy stood watching as they ran off into the smoke.

By the time Ham had arrived, forty or fifty attackers had already climbed over, but instead of fanning out immediately these had remained on the catwalk to help the others. Ham ordered the hundred men under his command to spread out into a semicircle, then they closed in.

On the south side, which had borne the brunt of the main attack so far, the defenders, with the help of Bryant, were gaining the upper hand, mopping up the attackers who had managed to gain the catwalk and dislodging the remaining ladders. Preston turned to see his youngest son dragging himself up the ladder toward him. He hurried to help.

"Jacy, are you all right?" Preston steadied him up the last few rungs then onto the catwalk itself, where he stood gasping for breath.

"Father . . . they've broken through," he managed at last. "Ham has gone."

Jem came to join them. "How many?" he demanded, but Jacy shook his head.

"I don't know," he said faintly, then suddenly collapsed at their feet.

Jem bent down quickly, then looked up. "He's

all right," he said. "Just fainted with the heat. I'll see to him."

"No, leave him," Preston began. "Take men from the west—" But before he could finish, a new attack came in, heavier than before.

"Wait!"

Jem straightened up hurriedly.

Ngle raised his spear, sweeping it to the right, and more fresh troops rushed to attack the east side. He raised it yet again, sweeping it to the left whereupon still more broke from the forest to assault the west.

Preston looked around desperately. "They're attacking from all sides at once!" he shouted.

"Then God help us!" Jem cried as the first wave scrambled over the top of the stockade onto the catwalk, carrying the nearest defenders with them.

The numerical superiority Ham and his detachment had enjoyed tipped violently against them as fresh attackers climbed over the top of the fence to join those already inside. All this was seen by Alison who, with another girl, was trying to cope with a fire on a rooftop about a quarter of a mile away; seeing how desperate their position had become, she dropped the brush in her hand and shouted: "Never mind about this, come on!"

The two climbed down, then ran for all they were worth toward the two ships, where a large number of young women and older children still stood on guard. After a hurried consultation, they split into groups and ran to join the defenders at the stockade. A few moments later, the hatchways of the two ships began to open and most of the old people hurried after the younger ones, leaving only a skeleton guard behind.

Ham suddenly found himself reinforced by Alison and nearly two hundred of the young women and older children who armed themselves with spears from the fallen, and climbed the catwalks to prevent any more attackers from joining those already inside. Vastly encouraged, he and the others started to press in on those who were now surrounded and eventually he fought to Alison's side.

"What are you doing here?" he shouted.

The girl grinned. "Same as you!" she shouted back.

Side by side they turned to attack the surviving intruders, and simultaneously all around the camp the attack began to falter as willing defenders arrived on all sides.

Up on the hillside, the guard commander stood behind Ngle, watching the tide of battle begin to turn.

"We've lost," he muttered. "It isn't over yet, but they've beaten us."

Ngle answered without taking his eyes from the battle. "Yes."

The commander stared at him for a long time, then his eyes dropped to the water bottle strapped to Ngle's belt and he raised his spear. Although he must have seen something out of the corner of his eye, Ngle continued to gaze down at the battle as if in a trance.

"In which case," the other shouted . . . and brought

the spear around club-fashion in a terrific blow to the side of Ngle's head. The horse shied and made off as the general's body crashed to the ground, and the commander sprang to finish him off with a thrust through the chest. Then he fell to his knees alongside the body and tore the bottle from the dead man's belt. He removed the cork and upended it greedily . . . but it was empty. He looked at it for a moment in disbelief, then, giving a cry of rage, threw it as far as he could into the bushes.

The commander looked down at Ngle's face, which stared back at him calmly in death, and started to his feet. "You fool!" he shouted. "You could never win!" He looked around desperately and saw the horse trotting away into the distance.

"Come back," he called out, starting after it. "Wait." But the animal disappeared over the ridge.

"Damn you!" he shouted, his voice beginning to crack. Then he turned back, swaying and screaming at the top of his voice, "Damn you all!"

Preston and Jem stood with the others on the cat-walk of the southern stockade, looking across into the now silent woods. There had been no movement for the past two hours and there was so little sound that when Preston eventually sighed it was quite audible. The rest looked at him expectantly as he turned to Jem and gave him a weary smile, then he made his way down the ladder to where a large crowd of people stood waiting. He paused at the bottom.

"God held us in the palm of His hand today," he told them quietly. They continued to look at him in silence. "The enemy has torn itself to pieces in search of water," he went on, then spoke the words they had all been waiting to hear: "We are safe!"

A shout of joy went up and was caught by those too far away to hear what was said. Preston walked through the cheering crowd, which separated to let him through, and presently Sarah was waiting for him. He stopped, put his arm around her, and walked away until he was lost in the cheering mass.

Simon Bryant came to the foot of the ladder which Jem was just descending and turned, smiling to the rejoicing young people around him.

"What about Jem?" he called out. "If he hadn't got at their water supply, we'd be fighting yet!"

Another cheer went up at this. Jem held up his hand, but Simon Bryant shouted again, "Come on, lads, let's show what we think of him." So saying they hoisted him onto their shoulders and carried him away in triumph after his father.

When they had gone, Ham climbed up to the catwalk with two young men who had been posted to keep watch and looked up into the hills surrounding the camp as it began to get dark. A quick glance told little, but closer examination showed the hillside to be littered with bodies; under a tree just at the edge of the wood he saw something which related the whole story—two dead men clutching at the same water bottle.

The plain beyond the ridge was a litter of destruction, and the wind stirred eddies of dust between the carnage. In the far distance, a man cried out in despair.

174

## CHAPTER THIRTEEN

As Preston had predicted, the attackers never came back and work on completing the ships went even faster than before. They had lost several hundred—both men and women—but with the threat which had hung over them for so long lifted, the survivors went about the remaining tasks with light hearts and renewed energy.

"Will we stow the cutting machine in the command ship when we have it in pieces, Mr. Fearson?" asked one of the gang dismantling it under his supervision.

"No, Mr. Bryant wants it with him where he can keep an eye on it," Fearson replied and the man nodded.

"Very good, Mr. Fearson."

On the command deck of the first ship, Jacy and Alison were clearing up while Ham rolled some diagrams and stuck them under his arm. He looked around with satisfaction.

"Well, that's that."

Alison glanced at the roll under his arm. "Aren't you leaving them here?" she asked.

Ham shook his head. "No. I'd like another look at them after supper. Just to make sure."

Jacy straightened up with a grin. "Did somebody say supper?" he asked.

175

"Yes, it's about time." Alison smiled, then she turned back to Ham. "Unless we're going to wait for Father?"

"No, he won't be back until tomorrow."

Jacy frowned. "I don't like him going off like that on his own," he complained.

Alison agreed with him. "Neither do I, really," she said.

"He should have taken one of us with him," Jacy added, but Ham shook his head again.

"It's no good arguing," he said. "He has gone to meet Vicro."

Jacy paused for a moment before saying, "I wish we could have seen Vicro . . . just once."

Ham looked at him, then said: "As long as he brings the navigation tape; that's all that matters."

At the head of the valley the trees gave way to open ground except where a circle of pine trees had once crowned the highest point of all, but most of these had fallen before the prevailing southerly winds. From here Preston could see over to the end of the ridge which bounded the entrance of the valley on the south side and from which Ndrew had first seen the advancing army. It was only a few weeks—but it seemed a long time ago.

He sat on one of the fallen trees to rest. The climb had tired him more than he had expected. There had been no time to bother with himself during the past two years and the effort of binding ten thousand refugees into a self-supporting society had taken its toll. The iron-gray hair was almost white now, and the lines of his face were etched so deeply that the flesh folded in upon itself like the skin of a sun-dried apple. Preston's voice had lost none of its firmness but his memory sometimes let every-day details slip in a way that annoyed him, and his frame, which had once matched that of his eldest son, seemed to have shrunk so there was no doubt now as to who was the taller, even when he stood up straight, shoulders back, which he did less frequently than before. He sat looking out over the valley now, recovering his strength. It was getting dark down there now, but since the power lines had been led outside the camp had enjoyed electric light and power, and the floodlights erected on the stockade made it impossible for any night intruder to get closer than a quarter of a mile without being seen. Further lights illuminated the living quarters and work areas but the ships themselves, apart from the flight and observation decks, contained few windows, so although Preston knew that every light outside would be ablaze as last-minute checks and adjustments were made, it was only possible to make out the bulk of the fleet as individual masses of darkness against the lights behind. He made himself more comfortable and prepared to wait. Later, his eyes closed in sleep.

Preston's head nodded forward violently and he woke up. It was cold and he was stiff from sitting in the same position for so long. He stood up, painfully at first, and saw with surprise the sky in the east beginning to lighten with the gray of early morning. He felt he was getting old.

He saw the dark mass of a ship a few hundred yards away down the hill on the other side then,

177

sensing someone watching him, turned to see his friend standing a short distance away, smiling.

"Vicro."

The other moved toward him holding out both hands, with which he clasped Preston on each shoulder affectionately.

"Preston."

"You should have awakened me."

The two men smiled at each other. "You looked tired," Vicro told him.

Preston looked into the other's face. "You never seem to change," he said and Vicro smiled again. "The ships are finished," Vicro said. It was more a statement than a question, but Preston nodded.

"Yes."

"Good. Then come with me and I will give you the tape which shows the course you must follow." He held out his hand, and the two men walked toward the ship which Preston could now see was identical to those in the compound.

The control cabin was also basically the same, and there Vicro gave him the tape.

"Remember . . . whatever happens, you must follow it right to the end," he said solemnly, "or everything will be lost."

"I understand." Preston looked around the empty cabin, puzzled.

Vicro smiled. "No. I do not travel alone," he said to the other's unspoken question, "but it is better you only have me to deal with. It must be difficult enough as it is."

Preston returned his smile, then he asked: "Your ship will not be traveling with us?"

"No. But I shall be there when you arrive," the other told him. "You will know what to do, when the time comes."

"Very well."

Vicro held out his hand again. "Come," he said, "let us walk outside for a while together. You can ask me some of the questions I know are in your heart."

Preston hesitated. "It's difficult to know where to begin," he said, and Vicro nodded.

"And there's little I can tell you now," he admitted, "but I'll do my best."

They sat on a large rock talking and looking out over the valley. Now it was almost light.

"Once I brought my second son Ham up here when he was only five," Preston told him. "I had to carry him most of the way." He smiled at the memory, then added wistfully, "Everything was green then . . . and the sky was a blue canvas painted with small white clouds."

Vicro nodded. "I remember the Earth when it was like that," he said gently.

"We sat with our backs to one of the pine trees," Preston went on. He looked around. "They were all standing then, tall and green, and the smell of resin mixed with the scent of yellow gorse—alive with bees, I remember—which drifted up from the bushes a little way down the hill." He paused. "And the birds . . . some used to stay in the woods down in the valley but others seemed to spend all afternoon up there in the sky wheeling and turning, so high you could only see them when the sun caught the underpart of their wings."

He stopped suddenly, afraid that he had wearied the other, but after a few seconds Vicro said, "God has many heavens in His universe, but none was more beautiful than Earth in the beginning."

Preston turned to him. "Then there are other worlds such as this?" he said.

Vicro nodded. "Many, as this used to be. Many more, equally beautiful, but different."

"Inhabited by people such as ourselves?"

"Yes. But some have already passed the point of decision." Preston looked puzzled, so Vicro went on.

"Every race reaches a point, some time in its development, when it ceases to be simply a product of environment and takes command of its ultimate destiny. At that moment, it decides for itself which of the various paths it will take—and in every case the Creator reveals enough of Himself for even the least intelligent of His creatures to make the right choice. Most of them do; but a few do not."

Preston thought for a moment, then he said: "How is the choice made?"

"It's a matter of choosing those things which mean the most to the greatest number," Vicro told him. "Some choose the fruits of selfishness and violence . . . these soon perish. Others listen to His voice. My own race was one, although I can take no credit, for it began millions of years ago; to us, the Creator reveals a little more of Himself with each generation, so we are able to speak with Him and know His wishes, without risk of misunderstanding."

Preston looked at him amazed. "You know everything about God?" he said.

Vicro chuckled and clasped him by the shoulder. "My friend! Don't you see, if we knew everything about God, we should be gods ourselves? The Creator is infinite," he continued. "Although we continue to learn a little more as time goes on, there can be no end to our journey."

He got up to stretch his legs and Preston looked after him.

"A journey without end?"

Vicro turned. "There is no other way for us to live," he said simply.

Preston stood up and moved to his side. "You mean it makes you happy?" he persisted.

Vicro shook his head but smiled. "What your people call happy is only the heat from a distant star. How can I explain to you what it's like when that star expands to fill the sky, like the Sun at high noon? You must trust me when I tell you that it is a slow climb from night into day; but, having set out, there is no turning back."

Preston frowned slightly. "I know you're speaking in pictures to try to help me understand," he said, "but anyone who approaches a star is eventually consumed."

"That is so," Vicro agreed. "If everything remains the same; but in the world of the spirit, physical parallels don't always make sense. You see, we only learn to approach the Creator step by step. Each new generation is given a better start than the last received, so we are able to draw ever closer to the source of all knowledge, of love—what you call happiness—in a way that those who went before would not have found possible." He paused, then smiled.

"If you like to return to my original metaphor, as the Sun in our universe expands, so our universe expands also."

"Then it's never possible to get too close?" Preston said.

"No. Because the Creator, in His wisdom, only allows those to come near who are able to do so." Vicro glanced down at the tape in Preston's hands. "You should start back soon," he said. "They will be wondering what has happened to you."

"There is so much left unasked."

Vicro nodded. "And unanswered; there always is." Then he held out his hand.

"I'll walk back with you part of the way," he said.

The two men turned and started back down the hill. They walked in silence for a few moments, then Preston said, "Why is it necessary for this decision to be made? I don't understand why the Creator made it possible for so many to lose their way."

Vicro nodded sympathetically. "You must understand that in the final reality, as in the physical world, motion is relative," he explained. "That is to say, just as a physical thing cannot be said to move in a total void—it is always necessary to have at least one point of reference—so, in matters of the spirit, progress toward the Creator cannot have meaning unless the other alternative exists."

"Is that why the drought came?" Preston asked.

"No," Vicro told him. "Your own race—apparently alone among creation—has made no decision. Many times in the past it looked as though your ancestors would turn their backs on God forever, but always there was a small minority who set their faces against evil and prevented the worst from happening. In this way, Mankind is unique." He made a gesture approximating a shrug and continued. "On occasion, the balance has been held by only one man who, by some miracle—perhaps by some special quality implanted at the very beginning—achieved a spiritual development in advance of his contemporaries by as much as a hundred generations. This happened nowhere else. Usually a species moves in one direction or another with uniformity. Perhaps one or two individuals per generation leap in front by as much as five or ten steps, but nowhere else have good and evil existed beside one another for so long. For this reason, no other beings have caused so much anxiety."

Preston looked at him. "To God?" he asked.

"To the Creator, yes, I'm sure; and certainly to those of His servants who had advanced sufficiently close to understand a part of His thinking." Vicro paused again for a moment before going on. "At any rate," he said, "it's true to say that, while Mankind has been locked in a life-and-death struggle, most races which began at the same time have progressed far beyond your present state . . . while a few have dropped out of sight completely." He looked directly at Preston. "Do you understand?"

Preston nodded. "I'm beginning to," he said.

That evening Preston stood on the ramp of the command ship, facing all the people of the camp, and told them what Vicro had said. Then he bent his head to listen to a question from one of the older men standing just below him.

"What about the drought, sir?" the man had asked. "Why has it been sent? What is its purpose?"

Preston raised his head when the other finished. "To give us another chance," he told them. "To force a decision at last." He paused before continuing: "Vicro's last words to me were, 'Remember, no matter how alone you may seem to be . . . the Creator has always had a special affection for the creature He called Man.' "

Preston looked at those furthest away and went on more strongly: "We leave tomorrow . . . you know that already!" He smiled as a murmur of excitement ran through those in front of him. "So it is the last time we shall have the chance to meet together, all in the same place, until we reach our destination." His eyes ran over the sea of faces. "You know what to do," he told them, "what ship each of you will be traveling in, and what part you have to play—we have been through it all many times—so do not be afraid. My sons tell me the force which drives the ships acts on everything within so none of us will be aware of any motion, unless, of course, we look out of the observation windows. We shall not be able to communicate between ships when traveling faster than the speed of light—in some condition my son Ham has nicknamed 'hyperspace' —because, apparently, during these 'leaps,' when most of the distance will be covered, in theory we don't exist at all!"

Preston looked around to smile reassuringly. "However, most of the time we'll be traveling below that speed," he went on more seriously. "We'll be able to communicate and move from one ship to another in the small pods, or miniature ships provided . . . which is as well, as once we have settled down we must begin to prepare ourselves for our new life." He paused for the last time, then went on quietly: "Therefore let us ask God to bless us . . . and remembering always His servant's command to follow the course we have been given without faltering, may He grant that each one of us will meet again wherever He has seen fit to send us."

Protesting cattle were driven up the ramp of Ship Twenty by Dom, the chief herdsman. His helpers followed with domestic animals of all kinds, then came men carrying cages containing all species of birds and wild animals. Preston helped to drive the strays inside, enjoying himself hugely; all over the camp columns of people filed into their appointed ships.

Sarah paused at the top of the ramp of the command ship with Alison and glanced back. She looked sad and older, but the young woman put her arm around her. Sarah looked up into Alison's face and smiled bravely; then she nodded, and they joined the others going inside.

On the command deck, Jem was checking the controls with David, his co-pilot, while Jacy systematically verified communications with the other ships.

Ham satisfied himself that the navigation tape was properly installed in the computer before closing the side panel and throwing the activating switch. After a few seconds the computer chattered out some tape, which he tore off and fed into a tabulator. This in turn printed out some objectives and Ham swiveled his chair back to the table and began to sort out the settings.

The last animals disappeared inside and Preston jumped to the ground and waved to those standing in the hatchway, then it began to close, and the ramp retracted. Preston turned and made his way back to the command ship. He was the last to go inside.

"Are the controls of the other nineteen ships locked on?" Jem asked.

Jacy grinned. "Yes, eldest brother."

Jem looked down at his own instruments. "I wish we'd been able to make some practice flights," he said.

"Preston said it was not possible," David pointed out.

"Even so, machines have been known to go wrong."

"I agree," Jacy interjected. "If you're going to make a mistake, do it with a single ship."

Jem looked at him half angrily. "I didn't say anything about making a mistake," he retorted, "cheeky young devil. I meant I would prefer to have checked out the controls."

"Only one trouble," Jacy said, unabashed. "We don't know how they work!"

"That doesn't stop us from seeing *if* they work," Jem snapped.

"True."

"I'm sure it will be all right," David said soothingly.

One after another, the hatches of the twenty ships closed and the ramps retracted. Once this was done, there was no longer any visible movement within the entire area enclosing the stockade, for no living thing had been left behind.

"Panels eight and thirteen, fully open," Ham said, reading from his calculations. "Panel twenty-one . . . setting, point six, zero, sixty." David leaned forward, but Jem grabbed his arm just in time.

"Wait," he barked, "unless you want us all to go off half-cocked! The delay switch first."

David swallowed. "Sorry. Of course!"

Jem leaned forward and threw the switch. "Right," he said, "now." David automatically made the setting, repeating what Ham had just said, and Jem nodded his approval.

"Set for two, point three, zero, five, eight minutes," Ham went on when David had finished, and Jem adjusted the delay switch accordingly.

"Jacy, ask each ship in turn to read the setting on their instruments back to us as a check," he ordered when he had completed the setting, "beginning with Ship Two."

"Yes, sir." Jacy started to repeat the order into his microphone.

"I'll give you the next setting as soon as you've checked out," Ham called over.

"Right."

Preston came into the cabin and looked around. "Is everything all right?" At that moment a loudspeaker began to drone the other captains' confirmations of the original settings. Ham held a finger to his lips while beckoning his father closer.

"Everything's all right, Father," he said. "We're just checking with the other ships."

Preston grinned. "Good. Then you don't want me."

"We'll manage," Ham smiled back.

Preston hesitated. "I never got around to saying how proud I am of all of you," he said.

"Thank you."

"Well . . . in that case, I'd like to go back on the observation deck with Mother and see the fun."

Ham nodded. "Sure, Father. We have to change course almost immediately, then we're set for several days in hyperspace."

His father smiled again. "There'll be plenty of time to talk," he said.

"Plenty!"

Preston turned to leave, then turned back. "Oh, I nearly forgot," he said. "Valla asked if she could come up here for the departure."

Ham frowned slightly. "I haven't got time to explain anything."

"She knows that."

"She'll see more from the observation deck."

"She knows that too," Preston told him. "She just wants to be up here with you." He paused, then went on softly: "Things have been a bit strained between you two recently, haven't they? It's understandable . . . but now it ought to be better."

Ham looked at him, then grinned suddenly. "I hope so. All right."

Preston rested his hand lightly on his son's shoulder for a brief second. "I'll tell her," he said.

As soon as Preston had left the cabin Ham went back to his calculations, working against a background hum of checking and counter-checking from the others. A few minutes later Valla appeared and went at once to his side.

"Is it okay?" she said.

Ham smiled. "Of course. But you must be quiet."

"As a mouse!" she promised, and made herself inconspicuous behind the computer.

The observation deck ran around the circumference of the ship. On its outside was a continuous band of transparent material stretching from floor to ceiling. Preston walked out onto the deck through the entrance now facing south and found the windows crowded with everyone except those who had some specific job at that moment or who were too nervous to watch. They separated at once to let him through to where he found Sarah standing with Alison.

"Are you all right?" he asked. Sarah nodded and smiled, but he could see the strain in her eyes as she kept a tight rein on her emotions. Preston smiled briefly at Alison over Sarah's head, then he put his arm around his wife's shoulders. She seemed very frail beside him—even beside the girl whose right arm she clutched nervously with her other hand.

"Valla has gone up to the flight deck," Preston said to Alison. "Would you like to join her?"

She shook her head and gave him an appreciative smile. "No. I'd only be in the way."

Preston nodded. "Perhaps you're right."

Sarah looked up at him. "How much longer?" she asked.

"Less than a minute . . . but don't worry, nothing's going to go wrong now."

She smiled back at him. "I'm never really frightened when I'm with you," she said. "I never have been."

On the command deck the four listened in silence as the last ship confirmed settings; then Jem nodded.

"Right." He turned to Jacy. "Tell them to stand by, to take the next setting the minute we begin to move." Jacy started to repeat the order while Jem glanced briefly around at Ham and grinned. "Well . . . here we go!" he said. His eyes cut to Valla, but he did not acknowledge her. Ham smiled back and nodded. Jem swiveled his chair again and glanced down at the instruments in front of him. "All right, everybody . . . now we shall see." He reached forward and put his hand on the delay switch.

"Ten seconds," Ham said, and began to count down.

As he reached zero, Jem threw the switch to OFF. Outside, two complete panels suddenly turned white.

The twenty ships simultaneously leaped silently into the air and out of sight at a velocity that would have spread their occupants over the floor like jam with any other form of propulsion. A split second later there was an explosion of sound as the air rushed in to fill the twenty vacuum corridors thus created; half of the buildings and most of the stockade collapsed under the sudden multiple hurricane as twenty columns of debris were snatched into the air. The sound of chaos echoed over the surrounding hills like thunder.

Those on the observation decks saw the ground fall away at an incredible speed but, as Preston had told them, they had no sense of motion at all.

Some observed a huge fire far to the south, then

all vision was obliterated as they hurtled into the thick belt of cloud.

Alison clutched Sarah's hand, her eyes glued like almost everyone else's on what was happening outside, but Sarah turned to her husband and closed her eyes. He looked down at her tenderly and put both arms around her.

On the command deck Ham began to read the new settings which were to come into operation as soon as they were clear of the Earth's atmosphere. Jem carried out his instructions while David held the delay key and Jacy repeated them into the microphone. Valla stared at Jem, her eyes bright with excitement.

"Panel six . . . full," Ham said hoarsely. "Panel eight . . . full. Panel twelve . . . setting, point five, six, thirty. Panel twenty . . . setting point five, six, thirty. Panel twenty-six . . . full. Panel thirty . . ."

"My God, we must be going into hyperspace!" David said, white-faced.

"Quiet!" Jem barked. "Panel thirty?"

"Point three, six, fifty," Ham continued.

At that moment a sound was heard all over the ship which only Preston recognized immediately. It was like a solo violin holding an incredibly high harmonic and, although never very loud, it grew in intensity. Ham stopped, looking around, then he forced himself back to what he was doing and cleared his throat. "Panel thirty-one. Point seven, zero, six, zero, three."

Jem and Jacy mechanically repeated his instructions and went through the necessary motions, but

Valla's eyes never left Jem's face and her breath quickened.

On the observation deck Preston raised his head to listen, for now, by some trick of mind or imagination, it seemed he could both see and hear his sons on the command deck superimposed on the scene around him like the twin images of a double-exposed negative.

"Panel thirty-two," he heard Ham say. "Setting, point three, zero, six, zero, seven." He heard Jacy repeat the order into the microphone and saw Jem's hands moving over the control keys.

"Release?" David turned to Jem.

"No . . . not yet. In ten seconds from . . . now." Ham started to count down to zero.

Preston could see everyone around him standing motionless. Outside it was quite dark. Then he became aware of Valla's expression as she looked at his eldest son and what he saw troubled him deeply. Almost immediately Ham reached zero. Preston saw David's hand release the delay switch, then a great light began to grow and he turned to the windows to see the daylight side of the Earth emerging from the darkness as it turned toward them.

The light grew in intensity, and with it the elemental sound, until they could see the whole disc; but even as they watched it diminished in size, ever more rapidly, and the Sun itself shrank, until this too was just another point of light, undistinguishable from a million others in the black immensity of deep space.

# BOOK TWO — EXODUS

# CHAPTER ONE

In the void of intergalactic space, the fleet of twenty ships condensed like huge black crystals from an invisible medium. On the command deck of the leading ship, Jacy let out a whoop of joy and dashed to the window, leaning over the two pilots and gazing outside.

"We've done it," he shouted.

Ham got up and moved to join him while Jem and David grinned at each other. "Twenty days without being able to see anything," Jacy went on. "What a relief!"

"I can see the other ships," David pointed, equally excited. "Look there . . . and there . . . and another there, look."

Jem looked up at his youngest brother. "See if you can establish communication with them," he said.

"Yes, sir." Jacy dived backed to the radio set and gleefully started to call up the other ships one by one.

Jem turned to Ham. "What now?" he asked.

Ham glanced across at the computer. "Nothing for ten days," he said.

"Just stay as we are?"

Ham nodded, smiling. "I don't suppose Father will let us do that; but there's nothing more to do here."

People gathered excitedly on the observation deck as Preston strode through and glanced outside.

"Good," he observed.

"What happens now, sir?" a young man standing near him asked.

Preston smiled quickly and clapped a hand on his shoulder. "Now we get down to work!" he told him.

"There's little enough to do," an older woman remarked.

Preston grinned. "Don't be too sure!" he said. Then he turned and walked through the doorway leading back to the center of the ship. As soon as he had gone, the others turned to each other, wondering what he could mean.

While Jacy was reestablishing communications, Ham set up the small navigation telescope.

David turned to Jem while the two of them waited. "Do you think we're moving?" he asked.

Jem shrugged. "Probably," he said.

"I'll be able to tell you in a minute," Ham called across, and began to look through the eyepiece.

David turned to look outside. "I suppose it's because everything's so far away that we seem to be standing still."

Jem nodded. "I imagine so."

Ham pointed the telescope to the extreme bottom left of the window and after a few moments gave a loud exclamation. The others turned to look at him.

"What's the matter?" Jem said. Jacy also fell silent, looking at him.

Ham tried to push the instrument further to the left, but it wouldn't go. He groaned with frustration.

"What?" Jem demanded. "For heaven's sake!"

Ham glanced across at him. "Can you turn the ship to the left about forty-five degrees and down about ten degrees?"

"Of course."

"Then you'll see for yourselves."

Jem glanced at David. "No need to touch the panels," he said.

"No. Whatever you do, don't do that!" Ham put in hurriedly.

"Relax," Jem smiled. "We can use the gyros." He reached forward to touch a switch, and a faint hum started somewhere in the center of the ship. He maneuvered a lever and the star field outside began to slip upward and to the right so that after a few seconds a huge cartwheel galaxy swam into view and settled roughly in the middle of the center windows, filling about a quarter of it.

"Stand by. I'll call you back in a minute," Jacy blurted into the microphone, and stood up to move behind Jem's shoulder.

Ham centered the telescope, then looked up after a few seconds. "We are moving," he told them, "but it'll take some time to work out how fast."

"What is it?" David asked breathlessly.

"A galaxy."

Ham left the telescope and came to stand beside them. A few seconds later Preston entered from the back and joined them. Jem turned to look at him.

"Father?"

"Everything's all right."

They gazed in silence for a time, then Preston said, "We shall see many wonders before we reach the end of our journey."

"Maybe it's our own galaxy . . . the Milky Way?" Jacy said.

Ham turned to him. "Maybe. There's no way of telling. No one has ever seen it from outside before."

"No man," Preston corrected him, and Ham nodded. "That's true," he admitted.

"Can't we tell where we are?" Jem demanded after a few more moments of silence.

"We have no maps," Ham told him. "Only the course we have been given."

They looked at each other for a few seconds, then Preston said, "As long as we stick to that, we have nothing to fear."

Ham smiled. "It seems we have no choice," he said. Jem gave him a quick look as their father turned to Jacy.

"Have you reestablished contact with the other ships?"

"I was just doing so, Father."

"Good. Tell all captains and leaders to join us here on the command ship as soon as possible. I'll be back in plenty of time."

"Where are you going?" Jem said, looking up at him.

"Just across to see how my other children are getting on," Preston told him with a grin. Then he turned on his heel and walked out of the cabin while the four of them looked at each other in puzzlement.

Preston made his way down to the pod bay and was helped into one of the small craft—shaped as the name would suggest—by a young woman dressed in white overalls. The light was green above the outside air lock. He made himself as comfortable as the confined space in the front seat would allow—behind were five others in a row—then the girl looked through the hatchway.

"You know what to do?" she asked respectfully.

Preston looked down at the row of twenty numbered buttons in front of him. "Just press the number of the ship I want to go to?" he said. The girl nodded. "That's right. The rest is automatic."

"Thank you?"

The girl smiled. "At least that's what we were told," she said. "You're the first to try it."

"That's as it should be." Preston smiled back at her.

"Have a nice trip."

"I shall be on Ship Twenty if anyone wants me."

"Yes, sir."

"You can shut the hatch now."

The girl did as she was told, then waved through the window before disappearing through the inner air lock.

"Ship Twenty," Preston murmured to himself, and pressed the appropriate button.

The light above the outer air lock turned red and there was the hiss of escaping air. As the sound died, the hatchway opened and the pod floated out gently, then turned and made purposefully toward the designated ship. There, another part opened and the pod glided inside; the big door closed behind it.

As soon as he saw the light above the outer air lock turn green, Preston opened the door of the pod and climbed out. The inner door opened and closed automatically as he walked through, then he stopped for a moment, looking around, and took a deep breath.

The internal design of this ship was entirely different from the other nineteen, being given up almost exclusively to housing the thousands of species of animals and birds which had been brought along. Preston stood now just inside the tame animals' quarters, which occupied the whole of the lower half of the ship. Pens and stalls stretched around a great central arena in which several cows were munching their fodder, sharing the space with peacocks, ducks and rabbits. Flights of small birds wheeled around the far end where one of the keepers was throwing food up onto special tables for them, and over the half-doorways of the stalls could be seen the heads of all kinds of other comparatively harmless creatures, both domestic and wild. The air was filled with the sound of lowing, champing, stamping and twittering as the keepers moved among them; the nearest of these, Dom, a short, wiry-looking man with a shock of red hair, saw Preston and hurried across immediately, arms extended and grinning from ear to ear.

Preston smiled. "Dom!"

"Lord, it's good to see you." The two men clasped hands warmly.

"It's good to see you, Dom," Preston told him, and the small man turned and called to the rest.

"Look, the master has come to see us!" The others shouted greetings and those who could hurried to clasp Preston's hand.

While trying to shake as many as he could, Preston turned to Dom and said gently: "Dom . . . you must not call me lord or master. I have asked you before."

"But you are our lord," the other said simply. "Isn't he?" The others nodded vigorously, murmuring their agreement.

"You saved us all," said one.

"Without you we would all have died," said another. But Preston shook his head.

"Without God's mercy . . . and the help of Vicro, His servant," he told them firmly.

Dom nodded vigorously. "Yes, sir. Them too. But you're the one we see. It's natural we should call you master."

Preston frowned slightly. "Perhaps," he admitted, "but wrong. Remember, the only difference between us is that I was lucky enough to be chosen to bring the warning."

"You did, sir," one of the others put in, "but we know you're better than we are."

Dom nodded again. "That's right, lord. So there's no sense in not admitting it."

The others clamored their agreement but Preston held up his hand. "Lucky, if you like," he said, "but no different." He paused for a few seconds while they looked at him, then he went on: "Please . . . there is only one to whom you should use the word *lord;* the one in whom we have all put our trust. Do not say it to me again, I beg you . . . or I must be angry."

Dom looked at him solemnly. "That's the last thing we want, sir. Very well."

Preston smiled and clapped him on the back. "Good. Now show me around. How are they behaving themselves?" Dom was at once all smiles again.

"Remarkably well, lord . . . er, sir," he added quickly. He waved the others about their business and started to lead Preston forward. "But it makes extra work having to keep driving 'em to the exercise ground and back again."

Preston nodded. "I know," he said, "but it must be done or their muscles will become too weak to serve when we arrive and can start farming again properly."

"I suppose you're right, sir."

They walked down the avenue between the pens which stretched in a huge circle around the central exercise ground, both of them chatting companionably about the individual animals, and stopping here and there to give tidbits from their pockets. Finally they reached the foot of a narrow metal stairway and Dom stopped. Preston could now hear more exotic animal and bird noises coming from above.

"Would you like to see upstairs, sir?" Dom asked him.

Preston smiled. "Of course. Lead the way." The other nodded and started up the companionway followed by Preston.

Preston stopped when they reached the top. This half of the ship was arranged similarly to the one below, only there were cages instead of pens; also, the arena and the passages leading to it were enclosed. The air was full of jungle sounds and Preston saw that the exercise ground was occupied at present by a family of rhinoceroses.

The large half sphere above floor level was enclosed in netting from thirty feet off the ground up to the roof, two hundred feet above that. This area included cages containing all kinds of predator birds from small hawks to eagles, several sorts of which were taking a turn in the space available for wheeling and swooping from one perch to another. Preston nodded approvingly, but Dom looked at him, frowning.

"Sir . . . why did we have to bring the dangerous animals?" he asked. "The big cats, the alligators and snakes and so on?"

Preston turned to him. "Because we need them, as much as they need us now."

"How can we need poisonous snakes?"

"Dom, I don't know all the answers. I told you, I'm no different from you. But it was God's wish, so it must be obeyed. I can only guess that His purpose was to teach us to live again with other creatures different from ourselves."

"A snake will strike for food whether threatened or not," Dom pointed out mildly.

Preston paused for a moment, then he asked, "What do snakes live on?"

Dom looked at him. "Here? Why, the food we have made."

"What usually?" Preston persisted.

"Rats"—the little man shrugged—"things like that."

Preston smiled. "Then perhaps you should have asked me why we brought the rats; it would have been an easier question!" Dom grinned. "Come on." Preston put a hand on his shoulder and they started to walk toward a cage where a young lioness rubbed herself against the bars and purred in anticipation. "We have to start again," Preston went on after a moment, "so we must take most that we are told on trust. Perhaps one day we will understand for ourselves."

They approached the cage and stopped, then Preston reached through the bars and scratched the lioness' back. "Hello, Juno," he said apologetically. "Have you missed me? I'm sorry I've been so busy."

The lioness purred loudly.

Preston returned to the command ship with mixed feelings. He was never happier than when surrounded by animals and people like Dom, with whom he had an instinctive understanding, but it was essential to get the routine organized on a long-term basis. He had come to a definite decision concerning his own role in the future, so the meeting was also the obvious opportunity to make such an announcement.

They gathered eventually in the central hall of the command ship and Preston stood up to face them. "Everyone now has something to do with the actual running of the ships," he told them, "but I'm sure you understand how important it is to use the time we have been given to prepare ourselves."

"Excuse me, sir." Bryant interrupted. "Do we know yet how much time?"

Preston turned to him and shook his head. "We have no way of knowing," he said. "Maybe only a few months. Maybe years." At this there were gasps from several and Preston looked around. "Whatever it is, it will be for our own good," he told them.

"But is it not possible to judge from the amount of navigation tape used so far?" the Scot persisted. Preston glanced at Ham, who rose to answer the question.

"No," he said, "the tape simply gives each step at a time and there is no way of telling whether the next one will take a few hours or a month." He sat down and Bryant followed suit.

"So we must press ahead on two fronts," Preston continued, after pausing for a few seconds. "Everyone not too old will be expected to acquire some practical skill that will enable him to make a practical contribution to our new life; each person will also study an academic subject so the groundwork of knowledge can be relaid for our grandchildren and future generations, in the hope that with God's help—and our own willingness to learn from past mistakes—we can set them off on a road from which, this time, there will be no turning aside." He paused again for a few moments, then went on: "I'm afraid that to begin with the main weight of organizing the programs and keeping them going will fall on the shoulders of those of you here; but now the needs are clearly understood, and one difference will be that . . . this time, I must ask you to excuse me from assuming any direct responsibility."

There was a silence so deep that voices of children could be heard playing in another part of the ship. "I'm older than anyone else here," Preston went on, then smiled. "Probably older than most of you imagine, and recently"—he shrugged—"well . . . I've begun to feel my age a little." He looked around again at the worried faces in front of him, but took a deep breath and continued: "I suppose it's natural you should expect me to go on forever, but it has become increasingly clear to me that if a change is to be made, now is the time to do it."

"You're not leaving us?" David spoke without getting up and Preston looked in his direction for a moment.

"Of course not," he said. "In any case, it wouldn't be possible." Then he turned back to the others. "No, I'll be with you until the end of our journey. All I'm saying is that in the future I want to take things more easily. As some of you may know, Sarah has not been very well recently. She kept going as long as was necessary, but now I'll look after her and occupy most of the rest of my time in study." He glanced around. "I have to prepare myself too. So . . . I shall continue to be with you, but in the future, for everyday purposes, Jem, my eldest son, will act in my place, and Ham, his brother, will continue to be in charge of education and training."

And that's how it was. As far as the routine running of the fleet was concerned, Jem took command. David assumed more responsibility for the piloting of the command ship itself and Jacy and Ham, when not wanted on the command deck, plunged into the program of education after many long hours of discussion and argument.

As time went on, some preferred to take a greater share of routine tasks, once they had mastered some simple trade, leaving more time to others whose talents better fitted them for reaching into realms of knowledge; those who would teach had to give up an increasing amount of time to study themselves, in order to keep sufficiently far ahead. A few particularly clever students actually caught up and passed some of those who had had the advantage of previous education and these, while continuing their own studies under Ham, Alison or Jacy, swelled the ranks of those capable of helping the less gifted. The result was like a snowball gathering fresh momentum each day, but it contained within itself a special sort of danger.

"Why do you want to call a meeting?" Ham demanded. The two elder brothers faced each other angrily on the command deck while David and Jacy watched with worried expressions.

"To discuss how we're going to split up the people from Communities into family groups, once we get wherever we're going," Jem snapped back.

"You have no right to do such a thing without asking Father first."

"He doesn't want to be disturbed. You heard what he said."

"He left the day-to-day running to us," Ham persisted. "That doesn't give us any right to discuss such a thing without him being present."

"All right, then, if you want to bother, ask him to come along."

"Ask him to come along!" Ham repeated incredulously. "Who do you think you are?"

Jem glared at him. "I'm in command," he said.

"Not once we land, you aren't," Ham retorted.

"Who knows what the position will be then?"

"Father. That's why we ought to get on with what we've been told to do and leave the rest to him until he's ready to tell us."

Jem made a face. "Why do we always have to wait to be told?"

Ham paused for a moment, looking at him; then he said quietly. "You should ask such a question?!"

Jem flushed angrily and turned to Jacy. "What do you think?" he said.

Jacy shrugged. "As long as we just talk, I don't really see what harm it could do," he said unhappily.

"It can do harm, because I know our elder brother better than you do," Ham told him.

"That's not true," Jem put in.

"I know that, given half a chance, he won't be content just to talk."

They stood looking at each other in silence for what seemed a long time; then Jem turned to Jacy. "Tell all captains and leaders to be here this time tomorrow, ship's time."

"Right." Jacy nodded, but didn't move, except to look at Ham. Jem also turned back to look at him.

"You can do what you like about it," he said defiantly, "Come—or stay away. Tell Father—or leave him in peace as he asked."

## CHAPTER TWO

Ham lay on his bed looking at the ceiling of their cabin while Valla sat, brushing her hair in front of the mirror.

"You didn't tell your father?" she said after a while.

Ham paused before answering. "I went to see him," he said eventually.

"But you didn't tell him?"

Ham shook his head. "He was sitting in a chair beside Mother's bed, holding her hand. They had both fallen asleep." Valla stopped, watching him in the mirror. "She looked very frail," Ham went on, "and Father has aged a lot; but there's something about him now . . . some quality it's hard to define." He turned and looked at her reflection. "He seems . . . so at peace. As if he had found something, at last, that he had been looking for all his life."

"He's a good man," Valla said softly, avoiding his eyes. "He makes the rest of us seem like nothing."

Ham moved into a sitting position on the edge of the bed facing her. "I think he's gone ahead so he can show us the way . . . like he always has." Ham paused. "But differently this time," he went on eventually.

Valla looked back at him. "You didn't disturb them?"

"No." Ham shook his head. "I closed the door and came away . . . but I felt more at peace myself." He looked directly into her eyes in the glass. "It's strange how feelings pass from one person to another, without anything being said."

Valla dropped her eyes, then Ham got up and moved to stand behind her, resting his hands lightly on her shoulders. "You're very beautiful," he whispered. "I love you very much." After a few seconds she looked at him and he was shocked to see her eyes swimming with tears. Then her face contorted and she buried her head in her hands, weeping.

"Valla!"

She turned and wept against him while he cradled her head in his hands. "I'm so unhappy!" she choked. Ham didn't say anything but stroked her hair gently. "And frightened," she said desperately.

"I'd do anything for you."

"Oh . . . don't!" Valla wept more bitterly until she managed to say, "I love you, but I can't help myself."

Ham froze, but he continued to hold her until she looked up, tears streaking her face. "I feel myself being pulled away from you," she whispered, "where I know it's safe—to I don't know what."

Ham's lips tightened and, seeing his expression, she turned away suddenly and began to dry her eyes with a handkerchief. "I'm sorry," she said. "I'm being stupid."

Ham looked at her for a long time. "We can't go on like this."

Valla looked up at him. "What choice have we got?" she said hopelessly. "You can't help me; I can't help myself . . . and none of us dares admit it, because it would kill your mother and father . . . and ruin everything!"

Jem's meeting was not a success. He watched sourly as the various leaders filed out of the library. Valla remained sitting at the back of the room waiting, but Jacy moved to his side.

"Well, I still think it's a good idea trying to make the ships' dormitories into family units," he said. "It just needs a bit more thought."

Jem didn't look at him. "We can have another meeting later," he said.

"Which brings me to another point," Jacy went on. "You don't think it would be possible to run the navigation tape forward right to the end? That way we might work out where we're going—it might help." He looked doubtfully at Jem.

"Discuss it with Ham."

"I already tried," Jacy complained, "but he wouldn't listen."

By now the others had all gone. Jem turned to look at Jacy for the first time and gave him a quick smile. "We'll talk about it later," he said, and rose to his feet.

"Oh. All right."

"I'm off watch for a few hours. I'll be in my cabin."

"Right."

Jem made for the door and went out without looking at Valla. Jacy followed more slowly but stopped beside her.

"Maybe Ham was right," he said, raising his eyebrows slightly, but Valla shook her head.

"I don't know."

Jacy paused a moment longer, looking at her. "What's wrong between them?" he asked. "It's not just this; ever since Jem came back, it's been the same."

Valla looked away. "They just have different ways of looking at things," she said.

"I suppose so. Mother hoped it would be better once we set out but if anything it's got worse."

"I know."

"Anyone would think—" he began, but Valla looked up quickly and interrupted him.

"How's Alison?"

Jacy made a face. "She's all right," he said. "Busy as usual!"

"I haven't seen her for ages."

"She helps Ham most of the time, skipping from one ship to another while the rest of us slave away here."

"Surely she works hard though?"

"I suppose so. Somebody's got to coordinate things." Jacy grinned suddenly and his face was all boyish again. "Though what they'd do without me for help and advice, I'd hate to think!" Valla smiled, and he went on: "Are you coming for something to eat?"

She shook her head. "I'm not hungry."

"You should eat." Jacy paused to look at her, then he said, "Mother was asking after you last time I went to see her."

Valla looked down again. "I should go see her," she said.

"She'd like that. The rest doesn't seem to be doing her any good." He paused again, frowning, then went on more lightly: "Anyway . . . I told her you were getting skinnier than ever."

Valla looked up. "What did she say?"

"She doesn't say much these days . . . she just smiled." He frowned again for a moment, then went on brightly: "Well, I'm starving if you're not. I'll see you later."

He went out, leaving her completely by herself. After a while she got up slowly, paused by the door looking around, then turned off the lights, one by one.

Jem was washing in his cabin, stripped to the waist. He heard the door open and close behind him and reached for a towel to wipe the water from his eyes; then he saw Valla standing just inside the door.

"Valla!"

"Ham knows everything," she said, and moved toward him. "He knows I love him and that I hate and despise myself for coming to you like this." She stopped in front of him.

Jem looked worried. "What did he say?"

"Nothing." Valla shrugged. "He knows what it would mean if it became known Preston's eldest son betrayed his own brother, and the wife of his second son was without honor."

"He won't tell Father?"

"Of course not." Valla spoke almost contemptuously.

"Thank God for that anyway!" Jem went on drying himself. "How long has he known?" he said eventually.

"I don't know." Valla shrugged. "For some time. He's never said anything."

Jem hung up the towel, then turned back to face

her. "Why doesn't he say something? It might help if at least the three of us could talk about it."

Valla looked impatient. "He can't! He loves me . . . in a way you'd never understand. Don't you know him at all?"

They looked into each other's eyes, then Jem put out a hand to touch her. "I know you," he said.

Valla fell against him with a gasp, and Jem held her tightly. "I didn't ask to feel like this either," he said breathlessly. "If only he knew how my body cries out for you."

Valla looked up at him, her face contorted with her need for him. "I want you," she said.

"Valla!" Jem swept her up into his arms and put her on the bed. Then he began to undress her as she writhed and pushed her clenched fist against her teeth to stifle her cries.

The fleet hung in space, apparently motionless. In the remote distance a nova flared and died, and the twenty ships dissolved into nothing.

On the observation deck, a group of children watched the flaring patterns and splintering colors of hyperspace and one of the girls turned to the boy next to her.

"I don't like hyperspace," she complained. "It makes me feel dizzy."

The boy grinned. "Then don't look, silly!"

In Ham's office, Alison was sitting quietly, checking through some papers, but she looked up and smiled as he came in through the door. Ham was depressed but brightened as soon as he saw her.

"Alison!" He closed the door and went to her, smiling.

"Surprise!" Alison stood up and Ham kissed her cheek affectionately.

"How lovely to see you!"

"I slipped across from Ship Fifteen just before the leap," she told him.

Ham put the papers he had been carrying down on the table and frowned slightly as the girl perched on the end. "One of these days you'll be outside and get left behind."

"Could that happen?"

"We check that all pods are accounted for, but we could make a mistake."

"Couldn't you come back for me?"

Ham shook his head. "Nobody knows what happens in hyperspace," he said. "I was trying to explain that to Jacy a few days ago."

Alison looked at him eagerly. "How is he?"

Ham smiled. "Fine!"

"I couldn't bear being away any longer. That's why I didn't want to get stuck over there."

"I might have known it wasn't to come see me!"

"I came to see you first, didn't I?" Alison retored.

"Yes. To stop me from being cross with you for deserting your post."

"I'd almost finished."

"Almost?"

"I'll go back as soon as the leap's over," Alison said meekly; then they both laughed.

"Of course it's all right," Ham told her. "It's self-ish of me to keep you apart so much."

"As long as you don't mind my coming back like this when I get too lonely?"

Ham shook his head, still smiling. "Of course not."

"Then don't worry. I love the feeling I'm doing something really useful." She nodded at the papers on the table. "I brought the progress reports with me."

"Oh, good!" Ham glanced at them quickly, then turned back to her. "You go along," he said. "Jacy won't have much to do until we can reestablish communications."

Alison smiled. "That's what I thought." She turned for the door. "I'll come see you tomorrow."

"Please. I'll read the reports in the meantime."

"Right." Alison reached for the door handle but Ham suddenly called after her.

"Alison."

She stopped at once and turned around.

"Yes?"

"Could you find time to look in and see Mother?"

"Of course. . . . I was going to."

Ham nodded. "Thank you."

"How is she?"

Ham looked at her for a long time before answering; then he said quietly, "I think she's dying."

Alison dropped her hand and moved toward him at once.

"Oh . . . Ham!"

"Nobody says anything," he went on miserably, "but you'll see for yourself."

"Can't we do anything?"

Ham shook his head. "She's just worn out," he

said. "I don't think she minds, but she's missed you; you were always her favorite."

Alison's eyes swam with tears and she shook her head. "Jacy. Not me."

"That's different. You're the only friend she ever had. That makes you special."

"I'll go and see her at once." Alison made for the door.

"No." Ham called after her. "She'd want you to see Jacy first. He's your husband."

Alison hesitated. When she spoke it was softly, without turning. "All right."

Ham came up behind her and put a hand on her shoulder. "Besides," he said, smiling wryly. "She wouldn't want to see you looking like that."

Alison sniffed. "It's your fault!" But she returned his smile through her tears.

"I'm sorry." Ham paused, then he went on: "I don't feel I can talk to anyone else about her."

Alison looked at him, puzzled. She hesitated for a moment, then put a hand on his shoulder.

"We all love you," she said simply.

"I know." Ham spoke without bitterness and covered her hand with his.

After she had gone, Ham glanced briefly through her report, but he didn't feel in the mood to study it in any depth. Instead, he made his way up to the command deck, where he found David sitting in the co-pilot's seat staring out at the apparent confusion of hyperspace. He dropped into the seat next to him.

"Trying to work it out?" he asked after they had sat in silence for a while.

217

David smiled. "After listening to you and Jacy the other day?!"

"All I was trying to explain was why we would be no wiser if we ran the navigation tape forward."

David swiveled his chair to look at Ham more closely. "Because no one knows what happens in hyperspace?" he asked.

"That's right. We don't know how fast we travel, or for how long."

David frowned. "We know the last, surely?" But Ham shook his head.

"No. You're assuming time goes on outside the ship in the same way as it appears to us inside."

"Say that again?"

Ham smiled. "You know time slows down for the occupants of any ship approaching the speed of light?" he said.

David nodded. "Yes, I understand that much."

"That's right; we worked it out on the blackboard before we left. The dilation effect is proportional to the difference in speed between a ship and the speed of light; so at half the speed, ship time slows down by half, and at three-quarters of the speed of light, to a third . . . and so on."

"Yes, I remember. We worked out that a ship leaving Earth and traveling only a point of one percent below the speed of light for a year—"

"Ship's time," Ham put in.

"Would come back and find more than ten thousand years had passed while it had been away."

Ham nodded. "So what happens when we exceed the speed of light? And how is it possible when it has always seemed to be the limiting speed of the universe?"

"Because a ship's mass increases as it approaches the speed of light?"

"Yes. And at the speed of light its mass becomes infinite, thereby requiring an infinite force to move it any faster."

David paused for a moment before he said, "Perhaps we have an infinite force built into the ships?"

Ham shook his head. "No, I don't think so. I wouldn't say it isn't possible, but if it was true it would be miraculous."

"But God is helping us."

"That's true. He also created the rules which govern the universe."

"You mean He wouldn't like to break one of His own rules?"

Ham burst out laughing.

"What's funny?" David demanded, grinning without knowing why.

"I don't know," Ham answered. "It just seems a bit absurd trying to figure out things like this when we don't even know how the ships move."

David looked at him. "Don't you try to work it out?" he asked. "I do . . . even if I don't get anywhere. I can't help myself."

Ham nodded. "That's all right. God meant us to be curious; how else could we acquire knowledge?"

"Then what do you think happens?"

"When God seems to break one of His own rules?"

"Like helping us travel in hyperspace, yes."

"Well, I think—and this is only what I think—that when God seems to have broken one of His own rules, it only seems so to us because we're not advanced enough to understand the rule properly."

"But with Vicro it's different?"

"Yes," Ham said. "One explanation I thought of was that this force, which is harnessed by the panels in a way we don't understand, not only affects the speed of the ships, but also their mass, and everything in them."

"How would that help?"

"Well . . . say the entire fleet is reduced to zero mass? Then it might be possible to travel faster than light."

"You mean . . . you can't increase the mass of nothing?"

"That's right." Ham gazed outside. "Every ship, at this very minute, might have been reduced in size to less than the most basic particle." He pointed at the window. "I've been wondering about all that, because if what I'm saying happened to be true, and we are traveling at a thousand—perhaps a billion times faster than light—we might be passing through the heart of one galaxy after another right now. Out there might be the basic stuff of the Universe seen from inside." David turned to follow his gaze.

"As to time," Ham went on, "who knows what happens? The only thing we can be certain of is that, whatever it is, it won't be what we expect."

Sarah lay on the bed in the cabin downstairs, her eyes closed. She looked very frail, but at peace. Preston sat beside her holding her hand. In his mind they were young fugitives again, standing side by side on the hillcrest looking down at the plain beneath and the forest beyond, and the blue glint of the sea in the distance.

When they next emerged from hyperspace, people inside the ships were dazzled by a blaze of light from outside. Throughout most galaxies the average separation of stars is between five and ten light years, but here and there a system or cluster of between fifty to a hundred move in association with one another around the galactic center. In most instances, the associated stars are still hundreds of millions of miles from each other, but from the position the fleet now found itself in, there seemed to be ten or fifteen suns in the sky. Some were as bright as that familiar star when viewed from Earth; others were less so, although considerably brighter than any they had seen before.

For the first time, the ships were sufficiently close to be able to see marked changes in position as the hours went by. The observation decks were crowded and Jem relaxed the ordinary routine to enable as many people as possible to view the spectacle. A rumor swept the fleet that they were approaching their destination at last, but this was regretfully countered by Ham, who pointed out that most of the navigation tape still remained and another leap in hyperspace was scheduled as soon as the fleet was clear. Even so, excitement ran high and Preston saw no harm in it. Anything that broke the monotony was welcome.

During the second twenty-four-hour period of traveling through the cluster, it became apparent that their course would take them within sixty million miles of one of the stars, a yellow dwarf which now appeared almost immediately in front of them. Ham calculated that they would reach the nearest point in another twelve hours when, owing to its slightly smaller size, it would appear to be the same size as the Sun viewed from Earth and would give approximately the same amount of heat and light. On the command deck shortly afterward interest redoubled when Ham also detected the presence of a small planet orbiting the star they were approaching.

"What sort of planet?" Jem demanded.

"I can't tell yet. Perhaps like our own Earth—maybe completely different."

"When will you be able to tell?"

Ham shrugged. "It's hard to say."

Jem closed his eyes momentarily in exasperation. "Can't you give me a straight answer?" he said.

"Perhaps . . . in a few hours." Ham went on looking through the telescope, then he added, "Say, in a couple of hours. We should have moved enough by then to judge."

Jem nodded curtly. "Tell me as soon as you can say anything definite."

"Right."

As the distance separating the fleet and planet dwindled, surface details became increasingly visible until these were quite clear to the naked eye. Forests and mountains could be seen, and clouds bringing rain to warmer regions. There were no polar ice caps, but great rivers were seen making their way across fertile plains.

Jacy removed his headphones and swiveled his

chair around to face Jem. "Simon Bryant wants to know if we can change course and go into orbit," he said. Jem turned to face him, frowning.

"Why?"

"He says they have a bigger telescope than we've got. According to him, there are signs of people living down there."

"What are you saying?" Ham stood up and Jacy glanced at him.

"It's not what I'm saying."

"Go on," Jem cut in. "What else did he say?"

Jacy shrugged. "He can't see much point in going on if this planet is suitable." The four of them looked at each other for a long time in silence. "You must agree he's got a point," Jacy added, eventually.

Jem turned to Ham, the aggression gone from his expression. "What do you think?" he asked quietly —but unseen by any of them Preston had entered the cabin.

"It doesn't matter what Ham thinks," he said, coming forward. Jem turned quickly.

"Father!"

"What matters is what we've been told to do," his father went on, "and that is to go on until the end."

"Then why have we been brought so close?" Jacy said after a few seconds.

"Perhaps to learn something. Maybe to give the right answer to a question."

"What question?" Jem said impatiently, and Preston turned to him sternly.

"Whether you're still prepared to put your trust in the one who saved you in the beginning." They looked into each other's eyes, then Jem dropped his gaze.

"There are people living down there," Jacy pointed out.

"Then it's not intended for us." Preston turned to Ham. "How long have we got before we must go on?"

Ham glanced down at the instruments. "About fifteen hours," he said.

"Then there's plenty of time to see what we can learn." He turned back to his eldest son. "Give Simon and the others your answer," he said.

"Yes, Father."

"And be on your guard," Preston added. "Remember, much as we may pride ourselves on what is being achieved, an ignorant people will follow without question because they have no other way . . . but those with a little knowledge may be tempted to think they know everything." He turned for the door, but Jacy called after him.

"Father?"

Preston glanced back. "Yes, Jacy?"

"How did you know it was Simon's idea?"

Preston smiled faintly. "Simon is a proud man," he said. "It has always been more difficult for him than the rest of you."

When he received his answer Bryant walked back grimly down the deserted corridors of his ship through the empty public rooms, and eventually arrived on the observation deck, which was crammed with people gazing at the now shrinking planet. All heads turned to face him as he came through the doorway and stopped just inside. "The answer is no," he told them.

A sound like a drawn-out sigh came from those listening, and a man nearest to the window turned to look back. "But on the night side, we could see the lights of great cities," he protested, and several murmured their confirmation of this.

"There were lakes and rivers," said another.

"And oceans, blue with depth and fringed with beaches of golden sand," said the girl next to him.

Bryant shrugged uncomfortably. "It was inhabited already," he told them.

"But there were vast tracts of land without a sign of habitation," argued the first.

The murmur of protest grew stronger until Bryant held up his hand. "I've done what I can," he said. "I sense that some of the family secretly feel as we do, but Preston's answer to everything is that our journey is not yet completed, and that is the end of the matter."

"It never will be if we go on like this!" said one of those standing nearest him. The murmur suddenly died and everyone looked at the one who had just spoken, then they looked at Bryant, who stared back at them impassively.

"As long as we follow him, we must do as he commands," he told them.

Ham busied himself at his worktable; according to the tape, the next leap was due within a few hours. He had known from the first moment what the answer would have to be, but his own longing, when he had looked down from the loneliness of space at the richness of the world which had passed beneath them, had been as strong as anyone's. Once, when he had done something wrong as a child, his father's words had fallen on deaf ears and he had rushed out into the woods to spend the rest of the day venting his wrath on innocent treetrunks with a knife. Then, as it began to get dark and the shadows started to creep toward him across the clearing, his temper had suddenly evaporated to be replaced by an ache of self-pity. By the time he had returned to the farmhouse it had been completely dark and he had stood outside for a few minutes seeing his father and brothers sitting down to their supper while his mother moved quietly between the stove and table putting plates of hot food in front of them.

How much he had taken it all for granted. Apart from the obligatory word of thanks he had never glanced up to wonder at the woman who acknowledged him as her son and looked after him when the rest of her kind had abdicated to the Machines; or the miracle of home itself. When he had been in the dark outside looking through the window and struggling to swallow his pride, to come in from the cold and be received again, he had felt as he felt just now. He knew in his heart the time was not yet; but how could he blame those who longed for the things which sometimes it seemed they had lost forever.

## CHAPTER THREE

A few hours later the leap into hypserspace was completed, and for a few seconds the crew stared morosely out at the now familiar display; then Jem got to his feet.

"Well . . . that's that!" he said; but before he had time to move, the door at the rear of the cabin opened and Alison came in. He could see at once something was wrong and immediately the others turned to see what he was looking at.

Alison paused for a moment, then she said sadly; "Your mother died a few minutes ago."

"What!" Jacy stood up, and Alison moved to him at once.

"I'm very sorry, darling," she said softly, and hugged him gently; then she turned to the others. "I know how much you all loved her."

Jem looked the most shocked of all of them. "I didn't know she was so ill," he stammered. "Why didn't Father tell us?"

Ham also stood up. "Didn't you know?" he asked.

"Of course I didn't know," Jem said, turning on him. "How could I?"

"You could have gone to see her."

Jacy hung his head in misery and Alison stepped between them. "Please—this is no time to start quarreling."

Jem turned to her. "Father could at least have told us, so we could have been there."

227

"Your father didn't know. There has been little change in the past few days. He meant to call you just before the end, but she slipped away so peacefully, he thought she was still asleep." Alison paused for a few seconds, then she said quietly, "If you would like to come and see her now . . . your father is waiting for you." She turned and led Jacy out of the door.

When she had gone, the two brothers stared at each other. "You go," Jem said eventually. "It's only a small cabin. Tell Father I'll come later." Ham nodded.

"All right." He moved to the door, but paused when he reached it and turned back to face Jem, who was still watching him. "I'm sorry," he said. "I know you loved her as much as the rest of us; forgive me."

Jem almost wept. Suddenly he moved to Ham and put both hands on his brother's arms in an agony of remorse. "Should you ask forgiveness of me?" he said hoarsely.

Ham covered his hands with his own for a moment, then he turned and went out.

Jem turned back to the window and saw David looking at him. "Ham always said none of us realized how much we depended on her," he said, trying to swallow his grief.

An hour later Ham came out onto the observation deck and looked around. When he saw Valla sitting alone in a corner, he came over to her at once. "I've been looking for you everywhere," he said.

Valla shook her head slightly. "I didn't want to

stay," she said. "I prefer to remember her as she was."

Ham stood, looking down, then he sat beside her. "It's strange," he said after a few seconds. "We loved her, but we always thought of Father as being the really important person in our lives."

Valla didn't answer immediately, then she said, "I remember the first day you brought me to the farm. Your mother gave me a lovely feeling of being wanted, just for myself. You were in love with me, I know; but I didn't realize then it would grow into anything more than the feeling many of the boys at the Community said they had for me. They called that love. All it meant was they wanted my body until they got tired and went on to someone else. Sarah showed me real love for the first time in my life."

Ham nodded. "It's only these past few months I've realized how important she was," he said. "We took her so much for granted."

"Without her, the rest of us wouldn't even know what being a wife meant."

Ham paused for a few seconds, then he said: "Her whole life was based on her love for Father, and her faith that what he was trying to do was right. Imagine what it must have been like at the beginning . . . as a young girl, knowing nothing of life outside the Community, except what he had told her."

Valla nodded. "She must have been very frightened."

Father always said this journey was a test of

faith . . . but the same was true of her whole life. Perhaps that was her greatest gift to us."

After the others had gone, Preston sat down beside the bed looking at his wife's face, calm in death. His hand was big and roughened by a lifetime's work, but when he leaned forward to touch her cheek it was with the lightness of thistledown.

"Sarah!"

He remembered how he had looked down at her sleeping peacefully with their first newborn son, and how he had to rush outside to run and jump into the air, shouting for joy.

He remembered the first stallion they had ever seen, rearing on its hind legs and setting off across the plain like the wind. How the two of them had run, hand in hand, after the wild cattle, laughing; and how she stood breathlessly with her back to a tree, waiting for him to take her in his arms.

He remembered how he had stood on the high ground, aware for the first time of the one who had waited so patiently for his understanding. Surely he would not let the love they had borne for each other dissolve into nothing.

The three watched Ham go back to the telescope, take a sighting, then return to his table.

"Are you sure?" Jem demanded. "Just the one star directly in front of us?"

"Not another, as far as I can see, this side of the nearest galaxy," Ham told him without looking up.

David frowned. "What would it be doing right out here by itself?" he asked.

"Has it got any planets?" Jacy said without giving Ham a chance to answer.

His brother smiled. "Yes," he said, "one; but nothing to cause any trouble this time. Judging by the gravitational pull on the parent star, it's at least seventeen times bigger than Jupiter."

"What does that mean?" Jem asked.

"It means the gravity would spread us like jam under our own weight if we tried to land."

"I see." Jem stood up and stretched. "Well . . . I'm going to get some sleep," he told them.

Jacy yawned. "Me too."

Ham nodded. "Right. I'll let you know if there's anything else to report as we get closer."

Jem left the cabin followed closely by Jacy. The two walked along talking companionably until they reached a corner, then they separated and Jem went on toward the center of the ship where his own quarters were situated. On the way he passed several people who all nodded and smiled, greeting him with that mixture of affection and respect to which he had become accustomed.

Nearing the center, the corridors became more deserted and finally completely empty. Jem was about to enter his cabin when he paused and, on impulse, closed the door again and walked to the very heart of the ship, stopping outside the door leading to the annihilation box. He looked around, then got a key out of his pocket and unlocked the door . . . opened it and stepped through.

Jem moved onto the catwalk, shutting the door

behind him. He looked down, shading his eyes as the light from the swirling liquid made patterns on his body. He watched for a few seconds, then climbed down the iron ladder to the lower part of the chamber, in the center of which was the tank itself. He walked around slowly, examining the cell, until he heard a sound. He looked up to see Valla standing just inside the doorway.

"What are you doing here?" he said after a moment.

"I came to your cabin." Valla closed the door behind her.

"How did you know I was here?"

She turned back to face him and shook her head briefly. "I guessed," she said.

They looked at each other for a long time, then Valla said, "Can I come down?"

"No."

"Why not?"

"It's dangerous."

"You're down there."

"That's different. I know what I'm doing."

Valla smiled. "Do you?" she said, and started to climb down. When she reached the bottom she turned to face him, a little breathless. The light made strange images appear to float across her face, but her dark eyes never left his.

"I thought we had agreed not to see each other," Jem demanded.

Valla took a step toward him. "It's hopeless, cooped up like this," she said. "If I never had to see you again it would be different. Have pity." Her eyes sought his face for some softening of his expression.

"Have pity on us both," Jem answered. "How can I face my brother?"

"We didn't ask for this to happen," Valla persisted desperately. "It destroys me as much as you, probably more—I still love him—but I can't go on denying the need I have for you."

"Valla!"

She moved toward him again but Jem backed away. "It's as simple as that," she continued. "I know something terrible is going to happen. We'll be punished—but I don't care. God made me what I am, so if He wants to destroy me, it's His own fault."

"Don't talk like that," Jem begged. "We don't have to do this. We have a choice."

"I suppose so. Like a man who dies of drinking water from a poisoned oasis. He can choose to die of thirst." Her eyes held his and she began to unfasten the front of her tunic. When it dropped to the floor she was completely naked. "Make love to me here," she whispered, "where it's dangerous."

Jem suddenly gasped and reached out for her, crushing her body against his own and burying his hands and face in her hair. Valla laughed breathlessly and tore open his shirt, covering his chest with kisses.

"My darling . . . my big strong darling. You see . . . you're as weak and wicked as I am. But it doesn't matter now. It doesn't matter!"

Jem walked back to his cabin alone. He paused in the empty corridor, looking up and down, then opened the door and went inside.

He found the lights on already and stopped dead

just inside the door as a familiar figure got up
from the chair to meet him.

"Simon Bryant!"

"Aye." The Scot smiled.

"What are you doing here?"

"Waiting for you."

"Why?"

Bryant glanced behind him. "Will you not close
the door first?" Jem did so. "Thank you," the other
then continued: "They told me you were resting; so,
being a tactful man, I decided to wait when I didn't
find you . . . rather than raise a hue and cry." He
smiled thinly.

"What do you want?" Jem said shortly. He had
never particularly liked Bryant, and found him even
less welcome at the moment.

"Shall we sit down?" Jem nodded briefly, and tried
to keep his impatience from showing too much.

"Thank you." His visitor sat down again, perfectly
at ease.

"Well, now . . . I should tell you first, we have a
much bigger telescope on our ship."

"I know."

The other nodded. "That's right. And we've been
observing this giant planet which lies almost directly in our path."

Jem held up his hand with a mixture of contempt
and relief. "Before you say anything else, we couldn't
possibly land there."

"Because of the high gravity . . . yes, I know. But
if I may continue . . . with our bigger telescope, we
have observed something else that may have eluded
your brother."

"What's that?" Jem looked at him sharply.

"A moon or satellite . . . approximately the same size as Earth." Jem stared at him.

"Of course," Bryant went on, "it's possible he has already found it for himself—I understand you've been off duty for some hours—but when we realized the significance of the discovery, I decided to come straight over and tell you before anyone else."

Jem thought for a few seconds before answering, then he turned to look directly into the eyes of the other.

"Why me?" he said.

"Because you have it within your power to save the situation."

Jem began to look impatient again. "Stop talking in riddles."

"Very well. Let me put it this way: with very few exceptions, the people are not prepared to go on wandering the universe indefinitely. The young are restless to put their new skills to use, and the old don't want to die out here—as some are beginning to do already."

"It won't be forever."

"But can any of you say for how long?"

Jem shook his head. "There's no way of telling," he admitted.

"Aye!" The Scot nodded. "That's the answer we always get . . . but I'm telling you, it's no longer good enough."

"That's too bad," Jem retorted. "Nobody can do anything about it."

Bryant leaned forward. "They can," he said. "You can, if you have a mind!" Jem stared at him, and the other continued: "Some people say it might suit the Preston family to keep us wandering in space forever."

"What are you saying?" Jem demanded angrily.

The Scot shrugged. "It's obvious your father won't be needed, once we've found a suitable home."

Jem sprang across the cabin and seized the other by the front of his tunic. "How dare you say such a thing?" he blazed. "I should kill you!"

"Wait a minute," Bryant said breathlessly. "I agree. . . . Such a deliberate act on Preston's part is unthinkable—don't be so hasty! I was only telling you what I've heard others say."

"Why?" Jem demanded, without letting go.

"Because I want to avoid bloodshed, if it's possible."

"Bloodshed!" Jem loosened his grip slowly.

"Aye!" Bryant straightened his tunic. "Now calm down and listen to what I have to say without leaping at my throat."

Jem looked at him hard for a few seconds before saying, "Go on."

"As far as we can see," Bryant said, "the satellite is not only about the same size as Earth; it appears to resemble it in many other ways. The clouds and predominantly blue color indicate the presence of water . . . and there are other signs. Of course, we can't tell from here if the planet is suitable. . . . Only close inspection would reveal such a thing." He paused for a few seconds, then went on slowly: "And it is for this I have come to ask."

Jem shook his head after a moment. "It's no good,"

236

he said. "Father would never agree. The navigation tape still has more than halfway to run."

Bryant paused again for a moment, looking at Jem carefully, then he said: "I mentioned one opinion just now. Now, here's my own: your father is no longer young. No one knows better than I what we owe to him, but the strain of the last three years —and now the tragic death of your mother—have taken their toll."

"Come to the point."

"Very well. I think that perhaps your father may have misunderstood Vicro's instructions."

Jem looked at him, amazed. "How is that possible?"

"Not difficult . . . when you've been carrying that sort of responsibility."

"Misunderstood in what way?"

"Might it not be possible that we are being presented with a variety of alternatives from which to choose?" The incredulous smile which had been gathering at the corners of Jem's mouth faded suddenly. "You've heard him talk often enough about making a decision," the Scot went on. "Well . . . what sort of decision are we making if we turn our back on all the possibilities?"

Jem frowned. "We've decided to stay with the course we've been given . . . to the end," he said defensively.

"And what if, when we reach the end, there's nothing?"

"And what if you're completely wrong?" Jem countered. "What if Father has understood Vicro perfectly well, and by disobeying him we ruin everything?"

Bryant nodded. "I'm not saying that possibility

doesn't exist. But if we never pursue the matter we'll never know . . . maybe until it's too late."

Jem paused for a long time, then he said, "What do you want?"

"What we want," Bryant said, "is for you to organize an expedition to examine the smaller planet." Jem's eyes widened. "If it's unsuitable," the other went on, "then your father's view is vindicated and no harm's done; but if it is suitable, then he was mistaken."

Jem paused for a few seconds, then shook his head. "It's no use," he said. "I've told you, Father would never agree. You're wasting your time."

"Then you must take command as long as it's necessary," Bryant answered quietly. "You are the only person everyone would follow without a fight."

Jem thought about this for a few seconds, the idea growing in his mind, but then he said half-ruefully, "Ham would never agree."

"Then Ham, with one or two others, will have to be restrained long enough for us to find out."

Jem hesitated again before saying, "What about Father?"

Bryant smiled gently. "He will be . . . asked to stay in his quarters until the results of the expedition are known." He saw Jem's face and went on with even more determination.

"If I, or anyone else, tried to take the law into our own hands there would be chaos; but you have already been placed in command . . . And one thing I can promise: if we sail on past this opportunity without even looking, there will be bloody revolution."

Bryant paused, looking directly at Jem, then he said solemnly, "You alone can prevent this."

Jem slumped on the edge of the bed. "I don't know," he said.

"It's a heavy responsibility," admitted the other, "but you are Preston's son, and I think I know what he would have done at your age." He paused again, then went on more softly, "One last point: how long do you think you can go on with things as they are between your brother and yourself?" Jem stared at him. "You need to be able to get away from each other so the girl can choose freely before something more terrible happens."

## CHAPTER FOUR

The rebellion jumped from one ship to another like high-tension electricity. In less than an hour, Jem's supporters had taken control and, as Bryant had predicted, the vast majority were in favor. There were some points of resistance, however, and three died in the fighting which followed.

While Jem went to see his father to inform him of their decision, Fearson led a detachment up to the command deck to arrest Ham. They burst into the room but found Jacy the only person in there.

David dodged around a corner, just avoiding being seen by Bryant and another group of his supporters. He paused for a few seconds looking up and down the corridor, which was fortunately deserted, then ran to the far end; he checked to see if the next was also clear before hurrying toward Ham's cabin, conscious of shouting in some other part of the ship. He reached the doorway just as Fearson and his men appeared around the corner at the opposite end and started to run toward him.

David tore open the door and leaped inside; he slammed and bolted it behind him. He switched on the lights and turned to shake Ham, who was sleeping on the near side of the bed with Valla on the other.

"Ham!"

There was loud banging on the door and David heard Fearson's voice on the far side. "Come on, open up. We know you're in there!"

Ham stirred before David reached him, but the younger man shook him urgently. "Ham, for God's sake wake up!" Valla looked up in alarm, still half asleep, but Ham's eyes snapped open. He was fully awake in an instant.

"David!"

Again Fearson's voice could be heard. "I'll give you a count of ten, then we'll break down the door."

Ham jumped to his feet. "What's going on?" he said.

"Jem . . . Bryant's persuaded him to rebel against your father."

Ham looked at him incredulously. "What?!"

"There's no time to explain. They waited until you went off duty. Now they've come to get you."

"Is Father all right?"

"Yes . . . but captive."

Valla came around the bed toward them. "What?!"

There was a volley of blows on the other side of the door. "All right," Fearson shouted. "If that's the way you want it." A second later there was a crash which nearly took the door off its hinges.

"They're armed," David said hurriedly.

"Who?"

"Fearson and the others."

"Bryant's men!"

Another crash loosened the door still further and David looked around desperately. "Have you got any weapons?"

"Of course not!" Ham snapped, but he glanced around quickly, then seized the end of the bed. "Here, help me pull this against the door."

The other two jumped forward and they moved the bed so that the next assault was not so effective.

"What now?" David asked breathlessly.

"I don't know . . . but it gives us a moment to think."

"What are we going to do?" Valla said, frightened.

David gave her a look. "You're in no danger," he said. "It's us they want. Particularly Ham."

Ham seized his wife by the elbow and swung her around to face him. "Did you know he was planning this?" he demanded.

Valla looked up at him. She had never seen him like this before. "No. I swear!"

Ham looked at her a moment longer, then he turned to David.

"How did you get here?"

"I heard shouting down in the library. Burey was killed."

"Burey!"

"He refused to do what they said." David shrugged helplessly. "But the delay gave me enough time to get away. I knew they'd come for you next." There was a harder crash than before, and the door began to splinter. "Not that it's done any good!" he added.

Ham paused for a few seconds. "Yes, it has," he said suddenly. "There is a way out." He snatched the chair from in front of the dressing table and put it in the center of the room immediately beneath a small trap door. David looked up.

"The service tunnels!"

"Right." Ham jumped up on the chair, knocked the hatch out of the way, then leaped for the edge of the hole and pulled himself through.

The next blow disintegrated the door and Fearson started to push his way through as Ham reached an arm down through the trap.

"David . . . come on. Valla, you stay where you are."

David leaped onto the chair and jumped for the space almost in one movement. Ham pulled him through just as Fearson cleared the last obstacle. While Valla watched helplessly, the trap door fell into place just in time to block a thrust from the spear.

Ham swung around in the half-light and pulled a crate of loose tools over the trap door. "That should stop them for a bit," he said, smiling grimly.

David looked around. "I've never been up here before," he said.

"It's like a maze," Ham told him. "Come on."

He started to lead David down the tunnel, which immediately divided, then divided again, but Ham chose without hesitation. "It'll take them long enough to find us in here," he said over his shoulder. "Not many people know their way around."

"Long enough for what?" David whispered.

"To decide what to do."

On the command deck Jem sat at the controls giving orders to Jacy, who repeated them over the radio. Bryant watched as the planet loomed large through the observation windows.

On the word *mark* it started to drift in a different direction, then Jem stood up. "Stand by while I check our position," he said, and moved across to Ham's usual position to check the navigation instruments. On the way he paused by the now silent computer for a moment, then went past; a few more seconds and he turned back. "That's all right."

Bryant smiled. "Excellent!"

Jem turned to Jacy. "Tell them to stand by for course correction in two hours from now." Jacy nodded, and Jem faced Bryant. "We should be in a favorable position to launch a pod to the surface in about five hours," he told him.

The other nodded.

"That's good. All observations so far indicate we are not mistaken."

"I hope not, for all our sakes!"

Bryant looked at him.

"How did Preston take it?" he asked.

Jem stared out of the window, then answered without turning his head: "I don't know," he said quietly. "He seems . . . stunned."

"It's better he stays in his cabin until we know one way or the other."

"I suppose so." Now Jem turned to face the other again. "What concerns me more at the moment is your men's failure to restrain either David or my brother."

Bryant held up a hand. "Don't worry," he said, "they can't do anything. Either we'll find them soon or they'll be forced to come out by hunger and thirst—by which time everything will have been decided."

"Even so, I'd feel more at ease if I knew that brother of mine was where he couldn't do any harm!"

Bryant shrugged. "He is."

"Not until we've got him locked up. You don't know him like I do." Jem continued to look at the other for a moment, then he turned away and yawned.

"Will you rest now?" Bryant asked.

Jem nodded. "I think so. There's nothing more to be done for the time being."

"We'll see you're not disturbed." When Jem turned for the door Bryant smiled thinly behind his back.

Jem did not awaken when the trap in the ceiling opened and Ham, holding a knife between his teeth, lowered himself through and dropped silently to the floor. He took the knife in his right hand and moved to Jem's side as David followed, equally quietly, carrying a spear.

Ham put the blade of the knife within an inch of his brother's throat and whispered, "Jem, wake up."

Jem's eyes opened sleepily but started wide as he saw who was bending over him.

"Ham!"

Ham held a finger to his lips. "Quiet. If you want to live."

Jem glanced down at the knife. "You wouldn't!"

"Perhaps not before; but if I have to kill you now, I will." Jem saw the expression in his brother's eyes. His mouth opened to say something, but he closed it again and Ham smiled grimly. "I'm glad," he said. "I didn't say I'd enjoy it." Jem swallowed.

"What do you want?"

"Listen carefully, and I'll tell you."

A minute later, the door opened halfway and Jem stuck his head out into the corridor to speak to one of the two men standing guard.

"I want to have a meeting," he said shortly.

"Yes, sir."

"Fetch Bryant, Fearson, and my brother Jacy."

"Right away, sir." The man started to move away, and Jem's head disappeared for a moment, then it reappeared quickly and Jem called after him.

"Wait. First I want you to bring the six young men we locked up a few hours ago. I will see them here. Then you can fetch the others."

The man hesitated, frowning slightly. "Yes, sir."

"I want to speak privately so tell everyone else to stay at either end of the corridor—and see that we're not disturbed."

"Yes, sir."

"Go on, then," Jem barked.

"Right away, sir. You want me to bring the prisoners here first?"

"Then the others."

"Yes, sir." He turned and made off down the corridor hurriedly. When he was out of earshot, Jem turned to the man standing on the other side.

"Ask my father to come here," he ordered. "Tell whoever is in charge I said so." The man hesitated.

"What if he won't come?"

Jem paused. "Tell him Ham wants to see him," he said eventually. Before the other could argue any more, he shut the door in his face.

Bryant and Fearson came, looking none too pleased. They marched around the corner of the corridor, followed by Jacy, past the guards now at the other end, then up to the door of Jem's cabin. Bryant knocked loudly and glanced impatiently at the man beside him.

"I suppose he's lost his nerve!"

Fearson nodded. "But we still need him."

The door half opened and Jem looked out. "Well?" Bryant demanded.

Jem stood back and opened the door; after exchanging a brief look, Bryant and Fearson walked inside. They were well into the room before they saw David and his six now fully armed supporters.

"What's this?" Bryant said, wheeling around just in time to see Ham pull Jacy into the room and slam the door. Then he saw the knife blade pressed to Jem's side.

"I see."

"Drop your weapons, if you want to walk out of here alive," Ham snapped.

"You fool!" Bryant glared at Jem.

"Do as he says," David ordered.

Jem shrugged. "I told you not to count your chickens," he said.

"Your weapons," Ham rapped. "I won't ask you again."

Both captives looked as if they were about to explode, but after a second's hesitation Bryant dropped his spear and Fearson followed suit. Ham nodded.

"What now?" Fearson demanded.

"Now . . . I will tell you what you are going to do," Ham said not unpleasantly.

"Which is?"

"You will come with me to the command deck, one at a time, and there record a message to be broadcast to all ships, in which you will inform the people that the rebellion is over."

"Never!" Bryant roared.

Ham shrugged. "It doesn't really make much difference whether you do so or not—it's over anyway. The alternative is to be dragged around the fleet in chains, to demonstrate what you will not admit." Bryant glared at him, but Ham returned his gaze calmly. "Jem will announce that he has handed back his command to my father," he continued, "who will then assume direct control until he appoints a successor."

"You, I suppose!"

"That is not for me to say. You will be locked up and guarded until Preston has time to decide what to do with you."

"Your father is a senile old man," Bryant began. Just then the door opened and Preston himself stood in the doorway.

Jacy's jaw dropped. "Father!"

"That's all right," Bryant went on, looking at the others, "I'll say it to his face. We won't follow him any longer."

"I think you'll find there isn't much choice," Ham told him.

"No!"

"Preston slammed the door behind him, then he looked at Ham, who was still holding the knife.

"What are you doing?" he said sternly. "Have I lived to see one of my sons kill his own brother?" Ham looked at him in astonishment.

"What do you want me to do?" he asked after a few seconds.

"First of all, put away your weapons—all of you."

"But if we do that, they'll take control again," David pointed out.

"They could have taken control at any time." Preston looked at Jem, then at Bryant. "You only had to ask. Haven't you understood anything I've tried to tell you?"

His eyes searched the faces of everyone in the room finally alighting on Ham, and his expression softened. "Please, my son . . . put away your knife," he said quietly. "I know you would defend me . . . but this is not the way; believe me, I know." Ham glanced at the others, then moved to obey.

"Thank you for that, anyway," Jem murmured.

Ham nodded at David and the others put up their spears. Bryant and Fearson exchanged glances.

"You may pick up yours, if it makes you feel any happier," Preston told them.

"Aye!" Bryant glanced at his companion and the two of them retrieved their weapons, but held them lightly.

Preston then turned to face all of them. "I tell you with all certainty," he went on more strongly, "and with every fiber of strength I have left, that I did not misunderstand what Vicro told me."

Throughout the fleet, people gathered on the observation decks and in the central meeting rooms—anywhere near a loudpseaker—standing or sitting silently to hear what Preston had to say. Most preferred to listen like this with their friends, but a few like Valla chose to be alone in their cabins where his voice could still be heard over the communications system.

"I knew from the beginning that our journey would be longer and harder than most of you imagined," he told them, "and I tried to explain that this was a test of our faith in the one who saved us from the drought and preserved us in the face of our enemies."

Preston sat at Jacy's table on the command deck speaking into the microphone. Through the windows he could see the surface of the planet drifting past, as the fleet was already in orbit less than a hundred miles up.

"Of course there are alternatives," he went on determinedly. "What merit can there be if there is no choice? But the intention from the beginning was that we should choose the right at last—trusting in the merciful love of the one who made us, and the good of His purpose for us."

Preston paused to clear his throat before going on with even greater intensity: "In the beginning, God gave us free will—so that we could soar like eagles and not be confined in a cage of virtue. Free also to turn our backs on the light above and choose the dark beneath . . . and this is the choice which faces us now. Life or death. It is one we make as individuals. That is why the rebellion had no meaning—because I was chosen to lead, and I choose to go on now, but I have no power, other than these words, to make you follow . . . nor ever had." He paused for a long time, then said quietly, "I have no more to say."

There was a moment's silence on the observation deck of Ship Eleven. Bryant switched off the speaker and turned to the others. "He is a gallant fighter, the old man," he said, "I'll say that for him —worth all his sons put together; but he's beaten . . . and he knows it."

He smiled suddenly and looked around, and those listening felt the unease caused by Preston's words begin to lift. "The expedition revealed a virgin land of forests and grass plains," Bryant told them, "with sweet water in abundance waiting for us to take possession. Furthermore, there are no people of any kind to disturb. It is better than we could have hoped for." He flung out an arm in the direction of the planet beneath them; when he spoke again his voice rang with confidence.

"I say the journey is over. . . . We will make our home here!"

There was a moment's silence, then they began to cheer.

Shortly afterward, Ham walked slowly toward the door of Preston's quarters. He knocked, then went inside and found his father sitting on a hard-backed chair by the small table. Now that Sarah had gone, the cabin looked bleak. Preston turned at once to face Ham, who closed the door quietly behind him. One look at his son's face was all he needed.

"I'm sorry, Father," Ham took a few steps into the room, then stopped. "On every ship, including this one, a majority has chosen to go with Jem. We're looking for a suitable place to land."

Preston nodded after a moment. "And you?" he asked.

"We'll go on together, of course."

"How many others?"

"It's difficult to say until we land. I expect some will change their minds at the last moment."

"But not you?"

Ham smiled gently. "No. We'll take as many ships as we need, and a proportion of the animals. It has all been agreed . . . everyone will choose for himself, as you said."

Preston paused for a moment, thinking, then he said: "Jacy will go with his brother—he has always followed him—but what about Alison?"

Ham shook his head. "I don't know," he admitted. "She sided with you in the rebellion, but she loves him." His father shook his head unhappily. "What's more," Ham went on, "she knows how much he depends on her—even if he doesn't know it."

Preston wearily covered his eyes with one hand.

"God help us!" he muttered. He remained in the same position for a while, then dropped his hand and looked up at Ham with tears in his eyes. "No," he said, "I have no right to say such a thing. We have been given the chance. We had to do the rest ourselves."

"Yes, I know."

Preston looked at him more closely. "And Valla?" he asked.

Ham hesitated for a long time, then he said almost inaudibly, "She has chosen to stay . . . with the others."

## CHAPTER FIVE

The fleet landed on a grassy plain not far from a river and half a mile from the edge of a forest. The hatches opened immediately and crowds of people poured outside, laughing and rejoicing in the fresh air.

Jem stood beside Ham on the command deck looking down at the scene below. "You can't blame them," he said almost appealingly.

Ham shook his head. "They've made their choice," he said. "It's certainly not for me to judge."

Jem hesitated, then he said urgently, "Come with

us. Try to persuade Father to change his mind. . . . He would listen to you."

Ham looked at him, puzzled, then he said not unkindly, "Sometimes I don't think you know him at all."

"I do," Jem argued. "He's proud. There's a lot of him in both of us." Then he smiled. "We hate to admit we're wrong—but you can see for yourself."

Ham shook his head again. "I'm sorry."

After a few seconds the two brothers turned back to the scene outside and remained in silence for a while. Jem spoke without turning his head. "I promise I'll go right away," he said. "Neither of you would ever see me again."

Ham turned to look at him. "Do you think that would make Valla happy?"

Jem closed his eyes. "I'm ashamed," he said. "Please forgive me."

Ham smiled in spite of himself. "Same old Jem!" he said. "Do you remember how you used to knock me about when we were little?"

Jem turned to face him. "Yes," he said. "You never told anyone."

"Then you'd be overcome with remorse and ask me to forgive you."

Jem nodded. "You're right. I can't help being what I am; but if you stay it will be different, I promise."

Ham paused for a long time, then he said quietly, "It's nearly time for the division."

They made their choice, one at a time—those going on stood by Preston, and those choosing to remain crossed over to where Jem stood with Simon Bryant and Fearson beside him. When it was over, Ham stood with his father, together with David, Alison and about two hundred others, but these were far outnumbered by the vast crowd which faced them. Preston spoke:

"The choice has been made," he told them. "We will take the command ship. It will be easier to move the small proportion of animals due to us than the computer and navigation equipment."

"You can have all the wild animals as far as we're concerned, and welcome!" Fearson called out, and some behind began to laugh, but Jem wheeled around on them quickly.

"Silence!" then he turned back to face Preston, who now spoke directly to him.

"Is that your wish too?"

Jem hesitated for a moment, then he said, "Take them . . . they mean more to you."

His father nodded. "Then we'll start at once," he said.

"Very well." Jem turned to the crowd behind him, which numbered more than nine thousand, and shouted, "Make camp."

An excited cheer rose in answer as they broke up, while the few opposite stood watching. Jem turned back and looked into his father's eyes for a moment, then he strode away in the direction of the command ship."

For a few hours the full significance of what had been decided was elbowed aside in the frenzy of activity. Small trees were felled and branches trimmed under Bryant's supervision. Some of these were used to make temporary shelters while others were driven into the ground to make pens for the domestic animals that would remain. Cattle, sheep, pigs, goats and horses were driven or led down the ramp of Ship Twenty and across the plain to the new pens, while Dom and Preston led the small group allocated to them up the ramp into the command ship. The wild animals had to be man-handled in cages, but eventually these too were installed in their new quarters—and the people gathered again to see the command ship leave.

Preston stood by the window on the command deck looking down at the sea of faces below. Ham was in his usual position, but David was in Jem's seat. "Take it up very slowly," Ham told him. "They're standing much too close."

"Right."

"I'll give you the correct settings once we're well clear."

Jem stood on the edge of the crowd with his arm around Valla. Jacy was a few steps away looking utterly lost. A few of the women wept, but for the most part they watched somberly and with growing realization that in a few minutes the one who had brought them so far would be gone forever.

Ham glanced at the clock on the instrument panel which had been recoordinated with the computer. "It's time," he said.

"Should I close the hatch?" David asked, glancing up at Preston, but the other held up his hand.

"Wait," he said.

Ham paused for a few seconds, then he said gently, "It's no good, Father. No one else is coming."

Preston shook his head. "Someone is still making a decision," he said. "We must not make it for them." Ham followed his gaze to Jacy, standing some two hundred yards from the ship, then glanced anxiously at the computer.

"Father, time is running out."

"One moment longer. Please." Ham and David exchanged glances.

Jacy looked from the ship to Jem, becoming progressivly more agitated; then suddenly he made up his mind and stepped forward. "Jem. I—" But Jem pointed in the direction of the ship.

"Look!"

Alison stood at the top of the ramp searching the crowd for her husband. When she saw him, she started to run down the ramp. David leaned forward in the pilot's seat, staring.

"Alison!"

"What?" Ham started to his feet.

The other looked around. "She's leaving the ship!"

Ham rushed to the window.

Jacy started forward to meet her as Ham turned to his father in horror.

"Father!" But Preston held up his hand.

"Wait!" He continued to look outside. Ham turned back to see what was happening.

Jacy and Alison fell into each other's arms, then hurriedly exchanged a few words. Jacy glanced in Jem's direction, then they both turned and started to hurry back toward the ship. Preston closed his eyes, while Ham turned to David in delight.

"She's bringing him back!"

They walked up the ramp into the ship, hand in hand.

David looked up at Preston grinning. "Now?" he asked; but Preston still shook his head.

"No," he said. "Wait."

A young girl started forward from the edge of the watching crowd and stopped, looking back. A few seconds later a young man broke through the front ranks to join her and together they ran toward the ship. This began a minor flurry in which twenty more, mostly young people, broke from the crowd to follow their example. Then there were no more.

Preston waited a while, then he turned to David. "Now!" he said.

"Yes, sir."

The hatch closed, the ramp retracted and the watching crowd fell silent.

Valla looked at Jem almost in panic as the ship rose slowly from the ground. The loudest sound was a gasp from those watching. One or two waved their hands instinctively but dropped them again as the ship accelerated upward, soon to become a bright dot glinting in the evening sky. Valla could not bear to watch and buried her head in Jem's chest, but he continued to look until it finally disappeared.

It was difficult to sleep the first night outside, but only a few chose to return to the ships.

Clouds rolled across a sky partially illuminated by the reflected light from the giant planet just below the horizon. Valla suddenly cried out in her sleep and woke up fearfully. "Ham!"

Jem awoke to find her sitting up trembling. "What's the matter?" he whispered.

"I thought I heard a sound," Valla told him, trying to stop her voice from shaking. Jem sat up listening, then he put his arms around her.

"It's only the cattle," he said, but she buried her head against his shoulder.

"I'm afraid," she whispered.

Jem began to stroke her hair. "There's no need," he assured her. "I'll always be here."

In the central meeting room of the command ship Preston faced the few who had stood by him.

"The education and training program will go on," he told them. "Fortunately, we still have our best teachers. First, though, we must purify ourselves in accordance with the law given to me by Vicro, who foresaw the possibility that some of us might be unwillingly defiled by the disobedience of others." So saying he led them to the big shower room where the central jets were already blasting so hard it was impossible to see through to the other side for steam and water.

Preston stood at the entrance, the others crowding around behind him. "We will walk through to the other side wearing the clothes we wore outside the ship," he told them, "and so our disobedience will be washed away. Follow me."

He plunged into the water and disappeared. Ham and Jacy looked at each other, eyebrows raised slightly, then they grinned and marched after him, followed by Alison, David, Dom and the others.

A while later, Preston and Dom looked down,

smiling as they inspected a stall containing three wet and rather irritated cows and a young bull.

"They'll be all right, sir," Dom assured him. "But they didn't like it much—an' I don't say I blame 'em!"

Jacy, Ham and two other young men, dripping wet, came up carrying some rather bedraggled and still protesting hens, which they popped into cages. Ham turned to his father.

"The ducks are the only ones who enjoyed it!" he said with a grin.

"If I get purified anymore," Jacy muttered, "I'll disappear altogether!" and the others laughed.

"We haven't started on the wild animals yet," Ham told him.

"How are we going to do them, sir?" one of the young men asked.

Ham turned to him. "Cages and all."

Jacy groaned. "Come on," Ham said. "It's the only way." He put a hand on his young brother's shoulder and led him away, followed by the others, both arguing good-naturedly. Preston and Dom turned back to look at the cows.

"They look well enough, anyway," Dom remarked. "All the cows are in calf. At this rate we'll soon make up the numbers." Preston nodded.

"Yes," he said, "they look fine!"

## CHAPTER SIX

Within two weeks the first granaries and store-houses had been completed and a small village of timber construction was well under way.

Jem stood looking up at some men on a half-completed roof with Valla standing beside him. "That's fine," he called up to them, nodding approvingly. "But don't forget to start laying the roof boards from either side working your way up to the top." The men smiled down at him and waved their acknowledgment. "I know it's tempting to start at the top," he went on, "but that way the boards overlap the wrong way and let the rain in."

"Like Fearson's house!" one grinned.

"Yes! The Scots don't know everything."

"They've built a marvelous boat for the river," Valla pointed out.

"I know. It's not often they make a mistake."

They started to walk around the house, Jem still inspecting the roof frame, but Valla saw something out of the corner of her eye and turned to see one of the stockmen running toward them.

"Something's wrong!" she said. Jem stopped to follow her gaze and the runner, seeing them looking in his direction, waved frantically. "Something is wrong," she repeated.

"How do you know?"

"I can tell."

A few seconds later the man arrived in front of them, gasping for breath. "Sir . . ."

"What's the matter?" Jem said.

"The cattle," he panted, "there's something wrong with them. . . . They all seem to be dying."

Jem called a meeting that night in the open space in the middle of the half-completed village. They built a fire and Jem stood in front of it explaining the position. When he had finished, Bryant, who stood facing him with Fearson at his side, turned to those who had listened silently.

"I said this was not a suitable place," he remarked. "We should have moved down to the sea; then we should not have been so dependent on the cattle."

"The land at the edge of the nearest ocean is unsuitable for farming," Jem answered, coloring slightly.

"So you said," Bryant retorted. "But now the cattle are all dead, and the other animals are sickly."

"We still have enough food to last until the first harvest."

"If nothing goes wrong."

"As you say," Jem agreed.

The two men stood a few yards apart staring at each other, and a murmur rose from the people surrounding them. The growing animosity between Jem and Bryant was already well known, but this was the first time the latter had dared bring his defiance into the open.

After a few more seconds, Bryant turned to the crowd and said in a loud voice, "I say we should leave this place." This drew another murmur but Jem shrugged.

"You can go if you want," he said. Bryant quickly turned back to him, looking surprised.

"Very well," he said. "Give us our fair share of food and seed corn."

"Food, yes—but the seed will remain under my control," Jem said firmly. Bryant flushed angrily.

"I must protest," he began.

"Protest until you're blue in the face," Jem told him. "You may know about the sea and fishing—if there are any fish to be caught . . ."

"There must be," Bryant interjected.

"Why? There are no animals on dry land!"

"Perhaps the ground you have chosen is poison; that's why the animals die."

Jem paused for a few seconds, then he said quietly, "I don't know why the animals are dying, but I do know it has nothing to do with eating the grass around here. It's as sweet as any I ever saw."

"Then why . . . ?"

"On the other hand, I have seen the land you prefer," Jem persisted, "and I tell you that neither crops nor livestock could prosper there."

Fearson spoke for the first time. "Why don't you give us our share of seed?" he demanded, and those around him murmured their agreement.

"Because I'm responsible for all of you," Jem replied. "It may interest you to know I have already ordered the animals which still survive to be rounded up and fed from the granaries until we find out what is wrong; but whether we're successful in saving them or not everything still depends on a successful harvest and I'm not going to risk wasting half our seed on barren land!" He paused for a few seconds, then went on more reasonably: "I don't mind you taking enough food to live on, and trying your hand elsewhere, but until there's enough to spare the seed will stay here so that enough food can be grown to feed any of you who want to come back." Valla looked at him quickly.

"Even though they've done nothing to help?" she questioned.

Jem turned to her. "Don't worry about that," he said. "We'll get on better without having to argue half the time." Then he turned back to Bryant and the others. "You may go, taking food and whatever you need," he told them, "except the animals and what I've already said. If you fail and want to return at any time, you may."

"Sir, that hardly seems fair to the rest of us who stay with you," a man standing close to him protested; but Jem gave him a quick smile.

"Better than have them all return and try to exist on half the harvest we could have had."

Bryant turned on his heel. "Don't worry," he said over his shoulder, "we won't fail.

"I hope not," Jem called after him; then he looked around at those who remained. "There's nothing more to be said," he told them. "Go to rest now. Those who want to can leave in the morning."

Jem was awakened in the middle of the night by shouting in the distance. He got up quickly, waking Valla, and went to the entrance of their tent.

"What's the matter?" she murmured.

As soon as he came outside, Jem saw the fire over on the far side of the village. He turned at once and called back into the tent, "Stay there. I'm going to see."

"Wait!" A few seconds later she joined him.

"I can't see properly from here but I think it's one of the granaries," Jem said quickly, "I put guards there just to be sure." He turned and seized a spear from just inside the tent, then ran into the darkness without another word.

When still some fifty yards away, Jem stopped and saw that one of the granaries was indeed burning fiercely; anticipating such a danger, though, he had ordered them to be well-spaced so there was no immediate risk to the remainder. He saw also that the big double doors of one of the other buildings were open and that Fearson was standing outside, apparently on guard with several armed men, while others loaded sacks of seed from inside onto improvised sledges which were being towed away into the darkness as fast as they were filled—others being brought back to take their place. The bodies of several men lay on the ground beside the doors. Jem looked around to see that the twenty men he had hastily summoned had caught up with him then he ran forward again and stopped about twenty yards from the double doors.

"Fearson!" Jem shouted. The other turned quickly, adopting a defensive position, but the loaders froze in their tracks.

"Stay there!" Fearson called back. "We're only taking what is ours."

"And burning the rest?" Jem challenged, advancing a few more steps.

"That was an accident." Jem stared pointedly at the men on the ground.

"And those men you've killed?"

"It was their own fault."

"They were trying to obey my orders."

The big Scot shrugged. "They got in the way. We warned them."

Jem smiled at him grimly. "Well, now you're in my way—and I'm warning you. Fetch Bryant, wherever he is."

"He's inside."

"Fetch him." After a pause, Fearson nodded at one of the men beside him, who ran inside.

"The rest of you stand still," Jem ordered.

A few seconds later, Bryant emerged with a drawn knife in his left hand and a spear in the other.

"It took you long enough to get here," he remarked. "We made enough noise."

"Never mind. I'm here now."

The Scot grinned back at him. "To do what exactly?" he asked.

"Give orders to replace the seed you've taken," Jem demanded. "You can still leave in the morning . . . except those who are responsible for killing my men."

"I'm responsible," Bryant answered, "and I don't intend to take any more orders from you." He nodded at the loaders. "Carry on," he said. "We'll see that you come to no harm." The men hesitated, then one braver than the others moved to obey.

"Stand still," Jem shouted and the man froze again.

"I'm warning you, Bryant. I don't want any more bloodshed. We've trouble enough." Then he saw the Scot was looking over his shoulder.

"More than you know." Bryant smiled, his lip curling. "Look behind you." In spite of himself, Jem glanced over his shoulder and saw a ring of fifty armed men closing in on them. Bryant threw his spear at the same moment and would have killed Jem outright if the man next to him hadn't pushed him out of the way and received the full impact of it in his side. A few seconds later, Bryant's men fell on them from all sides.

They defended themselves as best they could but Jem realized they hadn't a chance where they stood and encouraged those beside him to fight their way to the side of the building, which they did. Here, although still heavily outnumbered, they only had to face one way. Even so, more of Bryant's men came running back when they heard the noise and Jem knew they were soon bound to be overwhelmed.

Just when it seemed they were lost, Jem saw Valla run into the firelight, followed by several hundred of his own supporters, who immediately fell upon Bryant's men from behind—and the battle started to tip in their favor.

Bryant, realizing he had lost, managed to fight his way to the girl in the confusion and, knocking the spear from her hands, seized her by the hair and dragged her down on her knees, holding his knife at her throat. Jem heard her scream and immediately ran toward them.

"Don't come any closer or I'll kill her," Bryant shouted, holding the knife up for a second. Jem stopped at once, but one of his men came up behind Bryant and, before Jem could stop him, threw his spear into Bryant's back. The Scot shouted with surprise. Valla tried to break free, but just as Jem ran forward Bryant fell to the ground, his hands still entangled in her hair, and plunged the knife into her shoulder. Valla cried out in agony, but Bryant looked up at Jem defiantly.

"You fool!" he snarled.

Jem plunged his spear into Bryant's chest, killing him instantly.

The wounded were laid out on the open ground in the middle of the village and were attended to—at least to begin with—as well as largely unskilled helpers could; soon, however, everyone except Jem—wounded and non-wounded alike—was gripped with a high fever that made them sweat and tremble, and finally drained all the strength from their bodies. The injured died first, then the others started to follow.

Jem knelt beside a young man next to another who had just died. After a few seconds, the other shook his head and stood up so unsteadily he would have fallen if Jem hadn't stood and put out his hand quickly.

"What about the others?" he said urgently. "What's wrong?"

The young man turned his head slowly. "Before we landed here, I chose to study medicine," he said.

"Then why can't you do something?"

"I read that many years ago the Machines removed all harmful germs and viruses from the Earth's atmosphere."

"Yes."

"Then don't you see?" the other muttered hopelessly. "Our bodies have lost their ability to fight." He looked around slowly at the surrounding plain and forest. "That's why we should not have come. This is a new world . . . full of microbes which develop in the course of evolution . . . against which we have no defense!"

Jem looked at him, stunned, then he said, half to himself: "He must have known! Why didn't he say?" but the other shook his head.

"Preston?" he said, dully. "I don't suppose he thought of it any more than the rest of us. He told us to have faith, but we wouldn't listen." The young man closed his eyes for a few seconds. When he opened them again, Jem saw he had already accepted death. "I can't do anything," the other sighed—then he turned unsteadily and walked away.

Jem watched him go. He hesitated for a few seconds, then turned on his heel and strode purposefully back to his own tent.

Valla was lying on some blankets. Her shoulder was bandaged and when Jem knelt by her side he could see her face was bathed in sweat.

"Jem!" She half opened her eyes.

"It's all right," he said gently. "We're getting out of here." Valla looked at him uncomprehendingly.

"How?" she whispered.

"There's something in the air stopping you from getting better. It's affecting everyone." He put his hands under her to lift her up. "Just lie still," he ordered. "I'm taking you back to one of the ships."

As he lifted her up, Valla winced with pain, then she rested her head against his shoulders, her eyes closed. "How can we go?" she murmured hopelessly. "They took the navigation tape."

"We'll find some way," Jem answered with more confidence than he felt; then he swung around to take her outside.

Jem began the long walk to the ships. Everywhere people were lying or sitting around, their faces flushed with fever, eyes without hope. He half expected someone to shout curses after him for bringing them to this place, but if the thought occurred to anyone, they were too weak to do so.

He carried her across the deserted space in front of the granaries, past the animal pens—now filled with dead animals—then over the hundred yards of grass to the nearest ship. Jem began to walk up the ramp, but when he reached the top Valla suddenly put up a hand to touch his face.

"No . . . stop!" He paused to look down at her. "Don't take me inside," she begged. "It's too late." Jem hesitated. "Please!" she beseeched him again.

They looked into each other's eyes for a long time, then Jem bowed his head. "All right," he said. "I don't suppose it makes any difference now."

He carried her back down the ramp, but this time away toward a small group of trees standing by themselves out on the plain some three hundred yards from the edge of the main forest; there he laid her down gently in the shade.

Valla's eyes were closed. She seemed to be scarcely breathing as Jem lay down beside her. He looked at her fever-ravaged face and took a handkerchief from his pocket to wipe away the sweat, then she opened her eyes to look at him for the last time.

"I love you, Jem," she whispered. Her eyes were as beautiful as ever, and Jem groaned as he gathered her into his arms.

They lay there together the whole afternoon and eventually Jem fell into an exhausted sleep. He woke up just before it began to get dark—he saw at once that Valla was dead. He closed his eyes then opened them again and felt his own face, but he was still without a trace of fever. Jem looked at his dry hands and felt the first prickles of panic breaking through the misery. Was it possible that he alone would not die?

He ran out from the trees onto the plain, then stopped, first looking back, then all around him. Nothing moved—except the evening wind through the grass. After a few seconds he began to run back to the camp.

Jem ran between the sheep pens where nothing moved and into the open space in front of the granaries. He hesitated, then made off again in a different direction toward the half completed row of houses, and to one in particular he knew was already occupied. When he got there he tore open the front door and went inside.

Adults and children, about a dozen in number, lay or sat grotesquely crumpled in death. After a moment Jem turned and ran outside again. He stopped a few yards from the house looking around, then shouted at the top of his voice: "Hello! Can anyone hear me?!"

He waited for what seemed an eternity, then shouted again, even more desperately, "It's me . . . Jem! I'm here! Can't anyone hear me!"

His voice cracked on the last word; then he saw something move out of the corner of his eye in the shadow of one of the further buildings. When he turned, it was only a dead hen with its feathers fluttering in the wind. Panic now possessed him utterly.

"There must be someone!" he shouted, and began to run back to the main part of the camp, repeating the words over and over again.

Eventually he reached the place where the wounded now lay dead and stopped, gasping for breath, his eyes wide with horror. "There must be someone else!" he croaked; but after only a moment's rest, he began to half stagger, half run back in the direction of the ships.

Jem ran on, his eyes staring, terror giving strength —although his feet were numb and bleeding and his body bruised where he had fallen before picking himself up—and blindly rushing on again. At last he reached the ramp of a ship and a minute later flung himself into the pilot's seat and reached for a switch.

Outside, the hatch closed and the ramp retracted. Jem began to breathe more easily; now that he was doing something positive he felt the panic begin to subside. He turned on the instrument lights and stared outside but now it was almost dark and all he could see was his own image and the cabin reflected in the glass. He began to flick the panel control switches one by one, at the same time murmuring half to himself: "I'll beat you yet. You can take my life, but I won't be left here alone!"

Jem flicked the last of the sixteen switches controlling the panels on the lower half of the ship, then he reached forward and threw the delay switch to OFF.

The whole of the lower half of the ship suddenly turned white—but the ship itself remained motionless. Half a minute later the ramp extended again, the hatch opened, and Jem ran to the bottom. He wheeled around to look up. When he saw what had happened, his face became a mask of fear.

"Don't leave me here alone!" he screamed and raised both arms above his head, looking up into the evening sky.

"Father!"

## CHAPTER SEVEN

Preston stood on the observation deck talking to a group of children as they watched the star field drifting past the windows. "There can be no going back," he told them.

"Why not?" the boy next to him asked, and Preston turned back to the window.

"We can't change the things we've done," he told them. "We can try to do better in the future, if it's not too late. We may be given another chance . . . but we have to take it."

"How many chances?" a little girl asked, looking up at him.

Preston looked down at her and smiled. "That depends," he said. "God forgives our mistakes many times, but there may come a moment when we deliberately choose to turn our backs on him forever. If so, nothing can save us."

On the command deck, Ham automatically went through the motions of clearing the controls preparatory to setting a new course. He no longer had to think about this, having done it a thousand times before. David, now in his early thirties, sat waiting for his instructions in the place once occupied by Jem so long ago, and Jacy stood by the window, looking outside. None of them said anything.

Sometimes they still spoke of those they had left behind, but more often they kept their thoughts to themselves. As one year followed another, Ham wondered sometimes if perhaps Jem had spoken the truth, but there was no going back, no way of finding out if by now the beginnings of a new civilization were established. There was no alternative but to go on, scarcely admitting doubt even to themselves, let alone to each other.

The course spelled out by the computer month by month, year by year, had taken them close to so many other worlds that their number had been forgotten. They had seen life in never ending variety on planets similar to their own, to complex systems

of small and large worlds where life had burst
forth in a profusion of species which would have
been impossible under different circumstances . . .
but always the computer gave a new setting, and
the latest revelation was left behind.

After a while Ham began to discern a pattern in
what had at first seemed random instructions to
change course. He noticed that after passing each
new planet they spent a period in space too far
from any other star to be able to see anything,
and that these periods were almost always of the
same duration. It was as though, having spoken to
them through their eyes, the one who guided them
took them far away from any other distraction for
a while so they could assimilate what they had
learned thus far.

Every so often in the kaleidoscope of life, they
would be shown something they came to call a
black world. They came close to the first one six
months after the division. They found themselves
looking down on a planet which had once been like
the others, but was now black waste and ruined
cities. The mountains of the planet had jutted tree-
less into the sky like the exposed bones of a corpse,
and the sky itself was black where once it had
been blue and green and orange. The seas which had
been the womb of life were its final refuge, for there
bacteria, the last things to survive, fought to consume the floating debris washed down by the flood
waters of a thousand years, and to turn it into an
all-embracing scum which would eventually suffo-
cate even this activity. It was a long time before they saw another world which had shared a

similar fate, and they never approached so close again.

Ham gave the settings and Jacy slipped into the co-pilot's position.

"Stand by in . . . ten seconds."

David looked up. "Check."

"Check," Jacy repeated automatically, and Ham began to count down to zero.

A few seconds after the delay bar had been switched to OFF the cabin door opened and Alison entered. She gave the others a quick smile before turning to David. "That new wife of yours is wondering when she's going to see you," she told him with mock severity.

David grinned. "Tell her I'll be down soon," he said.

"All right." Alison nodded, then she turned to her husband. "The children want to see you before they go to sleep," she said. Jacy smiled.

"Have they done their lessons?"

"Come and see. They want to show you."

Ham stood up. "You both go," he said. "Everything's set up. I can manage now."

David turned to him. "Are you sure you don't mind?" he asked, and Ham shook his head.

"Of course not."

"All right, thanks." He got up and went out after smiling briefly at Alison.

Jacy moved to follow suit but paused in the doorway. "You go on," she told him. "They're waiting for you. I just want to have a look outside."

"All right." He turned to Ham. "See you later."

Jacy went out, giving his wife a quick peck on the

cheek. When he had gone, Alison walked to the window, looked outside for a moment, then turned to face Ham.

"How much longer?" she said quietly.

Ham frowned slightly. "I thought we agreed not to ask that question."

Alison shrugged. "There are children over ten years old with us who have never known anything but life on a ship."

Ham glanced at the computer. "Sometimes the tape unwinds quickly. Other times it hardly moves at all."

Alison glanced outside, then she turned back to him again. "Many of the older ones have died," she said. They looked at each other somberly. "Maybe it is intended that only those who were born on the journey should complete it?"

"I don't think so," Ham said.

"Then why so long?"

Ham stood up slowly, then moved to put a hand on her arm. "I know it's more difficult for you, having children," he said softly, "but I think it is to give us the best possible chance."

Alison looked at him, puzzled. "What do you mean?" she asked.

Ham paused for a few seconds, then lowered his hand and turned to the window.

"You remember what Vicro said to Father that last time?"

Alison nodded, looking at him. "That God always had a special love for the creature He called Man?"

Ham nodded and turned to face her. "Yes," he said. "Think of all the different worlds we have seen;

the beautiful—and the terrible; those just beginning, and those whose civilizations have passed our understanding." Alison gazed at him in silence, and he went on: "I don't believe the journey is just a test anymore; I think we've passed that. We are being given a privilege . . . to see for ourselves the possibilities of eternity, in a generation."

Seven months after this conversation took place, they emerged from fifteen days in hyperspace to find the ship just inside the outer rim of a large galaxy, with one star almost directly in front of them. This had an apparent brightness five times greater than any other, due to its proximity.

David cleared the controls and Ham went back to his worktable. Jacy took his place at the telescope.

"Don't point it directly at the star," Ham called over his shoulder. "It's too bright."

"I'm looking at a planet," Jacy answered after a few seconds. David activated the delay bar, then turned to him.

"Can you see anything?" he asked.

"Not yet. It seems to be covered in cloud."

Ham got up again and moved to the computer. David moved across to stand beside the telescope. "Let's have a look," he said after a few moments.

"Sure." Jacy stood to one side.

"You're right," David said after a while. "The cloud cover is too thick at the moment. I can't make out any features at all." He paused for a few seconds.

"We're going to make a near pass, though. It must have something for us to see."

He straightened up and looked across at Ham." Unless we're about to change course again?" he added.

Ham looked over and smiled briefly. "You go on looking," he told them.

David had another look, then Jacy took his place while the other walked to the window and stood looking outside.

Ham pressed the activating switch of the computer —but nothing happened. He frowned and pressed it again, but still the machine remained silent. Hearing his exclamation, the other two looked across at him.

"What's the matter?" David asked.

"It won't work."

Jacy looked alarmed. "What?" They both moved toward him. "Why not?"

Ham shook his head worriedly. "I don't know," he confessed; then, after a few seconds, he began to take off the side panel. "Something must have gone wrong inside."

Jacy turned to David in something approaching panic. "Some hope for us if it has."

Ham removed the cover, revealing the navigation tape, which was at rest. He stared at it, puzzled for a long time. Finally his eyes widened and he looked up quickly at the two anxious faces looking down at him.

"Don't you see?" he asked.

They both stared at him. "What?" David said uncomprehendingly.

Ham took a deep breath. "The tape has run out."

There was a long period of silence while they all looked at each other stupidly.

"Run out?" Jacy repeated.

Ham nodded, then suddenly he grinned and stood up. "Finished," he said. "Our journey is over."

Jacy swung around to the window: "Then that planet," he said excitedly, "that's where we're going!"

Ham nodded. "It must be."

"Oh!"

Jacy flung himself at the side window and looked out.

"Just a minute!" David threw himself into the pilot's seat and started the gyros. They heard the familiar hum deep inside the ship and, while he manipulated the controls, the star, which had grown appreciably even in the past few minutes, and whose brightness now all but obliterated their view of other objects, swung across the windows to the right and stopped just beyond the edge, so that the glow was still visible but other stars could be seen again. The planet, now a bright crescent lighted on the right-hand side, was brought directly in front of them.

The three stared at it in silence for a few seconds, then Jacy suddenly sprang for the door.

"I'm going to tell Father!" he shouted and dashed out. Ham looked after him, smiling, then back at the ever-growing image before them. He turned to David.

"What are you thinking?"

David paused for a while, looking outside, then he turned to face him. "I don't know," he said. "I'm not like Jacy. I suppose . . ." Then he shrugged. "I can't really believe it," he said finally; but his expression belied his words.

Everyone packed the observation deck, watching the planet in front of them. It almost filled their view now, but was still a featureless crescent. There was an atmosphere of almost unbearable excitement but little noise. With them stood Alison and her two sons, aged eight and five.

On the command deck, David peered at the rapidly oncoming layer of thick cloud. Ham and Jacy stood on either side of him. After a while he shook his head and glanced up quickly. "It's no use," he said, "I can't see anything.

Ham looked down at the controls. "You'll have to go on automatic," he said. "Let the ship choose a site." Jacy nodded quickly.

"We've no choice," he agreed.

"But the computer's stopped!"

"That shouldn't make any difference," Ham told him. They looked back at the windows and saw the layer looming so close that patterns in the clouds could now be seen quite clearly. "Hurry up or we'll crash!" Jacy begged, and David reached across for the switch.

As the ship plunged down through the clouds they began to hear a high-pitched whistling sound. On the observation deck, people looked at each other anxiously until Preston came in from the main part of the ship and stood beside Alison.

"Don't worry about that sound," he told him. "It's only the wind."

His youngest grandchild moved to him and took his hand, looking up confidently. "When will we be able to see our new home?" he asked. Preston looked down at him and smiled. He was an old man now, too old to pick the child up and had to be content with putting his hands on the boy's shoulders.

"Very soon," he promised. "You'll see."

Ham, David and Jacy searched the windows anxiously for any distinguishing feature as the wind noise rose even higher.

Suddenly Jacy turned to Ham. "It's not working," he said fearfully. "We're not slowing down."

David glanced across quickly. "Shall I take her up again?"

Ham shook his head. "No, leave it," he said. "We haven't been brought all this way to die." Jacy bit his lip.

They stood in silence for what seemed an eternity, listening as the wind noise grew louder every second.

"Ten thousand feet." Ham looked down at the instruments, then Jacy suddenly grabbed his arm.

"We're going to crash," he said hoarsely. Ham shook his head, but Jacy stared at the gauge, his eyes bulging. Suddenly his nerve snapped.

"*No!*" He snatched at the control key that would stop their descent. Before he could touch it, Ham seized his hands in a grip of steel.

"Stop it!" he said, shaking him.

"One thousand feet." David tried to stop his own voice from trembling.

Ham looked down at his brother's terrified face, not unkindly. "We can't do anything," he said.

Jacy groaned, looked outside, then turned his head against Ham's shoulder. Still the noise mounted.

"Five hundred," David said.

On the observation deck only Preston now looked calm. Alison clutched her eldest son with one arm, Preston with the other, while the younger boy hid his face in the old man's tunic.

"Don't worry," he told them. "We're nearing the ground. It's all going to be all right."

The screaming noise grew in a wooded valley shrouded with thick mist until an observer would have seen an object flash into the ground; then all was silence. There was no impact, no explosion— only where before there had been an open space, the ship now stood.

After a few seconds Ham and David sighed with relief, but Jacy didn't move until Ham shook him. Then he began to grin self-consciously, and tried to wipe the tears from the cornrs of his eyes without the other two seeing. After giving him an encouraging dig in the ribs, though, Ham had already turned to the window.

On the observation deck, Preston looked around smiling at the others, who stood awestruck at what had just happened. "Well, come on," he said cheerfully. "Don't just stand there. Let's see what the Lord has prepared for us." This broke the spell and everyone started to hug and kiss each other with joy. Alison and the boys crowded around Preston, all trying to hug him at the same time.

"Come on, come on," he said delightedly. "Save some of that for your father." A few seconds later he was swamped by everyone else who wanted to say something to him, or just touch him with their hand. So it was almost half an hour before the ramp was extended, the hatch opened, and everyone poured outside, rapturously ignoring the mist which still obscured their view of anything beyond fifty yards.

Preston was one of the last to leave the ship. He stood with Ham at the top of the ramp and took a deep breath. "Ah! The smell of woodlands," he breathed. "I think I've missed that more than anything."

Ham nodded, then he turned from watching the children who had begun to chase each other through the trees, laughing and shouting. "What about the animals?" he asked.

Preston shook his head imperceptibly. "Let the children stretch their legs first," he said. "Another hour won't make any difference."

By the time it got dark, a large fire had been built fifty yards from the ramp. Temporary pens had been constructed for the domestic animals and most of the cages of the wild animals had been moved outside. When they finished their evening meal, Preston stood up and spoke to them quietly against a comfortable background from the animal pens of munching, gentle lowing and other contented sounds.

"There are many things in my heart I could never express properly," he told them. "First . . . the love I bear you all." He looked around. "So much of our time together has been spent in struggling against one adversity after another . . . not the least ourselves; perhaps you thought, sometimes, that the affection and trust you gave me was taken for granted. If so, I want to tell you that many times, particularly after the division, I would have lost heart were it not for the love and strength we gave each other."

Some of the older ones smiled at this as Preston went on: "Secondly, I would have expressed better, if I could, my joy at God's gathering presence to us, which is both the source of our love for each other and our hope for the future." He paused now. "I should have said . . . your future," he went on eventually, "because I shall not be with you."

There was a moment's stunned silence, then a murmur of anguish arose from everyone listening. Ham stood up quickly.

"Father! Why?" he said, his voice half choked, and Preston held up his hand.

"I've dreaded telling you," he said, "but try to understand, and do not be sad. I'm an old man. I don't know what God has in store for me . . . but whatever it is, I cannot believe that the one who made Himself known to me so many years ago— and who has filled my heart with happiness so many times since—can have any purpose that will not be good for me." His eyes moved from his son to the others and he saw how some wept openly.

"Think how far we have come together," he reminded them vigorously. "Not just in space and time, but in our development as human beings. When I was my grandson's age we were rapidly becoming extensions of the Machines we had created. No one gave any thought for another, except the gratification of his or her needs, and we had pushed the source of all life so far away that our souls had shriveled almost to nothing. But in His infinite love for us, God sent His servant to give us another chance. So why should I be sad because my life is nearing its end?" He looked around at them all, his arms out-

stretched in a gesture which begged their understanding. "He chose to use me as well, and there
could have been no greater privilege."

Preston let his hands fall to his side and he paused
for a moment again before continuing. "Do not
weep," he said, "because if I stay it will only delay
the moment when you must take your lives fully
into your own hands."

"Where will you go?" Alison, who was standing
nearest to him asked tearfully, and Preston turned
to her. "I'm going to meet Vicro for the last time,"
he said calmly, then turned back to the faces in
front of him, lighted by the fire.

"The mist will lift tomorrow," he told them, "and
you will see the beauty of the place that has been
made ready to receive you." He looked over their
heads as if his eyes could penetrate the darkness
before coming to rest on his eldest son. "Ham will
come with me part of the way," he went on softly,
"and as we walk together, I will give him a message
to bring back . . . then he will remain with you
always, as a reminder of the best that was in me."

The following morning, Ham followed his father
through the trees and up a hill still shrouded in
mist. When they left the wood behind, they had to
scramble up a steeper, grass-covered slope and eventually reached a ledge.

Preston rested on a large boulder while Ham
stood beside him; presently the older man rose to
his feet again and said, "This is as far as you must
come."

Ham was stricken. "Father. Don't leave us," he

begged, but the old man put a hand on his son's shoulder.

"I must," he said. "Please don't look like that. We'll be together again, I'm sure."

"How?"

Preston smiled gently. "With God, all things are possible."

Ham took a deep breath. "Then there is hope?" he said.

His father nodded. "Much more . . . a promise fulfilled." Ham saw he was looking past his shoulder down the way they had come. "Look behind you," Preston said, and Ham turned to follow his father's gaze. Already the mist was beginning to lift, revealing first the woods they had just left, then the clearing with the ship on the far side—and finally the far edge of the woods, where an undulating plain of waving grass stretched away to a ribbon of blue sea in the distance. As they looked, the sun broke through and was warm on their backs.

After a long time, Ham turned to his father, his eyes glistening with tears.

"We've come home!" he said, and Preston nodded.

"There was no other place for us," he said, "and look . . . in all God's creation . . . was anything more beautiful than Earth . . . as He intended it to be?" Ham shook his head in silence. "Then go back and tell them," Preston commanded, "and make them understand."

"I will." Ham looked around again, his eyes still wide with joy and wonder. "How long must it have taken?" he asked at last.

"As long as we were away," his father told him.

"But how long was that, really?"

Preston shook his head. "I don't know," he confessed, "but it doesn't matter." He paused for a moment, then he said, "Somebody wrote once: 'A thousand years are but as a day in Thy sight, O Lord.'"

Ham turned back to look at him.

"Father."

"Goodbye, my son." They held each other close, then Ham looked into his father's eyes, dimly conscious that for the first time in years he had to look up to him.

"I love you," he said simply. "I don't know how it's going to be without you."

Preston smiled down at him gently. "Better than you think," he said. "I made no exaggeration when I told them I was leaving you as a reminder of the best in me." Then he dropped his arms and said quite gaily: "I must go now. Vicro is waiting for me."

"Can I come a little further?" Ham begged, but Preston shook his head.

"No." Then he looked up to the brow of the hill and said, "Wait here. When I reach the top, I'll turn and wave . . . and that will mean I shall be thinking of you always."

He paused for a moment and Ham nodded, then Preston turned and started up the hill.

Ham stood watching, occasionally glancing up at the vault of deep blue overhead which faded almost to white at the horizon. Then he looked back and saw his father only had a few more yards to the summit. There the old man stopped and turned to raise his right arm in a last farewell. Ham raised his own in return. He saw his father look back for a moment down to the ship, then raise his head to the distant horizon, still keeping his arm outstretched as if in a gesture of blessing; then he lowered it to his side, turned, and walked out of sight over the crest of the hill.

Ham remained for a moment, then started slowly back down the hill. He reached the edge of the wood, then looked back.

Just below the ridge, a skylark suddenly rose into the air and climbed high into the morning sky, singing. Ham watched the bird rise higher and higher until it was a mere dot, but the sound of its music filled the whole world.